JOSIE BONHAM

A Good Match For The Major

First published by Pitcheroak Press 2020

Copyright © 2020 by Josie Bonham

This novel is entirely a work of fiction. The names, characters and incidents portrayed in it are the work of the author's imagination. Any resemblance to actual persons, living or dead, events or localities is entirely coincidental.

Josie Bonham asserts the moral right to be identified as the author of this work.

First edition

ISBN: 978-1-913856-00-7

This book was professionally typeset on Reedsy. Find out more at reedsy.com

Chapter One

January 1800 Kent

Eliza Wyndham smiled at her brother as he sat down at the breakfast table. She handed him the coffee pot and he grabbed it like a drowning man seizing a piece of driftwood.

Eliza's smiled deepened. "You must have found some convivial company last night."

The Marquess of Hargreaves, Max to his friends, groaned. "I did. Two old soldiers with heads of oak. It takes a lot to out-drink a Lovell."

Eliza blinked away a tear. "You're short of practice. You haven't enjoyed many evenings out since Mama died."

Max tossed back his coffee and refilled his cup. He caught her hand. "Augusta is right you know. You should go to London with her now we are out of mourning. A change of scene is exactly what you need, at least for a while. There are too many sad memories for you here."

Eliza snatched her hand away. "How many times have we been over this? I don't want to marry again and risk ending up with another fortune hunter like Miles."

"Not all men are fortune hunters. Besides, Augusta swears she has no intention of trying to find you a husband."

"And you believe her?" Eliza glared at him. "She wouldn't

be able to help herself. I am not going to London with Augusta. You may be my brother and Augusta may be the eldest but that doesn't mean the two of you can tell me what to do. I will never agree to become the legal property of a man again. Now, if you will excuse me, I've promised to visit Lord Overton this morning."

A few minutes later Eliza accepted the reins of her gig from a groom but refused his offer of escort. Footsteps thundered down the steps from the house.

"Eliza, wait. I'll come with you. It won't take me long to get my horse saddled up."

"No thank you. I want some solitude."

She sent her faithful chestnut mare trotting down the drive, ignoring her brother's response. Apart from anything else Max had been so foxed last night he wasn't safe to ride down the drive, let alone all the way to Overton Grange and back. He was wasting his time trying to talk her into falling in with Augusta's plans. As a rich widow she could do as she pleased and another marriage was the last thing she wanted.

The heavy downpours of the previous few days had stopped but a murky mist clung to the bottoms of the rain-darkened beech trees lining the drive. Perhaps the sun would fight its way out later. Once she was past the trees the mist cleared. The gatekeeper opened the side gate for her and she waved to him as she drove through onto the lane. Moisture clung to the hedgerows and dripped off overhanging branches. She kept Maisie to a steady pace. Overton Grange was the best part of an hour's drive and she couldn't afford to tire her too much with the return journey to come.

It was mild for the time of year and she settled down to enjoy the drive as best she could. The rhythmic clip clop of hooves and the creak of harness were so soothing that it didn't seem long before she reached the spinney on the edge of the Overton estates. Flocks of birds twittered skywards out of bare branches as she drove past. The trees gave way to a long stretch of hedge bordering the lane. Maisie's ears twitched as if she could hear something Eliza couldn't. They neared the bend in the road that hid Overton Grange from view and Maisie threw her head back. Eliza leaned forward to take a tighter grip on the reins lying loosely in her lap but they slipped out of her hands.

The gig rounded the bend just as a massive grey horse cleared the hedge and landed in front of them. The normally docile Maisie reared up. Eliza made a desperate attempt to recapture the reins but they remained out of reach. Maisie caught a leg in the traces connecting the gig to her harness before trying to run away. The world moved around Eliza as she was thrown out into a muddy ditch. The gig landed with a crash nearby and settled into the mud with a sickening gurgle.

Eliza sat up, spitting out mud and wiping her hands across her face to clear her vision. The mud had softened her landing but she was lucky the gig hadn't landed on her. Her stomach lurched at the sound of Maisie's high pitched whinnies and she struggled upright. Somehow the mare was on her feet but she was still thrashing about, hopelessly entangled. Eliza waded out of the ditch towards her, calling her name. She would never forgive herself if Maisie was seriously hurt. Strong hands pulled her back as Maisie reared again in her panic.

A deep voice murmured in her ear. "Stand back. Do you want your brains dashed out? My man has got her."

The warmth from his hands seared through to her shoulders as their owner kept his grip. Who was he? Her breathing

3

quickened but Eliza was too concerned for her horse to struggle. She stood in silence, back ramrod straight, watching as a middle-aged, weather-beaten man grabbed Maisie's head collar and brought her to a standstill. He stroked Maisie's neck, chatting softly to her as he did so, until she was much calmer. He certainly had a way with horses.

The owner of the hands let go and marched past her. A soldier perhaps? He was a giant of a man, with broad shoulders encased in a tan coloured riding jacket and even taller than Miles had been. A shudder ran through her at the thought. He wasn't Miles and he looked concerned for her horse. She held her breath as he bent down to run long fingers over Maisie's legs, talking softly to her as he did so.

He straightened up and grimaced. "I thought so. I'm sure there is nothing broken but she's strained one of her hind legs badly."

Eliza ran forward and threw her arms around Maisie's neck. "Oh, my poor girl. That huge horse terrified you, didn't he?" She glared at the man. "What were you thinking of, jumping out at us like that? You could have killed us both."

"We weren't so close that you didn't have time to get your horse under control." His already deep voice became a rumble. "You were daydreaming instead of minding what you were doing. Either that or you are so cow-handed you shouldn't be let loose behind any horse. Now we had better free her from the gig." He strode away to consult with his servant.

Eliza was left shaking. He hadn't even had the decency to look at her when he was berating her. Yes, she had been daydreaming but that didn't excuse his dangerous action. Few horses were as placid as Maisie but even she had been terrified by that great grey horse landing almost on top of them. He

4

was the one who needed telling off but it was better to say nothing in case it provoked him. There was a breath-taking aura of power about him which was intimidating. She could only hope he meant her no harm. Eliza's heart beat furiously as she watched them calm Maisie and inspect the gig until the sound of the tall man's deep voice made her jump.

"These reins are so tangled I'm going to cut through them. I don't want to risk any more injuries to this poor girl."

Before Eliza could respond he nodded to the stocky man. "Hold her tight."

He pulled out a folding knife and sliced through what was left of the traces. A quivering Maisie was led slowly away from the gig.

"Thank you, Bright. We need to get her to a nice warm stable as quickly as possible."

Bright tugged gently on Maisie's head collar. She hobbled after him.

Eliza gasped and her hand shot to her mouth. "She won't to be able to walk far like that."

"We'll soon have her settled in a stall at Overton Grange."

Eliza took a step back. "How did you know I'm going to Overton Grange?"

Nat eyed the woman in front of him. Was she the Lady Eliza Wyndham Uncle Henry was waiting for? She appeared plainly dressed for a Marquess's daughter but her bearing was definitely regal. She was quite a looker too with that glossy dark hair and deep blue eyes. Not that looks were everything.

"I didn't. It's where I'm staying and there is nowhere closer."

Lady Eliza stared at him. "Lord Overton never mentioned

he was expecting visitors."

Nat leaned back to study her better and his breathing quickened. She might not be a classical beauty but with that tempestuous expression on her face she was quite lovely. Beautiful or not, what right had she to question his movements? He raised his eyebrows at her and she had the grace to blush. With pink cheeks topped by sparkling blue eyes she was stunning.

"I've been here a while. Perhaps he thought he had already told you. I'm sorry if I seem to be ordering you about. It comes of being an army officer."

The anger in her eyes faded. "Overton Grange is the obvious choice to take Maisie."

He focussed on Bright, now mounted, leading the little mare. They were making slow but steady progress. He brought his attention back to Lady Eliza.

"Your horse seems happier with Bright's horse alongside her."

"Yes, she does. Your groom knows what he's about."

Her expression was calm enough but there was defensiveness about the way she was standing. Was she afraid of him? He had been abrupt with her. Even thinking about the moment when he'd been sure one of the mare's flailing hooves would land on her head, if he didn't reach her, made him feel sick. He had seen too much death and destruction in the army to want to face it on a quiet English road. He stepped forward and bowed.

"Major Nathaniel Overton, at your service. Since my uncle said he was expecting Lady Eliza Wyndham to call today, I presume that's you."

She nodded at him. "It is."

He saw a surge of curiosity in her eyes. How much did she

know about the family and why the devil was he spending so much time looking at her eyes? He failed to stop his gaze travelling down her shapely figure. She was lovely, but not for him. And she was shivering.

"You'll catch a cold standing here. Let's get you up to the house."

She glanced down at her mud spattered clothes. "I can't argue with that. I need to get out of these wet things. There should be a basket somewhere with one of Lord Overton's favourite pies in it."

She walked towards the gig and stopped short. "Oh."

Nat followed her. A wicker basket lay smashed to pieces. Next to it a brightly coloured cloth fluttered in the breeze, the edge of it held by the mud. The broken pie dish lay to the side and pieces of meat and pastry were scattered around the sorry mess.

"Your mare's hooves must have caught it." He pointed to the remains of her hat lying nearby, the feathers bent in two. "I'm sorry I pulled you back so roughly but that could have been your head."

Bile rose in his throat. He stood, head bowed, unable to tear his eyes away from the wreckage as a fleeting memory of the broken carriage his parents had died in hit him.

"I never thought of Maisie harming me, but she was in a panic and I ran right under her hooves, didn't I?"

"Yes." He hesitated. "That's why I pulled you back so hard."

Bright was out of earshot but Nat could see Caesar standing patiently waiting further along the road. He whistled and the grey trotted towards him. Another whistle stopped him by a flat rock that looked high enough to allow her to mount.

He lifted her onto the rock and helped her scramble on to

the horse's back.

"You will have to lift a leg over the saddle. I'll keep Caesar steady."

Lady Eliza stared at him. "I'll do nothing of the kind."

The horse fidgeted and Nat couldn't suppress a smile. "You have no chance of staying on this fellow sitting like that."

She blushed beautifully but this was no time to worry about the proprieties. He could see her teeth chattering. "You will freeze to death in those wet things if we don't get you to shelter soon."

"I'm not riding up to Overton Grange with my legs on display for everyone to see."

Nat sighed. "I'll lend you my jacket to cover them."

Still she hesitated. He wriggled out of his jacket, one arm at a time, and held it up to her, juggling the reins from hand to hand. Caesar took advantage of the temporary lack of restraint to jig around and Nat whistled at him to stand still.

"Before we both freeze to death, get astride this horse. I'll look the other way until you tell me you're decent." A gust of wind had him shivering nearly as much as Lady Eliza.

She glared at him but accepted the jacket and threw it over her knees. He turned away.

"There, I'm astride now but the stirrups are too low down for me." She held her hand out for the reins.

Nat moved them farther away from her. "I'm not letting you loose on this fellow."

He jumped on the rock with the reins in one hand. His foot found the stirrup straight away and he mounted behind her.

She moved forward until she was almost sitting on Caesar's neck. The horse shied in annoyance.

He grinned at her. "Do you always have this effect on

horses?"

"I never had any trouble with them before you came along."

"That's as may be, but if we are ever going to get you into the dry, you will have to sit on the saddle in front of me."

She turned around to glare at him and he saw her shudder.

"I'm not going to ravish you if that's what you're worrying about."

She flinched away from him. A flush burned his cheeks. He should have thought about how a lady would react to sharing a horse with a man. He'd been in the army too long.

He tried for a more conciliatory tone. "There is no one about to see us and we need to get you up to the house before you freeze. I'm sorry, but there is no other way."

She huffed out a breath and wriggled backwards until she was sitting almost on his lap with her body firmly pressed against him. He jumped as the feel of her soft bottom wedging itself firmly between his legs had the inevitable result on his male anatomy. At least they didn't have far to go. This was going to be torture.

"Are you ready to set off? These things aren't made for two people."

"It feels reasonably secure."

She sounded nervous but there was no other option. He wrapped an arm about her waist. "Don't worry. You will be perfectly safe with me."

Caesar broke into a steady trot at his whistle and headed for home. Home. That was a word. He hadn't had a home for a decade and yet here he was agreeing to stay in England and take up the running of the Overton estates. It felt like the right decision. For now, he needed to concentrate on getting Lady Wyndham to warmth.

"We'll take a different route to Bright. I don't want your mare spooked by Caesar again."

She twisted around for a few seconds and glanced at him with an unreadable expression on her face. Was she still angry with him? She ought to have been paying more attention but he should never have jumped onto a public road where he didn't know the terrain. Coming around that bend she wouldn't have seen him until the last minute.

He willed his body to stop reacting to their forced proximity but thinking about his physical state only made it worse. Damn. Hadn't Uncle Henry said she was a widow? She would feel his arousal pressed against her and understand the effect she had on him. She trembled in his arms. Was she cold or could she be afraid rather than angry? Perhaps it hadn't been such a good idea to take a different route than Bright.

Chapter Two

The heat from Major Overton's large frame, pressed up so close behind her, seeped into Eliza. The arm anchoring her against him felt strong enough to match the power of his horse. Her shivers subsided. He had a point. She would have struggled to control a powerful horse like this and if he had walked alongside she would have been half frozen to death by the time they reached Overton Grange. The movement of the horse kept throwing them closely together and she could tell he was aroused by her. Another shudder ran through her. It was a long time since she had been so intimate with a man. She had vowed never to get physically close to one again and now here she was sharing a saddle with one who clearly desired her. All she could do was pray Major Overton was a gentleman.

Miles would have forced himself on her as soon as he could, regardless of her wishes. A wave of nausea hit her at the unwelcome memory. She tried to remember the Overton family tree as a distraction. The only brother of Lord Overton who could have had a son was the one who had been expelled from the family. This man would be his heir unless he had an older brother. Was it a coincidence that he had come to see Lord Overton at last, now that he was ailing? She pursed her lips. Surely he could have come to see the old gentleman before now. He didn't look the sort to be worried by some old family feud. Perhaps Augusta would know what it had all been about?

Eliza sighed with relief when they reached Overton Grange and Major Overton called for a groom. The journey couldn't have been more than a few minutes although it felt like a lifetime. She shivered as he climbed down from his horse, taking his warmth with him. The feel of his hands around her waist made her catch her breath when he lifted her down. He reclaimed his jacket and threw it over one shoulder, sending lumps of mud all around them. Shivers racked her and she stumbled when she tried to walk. She hesitated when he offered his arm but the weight of the mud-soaked fur lining of her pelisse made walking difficult without assistance.

She placed an arm through his. "Thank you."

Her progress was undignified, even with her skirts held up by her spare hand. When they reached the steps to Overton Grange, she was forced to lean on him heavily to negotiate them. He rapped hard on the door knocker. For such a big man he had delicate looking hands, long and slender. He would make a good pianist. Why was she so intrigued by him? Had she never seen a handsome man before? A footman opened the door.

"Lady Eliza has been so unfortunate as to overturn her gig. I need Mrs. Ambrose to look after her. We'll go into the library, there's always a fire in there. Can you send a footman to stoke it up?"

"At once, Major."

The footman ran past them and added a log to the fire in the library. Major Overton guided them past the rows of leather-bound books to stand in front of its comforting warmth. He kept her hand trapped in the crook of his arm. She ought to protest but she didn't have the strength. He released her as soon as Mrs. Ambrose, the housekeeper, scurried in followed by a maid carrying some blankets. Mrs. Ambrose picked a blanket off the top of the maid's pile and threw it around Eliza's shoulders. She glanced at the major's jacket hanging over his shoulder.

"I'm sorry I'm in a state of undress but I used it to try and keep Lady Eliza a little warmer."

"I don't mind that, Major. I was wondering if those stains will come out. There's some on the rest of your clothes too. Once we've got Lady Eliza warm and dry, I'll have the laundry maids see what they can do with them."

"Thank you, Mrs. Ambrose. That would be most kind." Major Overton bowed his way out of the room.

The maid put her pile of blankets on a chair and grinned at Eliza. "Oh, my lady, fancy having the major's jacket around you." Her expression softened and she sighed. "He's so handsome and he looks wonderful in his shirtsleeves."

"Let's have less of your nonsense, Jenny. Lady Eliza has been in an accident and she doesn't want to listen to it." Mrs. Ambrose took Eliza's hand. "I thought so. You're icy cold. Jenny, go and ask the footmen to light a fire in the second best guest bedroom. Once that's going, tell them to bring up a bath and plenty of hot water."

She added another blanket around Eliza's shoulders. Eliza hid a smile when Jenny pulled a face Mrs. Ambrose couldn't see before skipping out of the room.

"Have you injured anything, my lady? Should we send for the doctor?"

"I assure you I'm quite well, Mrs. Ambrose. The mud broke my fall. I'm just cold and a little shaken."

Mrs. Ambrose looked unconvinced but didn't argue. "So fortunate the Major was there to help."

Eliza bit back an unladylike utterance. "Indeed."

"Such a lovely gentleman, I can't tell you what a relief it is to find Lord Overton's heir so considerate."

So she was right, Major Overton was the heir. She forced a smile for Mrs. Ambrose.

"I'm sure it must be."

Eliza followed Mrs. Ambrose to a well-appointed bedchamber. It was a beautiful room, although the red silk brocade curtains were a little faded by the sun. Lady Overton had always had good taste. Poor Lord Overton had become something of a recluse after her death. There was a knock on the door and two footmen entered with a bath. Mrs. Ambrose laid a sheet on the floor in front of the fire for them to leave it on. Eliza watched the steam rising as each jug of water was added to the bath. Once the last footman had left Mrs. Ambrose pulled a little muslin bag out of one of her pockets.

"Would you like this in your bath, my lady? It's my own concoction of dried summer flowers."

"That would be lovely, thank you. It will help get rid of the earthy smell of all this mud. It's even in my hair."

Eliza sank into the warm water with a satisfied sigh. Some of her tension eased. She was right to stay away from London. Her fear at being alone with Major Overton had been far worse than the shock of the accident. Strange that she should recognise how attractive he was even through the fear. Her hands trembled and she hid them under the water. Mrs. Ambrose stoked the fire up again and welcome warmth seeped through her until her hands stilled.

"There, you've got some colour in your cheeks now, my lady. You were so cold I was worried. I'll go and see what I can find to wrap you in."

Eliza thanked her and sat back. She gave the little bag a shake under water and set her mind to deciding which flowers' petals were in it. Anything to take her mind off the memory of the Major in his shirt sleeves. Miles had often wandered around without a coat when they were alone. There was a strong smell of roses and lavender or was it lilac? It was most likely both with, surely, a hint of summer pinks. What a delightful idea and the perfect thing to have her smelling sweeter. She must ask Mrs. Ambrose for the recipe. She sank under the water and washed the mud off her face and out of her hair.

Mrs. Ambrose came in with a pile of clothes in her arms.

"I've brought some of the maids' spare nightgowns for you to try for size and one of Lord Overton's dressing gowns which has just been laundered."

Jenny followed with some towels and they soon had her dry and ensconced in a nightgown which fitted apart from being too short. Like all her sisters, Eliza was tall compared to most women. The nightgown was covered by a fancy brocade dressing gown hitched up with a cord tied around the waist. Jenny found a dry towel and rubbed at her hair. At least she felt fresh now. She sat on a sofa placed near a blazing fire and luxuriated in the warmth it threw out.

Mrs. Ambrose went to open the door in answer to a firm knock. The familiar, deep tones of Major Overton came from the corridor.

"Lord Overton has had a visit from the doctor and he's sending him along to examine Lady Eliza."

Eliza sighed. The doctor was such a fusspot she didn't fancy her chances of being allowed home for a day or two. There was a knock at the door and Mrs. Ambrose ushered in the spare form of Doctor Munro, wrapped in a dark grey winter coat which owed more to warmth than fashion.

"I hear you were thrown to the ground when your gig overturned, Lady Eliza," he said, with a trace of a soft Scottish accent.

"Yes, but I landed in mud. I assure you there is no harm done, Doctor."

The doctor put his medical bag on the floor. "So you have no pain anywhere?"

Eliza shook her head. "None at all."

He nodded. "Mrs. Ambrose said you even had mud in your hair. Allow me to examine your head."

He ran gentle fingers over her scalp and the top of her neck. "I can't see anything obvious but we can't rule out the possibility of a head injury. I prescribe an overnight stay just to be safe."

Eliza hid her hands behind her so the doctor wouldn't see them shaking. "That's out of the question, Dr Munro. It wouldn't be seemly for me to reside in a bachelor establishment even for one night."

"Come now, I'm sure no one will take it amiss if you stay with Lord Overton at his age."

"Perhaps not, but with his nephew staying here my reputation would be at risk."

The doctor tutted and shook his head. "Better to risk your reputation than your life, my lady."

"I'm sure there is no risk, Doctor. I would be far more at risk from my sister's tongue if I don't go home."

"Couldn't a messenger be sent to ask the Duchess to come to you? There should be more than enough daylight."

"I'm afraid that wouldn't help. She is visiting friends today and staying overnight. I'll have word sent to my brother to come and fetch me home."

Doctor Munro pursed his lips. He looked across at Mrs. Ambrose. "Would you be able to accommodate two extra people? I would be much happier if Lady Eliza stayed here tonight."

"Of course we could, Doctor." Mrs. Ambrose smiled at Eliza. "It would be a pleasure."

Eliza started to protest but the doctor raised a hand. "Please be advised by me on this, my lady. If you have no after affects Lord Hargreaves can escort you home in the morning."

She hesitated. He was well intentioned and she didn't like to upset him. He had been so kind to Mama throughout her long illness.

"Very well, as long as Lord Hargreaves agrees."

"Good. Now I must get on." The doctor picked up his medical bag and strode out, escorted by Mrs. Ambrose.

Eliza lay down on the sofa and curled her feet underneath the dressing gown. Tiredness washed over her. She closed her eyes for a moment but she was too on edge to fall asleep. Mrs. Ambrose returned a few minutes later.

"Would you like to rest in bed once the maids have made it up. They shouldn't be long."

Eliza struggled upright. "That's kind, thank you. I need to have a message sent to my brother."

There was a knock at the door as she spoke. Mrs. Ambrose opened it to admit Major Overton.

"Doctor Munro says you are staying overnight, Lady Eliza."

His mouth was pulled into a straight line but the crinkles at the edge of his grey eyes gave away his amusement. How dare he laugh at her when it was his fault she was in this predicament?

"Yes, I am. I'm sure I could easily travel home this afternoon but I don't want to upset Doctor Munro."

Eliza glanced at Mrs. Ambrose. The woman was simpering at Major Overton in a manner worthy of Jenny.

"Would you mind sending a groom across with a message for my brother, Mrs. Ambrose?"

"I'll see to it at once, my lady."

"There is no need to send a note. I came to offer my services as messenger, Lady Eliza."

Eliza's eyes narrowed. As the heir he would soon be Max's neighbour, was he hoping to play down his part in the episode? "I wouldn't want you to go to so much trouble, Major Overton. A written message delivered by a groom will be sufficient."

"It might be safer for your reputation if I wasn't in the house until your brother arrives." His smile lit up his face.

It was a strong face with high cheekbones, firm jawline and a small cleft in the chin pointing to full lips. She found her eyes drawn to his lips. What would they taste like? This was ridiculous. She had promised herself she would stay away from men but she was as intrigued by him as the rest of them, even though he was making fun of her. He had a point and there was no way she could decline his offer without it looking too particular.

"Very well, if you insist."

"I will be on my way as soon as Caesar can be saddled up."

"But you've already ridden him."

"Not far and I don't have a spare horse. I imagine your

brother will stable him for me and transport me back."

"Of course."

Her gaze was drawn to his retreating figure as he bowed and followed a beaming Mrs. Ambrose out. Why did she have to meet him when she had a nice safe future mapped out for herself? If only Augusta was at home. She would feel much more comfortable with her for company. Augusta had a knack of spotting people to be wary of. For all she knew Major Overton could be a complete scoundrel. Miles had been so attentive and agreeable only to change completely as soon as they were married.

Chapter Three

Nat followed Lord Overton's groom onto the lane. It was still early afternoon but the leaden skies made it seem later. There was more wind than earlier in the day. With luck, it would stay dry. They cantered past the trampled area where Lady Wyndham's gig had overturned. His eyes felt drawn to the spot where he had pulled her back from under her horse's hooves. Uncle Henry's estate carpenter had moved the gig already. If it couldn't be mended he would buy her a new one. That would infuriate her. She seemed determined to think the worst of him. The first time she saw him after he'd heard Mrs. Ambrose tell her he was Lord Overton's heir, she had raked him down with contempt in her eyes. What were the words she had used?

"I wouldn't want you to go to so much trouble, Major Overton. A written message delivered by a groom will be sufficient."

Innocuous enough in themselves if they hadn't been delivered in such a haughty tone, with an accompanying look that would have curdled milk. Perhaps she thought he was visiting in the hope he was about to inherit. He shouldn't have lingered by the door when he heard them talking but he didn't regret it. He grinned to himself. Considering he had been largely responsible for her accident perhaps she had good reason to be cold towards him.

He ought to reserve judgement. His friend, Luke, was always telling him he was too sensitive. Uncle Henry was fond of her and it was good of her to spend time with an infirm neighbour, especially at such a distance. Most of the society girls he had ever met considered no one but themselves and how to make a good marriage. The likes of him had been of no interest to them, except for their amusement. He pushed the unwelcome memory away.

They came to more open country and the groom soon led him down a bridle path to their right. The ground felt much springier as they climbed higher. Caesar was taking it all in his stride but with nothing in his uncle's stables up to his weight he needed to look out for a spare mount. They settled to a steady pace and Nat enjoyed the ride. The long, low profile of a country house came into view. Even from this distance the tall chimneys marked it out as Elizabethan or even earlier. It was a beautiful building. He didn't need the groom pointing it out to him to know it was Hargreaves Hall. It was exactly the sort of aristocratic home he expected Lady Wyndham to come from. A double sided curving staircase, which looked as if it might have been added at a later date than the original house, ran up to what must be the main door.

The path dipped and the house largely disappeared from view until they came to the entrance to the grounds. He raised his eyebrows at the grandeur of the gateway. Two smaller side doors flanked a large middle door which spanned the whole width of the drive up to the house. A gatekeeper exchanged a few friendly words with the groom as they turned onto the drive and went under the stone archway of the main door. A knot of tension formed in his stomach. He didn't want any trouble with neighbours. He would have to admit his share of the culpability for the accident. Would the marquess be as autocratic as his sister, or worse and pompous into the bargain?

He had no time for these aristocrats who sat comfortably at home being waited on whilst other people worked hard. A few years in the army should be compulsory for all of them. On second thoughts that wasn't one of his best ideas. Some of the worst officers were sons of the aristocracy, often pushed into the army by older brothers. Then again some of the best officers were aristocratic. He was looking forward to visiting Luke. How would he be coping as Viscount Enstone? It was beyond him how some of the men could be congenial and yet he had never met an aristocratic female he would want to know better. All they were interested in were men with position, money and power. No wonder father had looked elsewhere for a bride.

He still didn't understand why the Overtons were so upset at him marrying a shipwright's daughter. His father's designs coupled with his grandfather's skill had taken the company to great heights. What was wrong with that? He stiffened at memories of his mother's distress every time his father tried to heal the family breach only to suffer another rebuff. He was glad he had accepted the invitation to Overton Grange. Uncle Henry's tearful delight at their first meeting had been enough to convince him that the rift had been none of his making.

Hargreaves Hall was even more spectacular as they drew closer. The honey coloured walls looked as if they were made of the local sandstone he had admired since his arrival in Kent. In fact the whole place had a homely feel to it despite its size.

They trotted towards the stables. Caesar stumbled and he felt his gait change. He pulled him up and jumped off. Grasping the head collar he set the horse to walk. He gave the command to stay still and walked around the horse to run a practised hand over his legs. Damn, he had strained his left hind leg.

The groom stopped by him and dismounted. "Is he injured, Major?"

"I'm afraid so. He must have caught a hoof in a rabbit hole or something. Nothing serious but he needs to rest his leg for a day or two."

"I'm sure Lord Hargreaves would lend you his spare until he is fully fit."

They walked their horses to the stables and the head groom took charge of Caesar and directed the stable boy to show Nat up to the house.

He ran up the steps and raised a hand to the door. It was opened before he could knock. The butler led him to the library and announced him. Nat's gaze was drawn to the blazing fire in the large chimney breast. A familiar figure rose from one of the sofas in front of it and moved towards him. Good Lord, it was his friend from the Golden Cross.

"Major Overton is it? I had you down as a military man last night. We must have both been well in our cups when we met, not to introduce ourselves properly. Max Lovell."

He held out his hand and Nat shook it.

"Come and sit down by the fire and tell me what has occurred. My valet has been to tell me some garbled tale he heard from a groom, about my sister overturning her gig."

Nat could see concern beneath Max's relaxed manner. He hastened to reassure him.

"She hasn't taken any lasting harm."

"I'm relieved to hear it. I blame myself. She went off in a temper after something I said."

Nat accepted the seat cleared of paperwork for him. "The doctor was visiting Uncle Henry and he has persuaded her to stay overnight but she wants you with her."

Max nodded. "Of course I'll go. Will you take some refreshment?"

"Would you think me odd if I asked for tea? It was one of the things I missed in my years abroad."

The butler entered as he said it.

"That can be arranged, Major Overton. May I bring anything for you, my lord?"

"I'll have the same. I don't know about you, Major Overton, but I find I'm hungry the day after a heavy night of drinking." He turned to the butler. "Perhaps cook could rustle up something for us to eat before we set off."

"I'm sure she will manage a cold collation, my lord."

"Thank you. Tell Jepson he's to select a few things for an overnight stay and ask Lady Eliza's maid to do the same. He's to order a carriage put to and set off for Overton Grange with the maid, as soon as may be."

"Yes, my lord."

"Oh and have one of the grooms follow them in my curricle."

The butler hurried off.

"Now, tell me how it happened."

"It was largely my fault. I jumped a hedge on my big grey, Caesar, without checking the terrain. We landed in the lane safely but Lady Eliza came around a corner at the same time and her mare was spooked at the sight of Caesar in front of her."

Max gave him a penetrating stare for a moment. "Even so I

would have laid money on Eliza to calm her down."

Nat hesitated. It felt rather like telling tales but the truth would come out eventually anyway.

"She must have been daydreaming and didn't have a hold on the reins."

He heard Max groan. "So it was my fault indirectly. Can the gig be repaired?"

"The estate carpenter thinks so but if not I'll buy her a new one."

"That might not be a good idea." A smile played around Max's mouth and his eyes gleamed. "There are some high sticklers in the neighbourhood and such an action might be misconstrued."

Oh Lord, he should have thought of that. A wave of heat washed over him and he turned his face to the fire to hide it.

"Lady Wyndham was furious with me for spooking her horse."

"She was in a strange mood this morning and with you being …"

Nat grinned. "Partly to blame?"

Max returned the grin.

"She didn't want to stay at Overton Grange overnight."

Max's lips twitched. "My youngest sister can be somewhat headstrong."

The butler arrived to usher them into the dining room. It was a fabulous spread for an impromptu meal, with a variety of cold meats and cheeses, fresh bread and even some apples and pears.

Max glanced out of the window. "The light won't last much longer with so much cloud cover. We had better be off as soon as we've eaten. It's a lot quicker on horseback. I'll have our horses saddled up, unless you want to rest yours."

Nat hesitated. Max raised an enquiring eye at him.

"Caesar picked up an injury on the ride over and I don't have a spare at the moment."

"You're welcome to borrow my second horse until yours is fit enough to ride."

Nat smiled at him. "Thank you. I must buy another mount soon but it's a job to find the right one for a large fellow like me."

Nat followed Max along the bridle path until it widened and he was able to ride up alongside him. Uncle Henry had mentioned what a good chess player Max was. He gave a wry smile. Since he hadn't won a game against his uncle yet he ought to ask Max for some lessons.

"Do you want to share the joke?" Max said.

Nat laughed out loud. "I was thinking about asking you to give me some chess lessons. Uncle Henry is too polite to say so but he is bored with beating me."

"I don't always beat him myself. I'll happily give you some tips. We have some good games. When I'm in residence at the Hall I try and ride over as often as I can."

Nat studied the Grange as they neared it. It was nowhere near as large as Hargreaves Hall and no more than a hundred years old. The Kent sandstone of its walls glowed more golden than honey coloured in the fading light. It was a charming house and perhaps he would be able to make a happy home here.

Eliza came to with a start. She must have fallen asleep, not surprising considering how poorly she had slept ever since

Augusta had started teasing her to go to London. Mrs Ambrose came into view.

"I'm sorry if I woke you, my lady. I was drawing the drapes to keep the warmth in. It will be a cold night tonight. May I get you anything?"

"A pot of tea would be lovely, if it's not too much trouble."

Mrs Ambrose called to a passing footman and sent him off to the kitchens. "It's gone dark early tonight. The maids have done their best with your clothes. We've steamed them dry in front of the kitchen range."

Eliza sat up startled. "Dry already. Lud, what time is it?"

"Nigh on four o'clock and the light is fading fast."

Eliza closed her eyes. What was keeping Max? Her stomach lurched. He had been foxed last night, after his convivial evening at the Golden Cross. Could he have met with an accident? The tea arrived and the routine of preparing it calmed her. It was more likely Max had taken the dogs on a long ramble to clear his head and was out when Major Overton arrived. He would be here presently. Within minutes the door opened and she heard the sound of her maid's voice.

"Put it over by the window, please."

Two footmen deposited one of her travelling trunks.

Alice opened the trunk and pulled out a selection of evening gowns. "Lord Overton is feeling better and the footmen are going to help him down for dinner."

"In that case I must make an effort to dress to mark the occasion."

Eliza ruled out a black dress. Perhaps it was time to heed Augusta's advice to start wearing colours again. The lavender dress was pretty but her eyes were drawn to a brilliant sapphire blue, her favourite before Mama died.

"That one I think."

It was the most expensive dress she had ever owned, bought at her mother's insistence just before she had become confined to the house. That was a comforting thought and the urge to wear it had nothing to do with a fine pair of grey eyes that looked at her with admiration.

Alice seemed to take longer than normal to dress her hair but at last she was satisfied. She pulled out a jewel case and selected Eliza's sapphire necklace, fastening it around her neck.

"There you are, my lady. You look lovely."

Eliza accepted a pretty shawl to drape around her shoulders and made her way downstairs. She entered the drawing room to find Max and Major Overton already there. The major's eyes lit up and his gaze swept over her before he lowered it. She felt her cheeks grow warm and stepped forward to place her hand through Max's arm before the Major could offer his.

Max smiled down at her. "You look well, Eliza. I heard some lurid tales that had me worried for your health."

"It was nothing, Max. I landed in mud and only my dignity was injured. I'm afraid poor Maisie came off the worst."

"I spoke to Bright when we arrived, Lady Eliza. He's confident Maisie will make a full recovery." Major Overton said.

"That's a relief. Would you thank him for his care of her?"

"Of course." He gave her a warm smile that left her breathless.

She was relieved at the arrival of Lord Overton on the arms of two sturdy footmen. One handed him a walking stick and Major Overton stepped forward to take his other arm. He looked so frail but at least he was well enough to come downstairs.

"Eliza, my dear, how dreadful for you to be thrown from your gig."

Even his voice sounded a little stronger than the last time she had seen him, although it still lacked power.

"I assure you I'm perfectly well, my lord." She smiled at him.

"You look splendid, my dear. I'm glad to see you out of those dark mourning clothes. They drained your complexion. You have much more colour in your cheeks tonight."

"I agree my sister looks much healthier in pretty colours, my lord. It's time for the family to return to normal life and I believe Eliza is feeling better now that spring is near."

"I'm glad to hear that but what a pity she should have had this set back today. Come we mustn't let the food go cold. Cook has been enjoying herself with a proper appetite to cater for." He leant heavily on the Major's arm. "Thank you, Nat." He smiled up at the Major and signalled to Max to lead them into the dining room.

Eliza took the seat to Lord Overton's right, with Max beside her and Major Overton opposite. She stole a glance at him. He settled his uncle in his chair and took a woollen throw from a footman to wrap around his knees. Major Overton seemed to have become a firm favourite with his uncle already. Lord Overton was no fool but he would be predisposed to like his heir so that proved little.

The conversation was lively between the three men and Eliza was able to relax. If anyone noticed she was quiet they would put it down to the after-effects of her accident. It seemed Major Overton had arrived nearly three weeks ago. If it hadn't been for the awful weather they would have seen him a lot sooner. Thank heaven for that small mercy. She found his company and her reaction to him unsettling. She had to admit Lord Overton seemed a different man because of the major's presence. He had been fretting about what would happen to his servants and tenants when he was gone and Mrs Ambrose seemed confident all would be well with the major. The men became silent.

She decided to probe. "Do you intend to stay in the area for long, Major Overton?"

He gave her a lazy smile. "I've promised Uncle Henry I will make my home here. I've done my duty by my country with ten years of service in the army and now I'm ready to settle down."

Lord Overton glanced around the table. "I can't tell you how happy I am to know the place will be left in good hands."

Eliza's stomach lurched. She could only hope her doubts about the Major were unfounded and he was everything his uncle clearly believed him to be. Not every charming man was a rogue. Her experience with Miles had left her particularly vigilant. Then again a true gentleman would have owned up straight away to his error in jumping that hedge rather than try and put the blame on someone else. She glanced up to find Major Overton lowering his eyes but not before she had seen the, hard, searching look he was giving her. The attraction she felt for him was stronger than anything she had felt for Miles. A frightening thought.

Max didn't seem to have any doubts about Major Overton. He slapped him on the back. "Now that is good news, Nat. I'm glad to hear it."

Major Overton gave him a charming smile. "I wouldn't be too sure about it if I were you, Max. I don't know the first thing about estate management. I'm hoping you will answer some of my questions from time to time. "

Eliza frowned and quickly lowered her eyes to her plate. So he was on first name terms with Max was he? Why couldn't Max be more careful? Surely Lavinia's pursuit of him, or rather of his money and position, had taught him something about caution. It had taken the combined influence of the entire family to help him outlive the scandal of jilting her. It had even been one of his so called friends he had found her in bed with. Had he learned nothing from that experience? Apparently not, one pleasant evening at the Golden Cross and 'Nat' was well on the way into Max's inner circle.

The footmen cleared the dishes from the main course and removed the tablecloth. They laid out a selection of jellies, pastries and creams. Eliza selected a pastry and Max passed the dish to Lord Overton who put a jelly on his plate and started to eat. He definitely seemed to have more appetite at last. The butler brought in a decanter of port on a silver salver, along with four glasses, and withdrew at a nod from Lord Overton.

"If you're both agreeable, I suggest we invite Eliza to stay and take port with us tonight." He smiled across at Eliza. "This is the good vintage Nat found in the cellars the other day. Lady Eliza will love it."

The Major turned to Max, as if she wasn't there.

"I have no objection if Lady Eliza cares to stay with us."

"Thank you, Overton. It would be a shame to leave my sister on her own and she has a taste for port. Good port was an indulgence of my father's he shared with us all. I should add that Eliza is the youngest of my seven sisters. It doesn't seem fair for one man to have to bear that does it?"

Major Overton laughed. "You do seem to have more than your fair share, would that I had one sister or brother."

31

Max grinned at the major. "I hope you don't mind our informality but Eliza and I have enjoyed many a good port with Lord Overton. If I remember I often bring one of the bottles my father put down. You will have to come over and try some with us."

"Now that's an invitation not to be missed, Nat. The old marquess was a real connoisseur."

Eliza clenched her hands under cover of the table. She must make sure to be out when he came to Hargreaves.

Chapter Four

L ord Overton poured out a good measure for Lady Wyndham. "Tell us what you think of this one, my dear."

Nat watched as she raised the glass to her lips. She looked magnificent tonight in a dress the exact shade of blue as her eyes. The light from the chandelier above them bounced off the curls arranged on top of her head. His gaze dropped to her throat as she swallowed. What would it feel like to kiss her there until she moaned with pleasure? She put down her glass and ran her tongue around her lips. He bit back a groan. Was she torturing him deliberately? Her lips were stained a luscious ruby red by the trace of port, eminently kissable. He tried to drag his eyes away but failed miserably. He had been without female company for far too long. She glanced around the table. He averted his gaze before she reached him.

"This is excellent, as good as some of my father's best. Where did you get it?"

"Nat found it tucked away in a cellar that hasn't been used for some time." Lord Overton smiled at her. "I have a feeling it's from a batch your father laid down years ago. There was quite a lot and he let me have some."

Lord Overton passed the decanter around and Nat concentrated on his own glass. The colour was excellent. He tried a sip. This was good.

Max replaced his glass. "I think I know which one this is. There is some left at Hargreaves as well. Beautiful."

The decanter went around again and Lady Wyndham had a second glass. The Lovell's must be the most informal aristocratic family he had come across. As the youngest perhaps she had been spoiled? Max said something to him.

"I'm sorry I was wool-gathering."

"I'm not surprised after tasting a port as good as this. Roberts, my land agent, is paying a visit next week. Why don't you come to stay and travel around with us? He's an excellent man, up to date with all the latest theory on agriculture."

Nat spotted a sudden movement opposite. He glanced at Eliza. For a moment she looked horrified before she quickly schooled her features into a neutral expression. The lady did not like him. He shrugged inwardly. He couldn't afford to give up an opportunity like this because of a silly, spoilt girl. He grinned at Max.

"That is a generous invitation. If my uncle can spare me I would love to." He glanced at Lord Overton.

"Of course you must go, my boy. The Hargreaves estates are some of the best run in England. I'm sure you will learn a lot."

"In that case I accept your offer gladly. I have so much to learn and the best place to start is always with an expert."

"Excellent. I shall be at Hargreaves for at least another two weeks, depending on circumstance."

Nat noticed Max glance at his sister before he continued.

"You are welcome to stay as long as you like."

"Thank you, Max. If I can absorb some of the basic knowl-edge I need it will be a weight off my mind. Uncle Henry is keen for me to look into ways of making the estate more efficient."

There was the scrape of a chair and Lady Wyndham stood up. "If you will excuse me, I'm rather tired. Goodnight."

Max rose and escorted his sister to the door. "You do look rather pale. Should I send for your maid?"

"No. I'm perfectly well, just tired." She turned on her heel and marched out.

Max looked almost sheepish for a moment but quickly recovered.

"I think the accident must have shaken Eliza up more than she would care to admit. I pray you will forgive her rather abrupt departure, Nat."

"Of course I will. I feel guilty because I was partly to blame for it. I hope she has no lasting ill effects."

Max nodded and started detailing some of the improvements they were making at Hargreaves. Nat tried to concentrate but the image of a pair of icy blue eyes kept intruding on his thoughts. Lady Eliza was angry at the invitation that much was clear. He forced his mind back to Max. He had more important things to worry about than what was ailing the wretched woman.

He relaxed as he listened to Max. He was a fount of knowledge. They had been chatting for some time when he noticed Uncle Henry nod forward over the table and then jerk upright.

"Would you like me to help you up to bed, Uncle? I'm sure Max will excuse us." He glanced at Max who nodded in agreement.

"I am rather tired. Don't bother to send for a footman, your arm will be sufficient."

They made slow but steady progress. Uncle Henry seemed much improved. Having company had lifted his mood. Nat opened the door of Uncle Henry's room to find his valet waiting for them. He helped his uncle into an armchair by the fire. The valet finished laying out Uncle Henry's nightgown and moved towards the dressing room.

Uncle Henry stopped him with a wave in Nat's direction. "I'll sit for a while and talk to my nephew, Blunt. Go and get your supper. I'll call for you when I need you."

Blunt bowed and went out.

"A good man, Blunt. Fusses too much mind. What do you think of Lady Eliza, Nat?"

Had his interest been so transparent? "I hardly know her but it's kind of her to come so far to visit you."

Uncle Henry gave a soft laugh. "Not one to give much away are you? She would be a good match for you, my boy."

Nat smiled and shook his head. "You're as bad as my grandfather. He was always trying to push me into the Ton and much good it did me. Aristocratic women are not for me."

Uncle Henry laughed out loud. "Care to tell me what happened?"

"Not really, I still cringe at the memory." Nat smiled. "On the other hand, if I tell you it might stop you matchmaking. Grandfather always told me to get myself invited to friends' houses in the holidays, apart from Christmas. He said it was because he was so busy but that wasn't the only reason. I think he paid someone a lot of money to get me in to a school for gentlemen."

Nat paused to add some wood to the fire. "It's getting chilly."

Uncle Henry sat back in his chair and allowed Nat to throw a blanket over his legs. "My father was much at fault, not recognising you. Mary and I tried so hard to make him see reason." He sighed. "She would have loved to help bring you up. It was your Uncle Charles's influence. Charles was not a nice man but he knew how to charm Father. I hate to think how much of the estate's coffers went into his pocket."

Nat put a hand on his arm. I told you not to fret about money. Grandfather left me a rich man and I have interests in several companies which bring in a good income. I'll soon be able to improve the estate with hard work."

Uncle Henry squeezed his hand. "I'm so glad I wrote to you. Now tell me what happened at friends' houses to make you wary of women."

Nat laughed. "I can see you're determined to have the whole story. I was just seventeen and I thought I was in love with a friend's sister. Her mother caught us together and the girl I thought loved me told her mother I had forced myself on her."

He hung his head. "The truth was she had tried to persuade me to take her virginity and I'd had the sense to refuse. Anyway, her mother had me thrown onto the roof of the next stagecoach home. Grandfather was furious and I was mortified. I vowed to stay away from society girls after that."

"That's a long time ago. Eliza is a lovely young lady."

"She is lovely but I think I would feel more comfortable with someone like a clergyman's daughter."

"Why is that?"

Nat sighed. "I don't want to risk marrying someone who is more interested in the title than they are in me. Aristocratic girls are brought up to care about nothing else."

"Even more reason to consider Eliza. She has never been ambitious for herself that I know of. She spends a lot of her spare time working for the charity her mother set up."

"What charity is that?"

"Can't remember what it's called but it runs an orphanage

37

and school in Hargreaves village."

Nat sat forward. "How interesting. I would love to set up a school in Overton."

Uncle Henry beamed at him. "There you are then. You're sure to have opportunities to get to know Eliza and judge for yourself. She deserves a good man like you after that scoundrel Miles Wyndham. I was glad when he was killed in a drunken brawl. Eliza's never been the same since her marriage."

Nat stroked his chin. So, she had been married to a drunken bully. Perhaps he had misjudged her?

Chapter Five

The next morning Eliza accepted breakfast in bed rather than face Major Overton. She couldn't feel comfortable in his company and yet she felt a strong tug of attraction to the wretched man. Alice arrived to tell her their carriage was ready.

"Thank you, Alice. Is Lord Overton up yet?"

"No, my lady. His valet said he was still asleep."

"I won't disturb him then."

She took a deep breath and followed the maid downstairs. She couldn't delay the moment of meeting Major Overton for ever. Sure enough he was waiting outside, talking to Max. He stepped forward to hand Eliza into the carriage before Max could. She gave him a tight smile and a nod of the head as she placed her hand in his. The heat of him burned through the fabric of her glove, taking her by surprise. She missed her footing and he caught her with both hands at her waist and lifted her into the carriage as if she weighed no more than a child. A flash of heat ran through her body and settled in her cheeks. With luck he wouldn't be able to see her blush, shadowed as she was by being inside the coach.

"Thank you. I'm clumsy this morning."

His deep voice flowed around her. "Think nothing of it, Lady

Eliza. It was my pleasure."

The words were polite but the smile he gave her set her teeth on edge. It was almost as if he knew the effect he had on her and was flirting with her. Her jaw tightened and she sank back against the squabs as Max saved her from the need to reply by engaging him in conversation.

"Your horse should be recovered in a couple of days. Why not ride over once he's fit and spend the day with us? I'll be able to give you a firm date for when my land agent is arriving by then."

They walked towards Max's horse and Eliza couldn't hear Major Overton's answer. She became aware of her maid's eyes on her. Jepson was riding on the seat beside the driver up front so they were alone.

"Ooh, my lady. Fancy being lifted into the air by Major Overton, all the maids at Overton Grange are a little in love with him."

"That will do, Alice. I hope I have more sense."

Alice gave her a sideways glance. Eliza pursed her lips and Alice subsided. All she needed was her maid trying to play matchmaker. She relaxed as the coach pulled away. Of course Alice had family in the area and would be pleased if she could stay nearby. She shouldn't have been so sharp with her. If her plan to buy Chesterton Court succeeded Alice would have her wish. In the meantime, how would she survive a week or two of Major Overton's unsettling presence at Hargreaves Hall? The idea was intolerable.

She stared out of the window but the passing scenery was a blur. Her instinctive reaction to Major Overton was disturbing. Even worse, after that ride with her in front of him it was clear he found her attractive. He said he was ready to settle

40

down and if so he would soon start looking for a wife. What if he decided to try and pay court to her? She closed her eyes and concentrated on calming her breathing. Her hands felt clammy. She could never trust her future to a man again. Major Overton would be out all day with Max but there would be the evening dinner to survive.

Eliza left her outdoor things with the butler when she arrived home and went along to the library in search of Max. If she could persuade him to help her deal with solicitors before she spoke to Augusta it would make it easier to put her plan into action. She was in luck. Max rose from his favourite sofa in front of the fire when she entered.

A smile lit up his face. "Come and get warm, Eliza. Let me get you a glass of port. You look a bit distracted."

"Thank you."

Eliza sank down on the sofa and held her hands to the fire. She stared into the flames. She had to bring Max around to her plan of setting up her own household. He returned with two glasses and handed one to her.

"Do you want to travel around the estates with us next week? I think Major Overton is taken with you. He seems a good sort to me and it would give you a chance to get to know him without fear of prying eyes."

Eliza gulped some of her port. "How many times do I have to say that I'm not interested in marrying again?"

"You're still getting over Mama's death but you'll soon feel differently."

Eliza ground her teeth together. "No I won't. I'm not going to risk ending up with another fortune hunter."

"I know I've said this before but not all men are fortune hunters. At least two of my friends sounded me out about you

41

before Mama died."

Eliza's eyes opened wide and her jaw dropped. "Really? I hope Peregrine Dempster wasn't one of them. He always used to hang around me."

"Certainly not. I should have put him to the rightabout before he could open his mouth. Two perfectly acceptable gentlemen have sought my permission to address you."

Eliza burst out laughing. "It's strange having you fend off my suitors considering you're a year younger than me. Some of your friends are lovely but most of them are still boys."

Major Overton wasn't a boy. How would she cope with spending weeks in the same household as him?

Max was watching her. "What is it, Eliza?"

Why should she have to explain herself? She was a grown woman. She shook her head. "Stop talking about Major Overton."

"I shouldn't say this, but you're my favourite sister. Lord we had some fun together running wild at Hargreaves didn't we. You were the brother I never had." He grinned at her. "Do you remember the time we climbed the big oak tree and dropped acorns on to old Pennyman?"

Eliza's lips twitched. "Lud, yes. I'll never forget the poor man's screams when his horse bolted. We should have thought of that. Mama was so mortified she invited him to stay for dinner."

"Yes, but we avoided having to talk to him when she banished us to our rooms."

Eliza laughed. "It wouldn't have been so funny if he had fallen off. When Papa heard about it he grounded us for a week."

Her smile faded. She was still shaken by the strength of her attraction to the major. How could she explain to Max the fear that shot through her if a man as much as looked at her?

"Stop trying to turn me up sweet. It won't make any difference."

Max captured her gaze. "I'm not trying to turn you up sweet, merely remind you how much I care about you. The last thing I want is for you to dwindle into an unmarried aunt. Come on, you can't deny you find Nat Overton attractive. So why not spend a week or two getting to know him?"

She tried another tack. "I don't see why he has to stay here. You could meet him at the farms. Augusta has already done her two month stint as my chaperone and Cathlay will arrive soon. He will be keen to get back to London. If she stayed here with me they would have to make separate travel arrangements."

Max sat back in his chair. "I can't uninvite Nat. You're a widow, not a green young girl and I'll be here. I don't see why you would need a chaperone."

Eliza gritted her teeth. There was only one thing for it if Max was determined to manoeuvre her into spending the days as well as the evenings in Major Overton's company. "I think it might be best if I go to London with Augusta next week after all."

Max gave her a sharp gaze but nodded. "I suppose I should be pleased. A pity though, I wouldn't think for a moment that Overton is a fortune hunter."

They were interrupted by the door opening to admit Augusta. Drat. Still she might as well talk to them both at once. Max stood and pulled up a chair for Augusta who smiled up at him. Eliza watched her with narrowed eyes. She looked pleased with herself. Had she overheard?

"Augusta, I've decided to go to London with you but don't

43

think I'm going to fall in with any plans to find me a husband."

"I never said I wanted to find you a husband."

Eliza raised her eyebrows. "You didn't need to. The others are as bad. I had a letter from Diana this morning inviting me to stay with them for the summer. I might have been tempted if she hadn't mentioned the widowed, Scottish earl they have coming for a long visit, complete with his two little children."

"You could fit in a season in London and summer in Scotland if you wanted to."

"No thank you. I was about to ask Max to instruct the family solicitor to buy Chesterton Court for me. I have a lot of friends around here so it's the perfect place to set up my own establishment. I'll only stop in London until that's done. In the meantime I think a change of scene might do me good."

Max sighed. "If buying Chesterton Court is truly what you want, Eliza then I will certainly speak to our lawyers."

Augusta gave her a bland smile. "You must do as you think best, Eliza. I shall be glad to have you in London for as long as you wish to stay." She turned towards Max. "I may be here for a while longer than we expected. Cathlay writes he has to stop off at one of his properties on the way down. He could be delayed for a few days."

That meant at least a week in Major Overton's company. A week of those intelligent grey eyes dissecting her. She had felt the evidence of his interest on the ride to Overton Grange. What if he wanted a serious dalliance? As Max had said, she was a widow. Beads of sweat dampened her forehead. She swallowed convulsively. Would he try and take what he wanted like Miles would have? Max answered Augusta but his voice was a long way away.

She straightened her spine. What was she thinking? He

would be mad to try and seduce her under her brother's roof. If he intended marriage then Max would probably encourage him. Panic threatened until Augusta's voice cut across her thoughts.

"Are you feeling quite the thing, Eliza? You have gone pale."

She snapped out of the spell and summoned a smile. "I'm perfectly well. I think I'm a little short on sleep that's all. I never sleep as well in a strange bed."

Augusta leaned towards her and caught her hand. "I promise I won't try and find you a husband, Eliza."

"Thank you." She ought to feel relieved, but men she had no interest in she could deal with. It was Major Overton who terrified her. He awakened feelings and needs she had thought long buried.

* * *

A quiet day at home did much to restore her spirits. The following morning, she was curled up in a chair reading a novel when Max strode into the library, still wearing his riding gear.

"You missed a great ride. Everything looks so much more cheerful with the sun out. I forgot it would leave you no mount trained to a side saddle, with Jemima retired, when I loaned out Jasper."

Eliza grimaced. "I can't even go out in the gig with Maisie injured. I'll ask Cathlay to look out for a horse for me when we go to London."

She glanced at Max and her mouth dropped open. "Why are you grinning at me like that?"

"Roberts has arrived early from Ireland. I've got a present for you. I didn't say anything in case he didn't have anything suitable. Come down to the stables with me and see for yourself."

Max's enthusiasm was infectious. Eliza threw a cloak around her shoulders and followed him, not even stopping to find sturdier shoes. When they reached the stables Max put a hand over her eyes and called out to the grooms.

"Bring her out."

"Ha ha, so it's a mare then."

There was a whinny and the sound of stamping hooves. Max removed his hand. The prettiest dapple grey mare she had ever seen pranced in front of her.

"Oh my. She's beautiful." She threw her arms around Max and hugged him to hide her tears. "Thank you my bestest of brothers. She's perfect."

Max laughed. "As I'm your only brother, that's not much of a compliment." He waved at the groom. "Walk her up and down for us if you would."

Eliza watched as the mare pranced along by the groom's side. "She's got a lovely action too."

A middle aged man emerged from the stables. "I can see you like her, my lady."

"She's wonderful, Mr Roberts. Which mare is she out of?"

"We didn't breed her, but Lord Hargreaves had asked me to bring a horse over for you. This one grew much taller than the owners expected. She was so pretty they still trained her to the side saddle but her size made it hard to sell her as a lady's mount." He smiled. "I didn't think that would be a problem for a skilled horsewoman like you."

"You made a good choice. She looks perfect. Spirited but good natured."

The groom brought the mare to a halt in front of them and

Eliza stepped forward to stoke her nose.

"My word you're beautiful. I'll call you Bella."

Bella's nose nudged at her arm and Eliza laughed. "I can see you are a spoilt young miss. Has anyone got a carrot?"

Bella nibbled delicately at the carrot Eliza held out on a flat palm. "I can't wait to ride you but I expect you'll need a few days rest first."

"We came here in easy stages, my lady, but yes I'd give her a couple of days before you take her out on a proper ride. You could trot her around the stable yard and along the drive tomorrow though."

"Thank you, Mr Roberts. I'll do that. What else have you brought?"

"A few assorted young horses and two bred by us which are up to Lord Hargreaves's weight. We didn't have a horse already trained for a lady. I was lucky to find the mare."

Eliza stroked Bella's neck before the groom took her back to the stables.

"I'm glad you did find her. Have you looked at the two for you, Max?"

"Not yet. Shall we have them out?"

"Yes please."

Max laughed. "You always were much more interested in horses than me. You can tell me which you think is the best."

Two grooms emerged from the stable block leading a large stallion apiece. They led them around the yard several times before returning them to the stables.

Max shrugged. "They both look good. I have no idea which one to choose."

Eliza shook her head at him. "Honestly, Max. You're hopeless. The grey is a good horse but the chestnut is exquisite.

I expect he is fast."

Mr Roberts nodded agreement. "Yes he is. I don't think there was a horse to beat him in Ireland. The grey is a perfectly acceptable mount but you would be well advised to have the chestnut, my lord."

"Perhaps you're right. I'll think about it. We'll see you for dinner at six o'clock, Mr Roberts. A friend of ours will be there. I've invited him to travel around with us. He's been in the army and has no idea of estate management."

Eliza walked back up to the house on Max's arm in a daze. Lud, she had forgotten Major Overton was spending the afternoon with them. He would be under the same roof soon, which didn't bear thinking about. What was Max saying?

He squeezed the hand resting on his arm. "Eliza, you haven't heard a word I've said have you? I sent a message over to Overton Grange telling Nat that Mr Roberts has arrived. I'm hoping he will be able to move over here today. I've been invited to stay with friends for a few weeks as soon as I'm free."

"Oh that's good. You'll get a change of scene too. I've felt guilty about tying you to Hargreaves. I was thinking about Bella. Thank you so much. I love her already." She summoned a smile.

Max gave her a quizzical look but let it go. They reached the house and Eliza excused herself to change her shoes. She ran up the stairs and slumped down on the bed as soon as she was sure Alice wasn't there. Her pulse thundered in her ears. She moistened dry lips with her tongue. The man hadn't exchanged more than polite conversation with her and she was terrified Major Overton might start to court her. Even if he wanted to, he couldn't try and seduce her with her family around. As long as she remained unmarried she was safe. So why did part of her want his advances, with an intensity that terrified her?

Chapter Six

Nat helped his uncle to a chair by the library fire. "Are you sure you'll be able to manage without me?"

"Of course I will. The staff can cope perfectly well for a few weeks. I feel so much better now I know the estate will be in good hands when I'm gone."

Nat smiled at him. "I hope that won't be for a long time. There is so much I don't know but Max Hargreaves is really helpful. I think I'll learn a lot from him and his agent."

"I'm sure you will. The Hargreaves are good neighbours. Eliza and Max have often taken pity on an old man and come over to see me." Uncle Henry's eyes danced. "You'll have a few days to get to know Eliza better at Hargreaves Hall."

Nat shook his head. "Uncle Henry I don't think for a minute she would be interested in me."

"I don't see why not." Uncle Henry smiled. "A splendid young man like you, fresh out of the army, will turn the heads of all the young women."

A rush of heat flooded Nat's cheeks and he looked away. It was time to change the subject. "I'm taking Bright with me. His father was a land agent and he's agreed to consider taking over when Hodge retires."

"I'm glad. I've enjoyed talking to him. He seems intelligent and might get bored as a groom."

"Oh he would. We'll go straight from Hargreaves Hall for that visit I promised my former captain. I'll try not to be away too long."

Uncle Henry caught his hand, with a reassuringly strong grip. "Hodge is happy to carry on until the autumn. Stay away as long as you like but don't forget to write."

"I won't. I had better be off."

They said their goodbyes and Nat made his way to the stables, where Bright was waiting for him with Max's spare horse already saddled up. Bright was quiet for the first part of the journey.

"Are you happy with my idea of training you up to take over as land agent?"

"I'm not sure. To my mind it's a small estate and even if you add to it there might not be enough for me to do."

"I know but I want you as my major-domo as well, amongst other things. I have this feeling our adventuring days are a long way from being over."

Bright grinned. "Your feelings are rarely wrong. That sounds much better. I don't mind doing the land agent bit as part of a bigger job. A good steward makes a huge difference to the people on an estate."

Nat turned in the saddle to look at him. "I saw so much suffering as a child. My grandfather always treated his workers well but some were ill-used. I trust you to always do the right thing and that means a lot to me. Thank you."

Max gave them a warm welcome when they arrived at Harg- reaves Hall. Nat couldn't resist looking all around the huge entrance hall in the hope of seeing Lady Wyndham. Max took them into the library and offered them a drink from the decanters laid out on a long side table. A novel was lying face down on a chair near the window and once again Nat found himself scanning the room.

A smile played around Max's lips. "My sisters have gone out to visit the squire and his wife. I'm not sure when they will be back but you'll see them at dinner."

Nat lowered his eyes. Could Max have noticed his interest in Lady Wyndham? "I'll look forward to it. I haven't found time to buy new clothes. I hope the Duchess won't object to me wearing my regimental evening dress?"

"Not at all. We're generally fairly informal at Hargreaves. My agent, Mr Roberts, will be joining us for dinner."

Nat grinned at Bright. "Mr Bright has agreed to take on the role as the Overton Land Agent in the autumn, so should we include him?"

Bright spluttered over his drink. "A duchess? I'll be much happier eating with the grooms."

Max grinned at him. "You might as well get used to your promotion straight away, Mr Bright. Mr Roberts often dines with us when he's in residence, as do his assistants."

Nat clapped Bright on the shoulder. "That's agreed then."

Bright glowered at them but said nothing.

"Come and have a look at the horses Roberts has brought over from Ireland. There are two for me to choose from. He'll sell the other one if you're interested, Nat. Your Caesar has recovered well but I remember you said you were looking for a spare."

Nat laughed. "Of course I'm interested. Finding a suitable horse when you're tall like us isn't easy."

Max introduced them to Roberts, who was in the stables,

checking on the new horses. "Major Overton is interested in buying one of the horses you brought for me to choose from."

Roberts nodded. "They've travelled well. I'll have the grooms walk them around the yard for you."

Bright checked over the horses with interest. "Two excellent horses, Major." He looked across at Max. "You'll want the chestnut, Lord Hargreaves. He's exceptional."

"That leaves Major Overton with two greys. I'm not worried about having the best one if you would prefer the chestnut. I'm sure either will suit my purposes. Eliza is the one who loves horses."

Nat studied the chestnut. "I'd love him but that doesn't seem fair."

Max shrugged. "Truly, I'm happy with the grey."

"In that case I'm happy to pay whatever Mr Roberts wants for him."

Bright stepped forward, shaking his head. "I might as well start work straight away, Major. That is not the way to negotiate buying a horse. Leave it for me and Mr Roberts to sort out."

Nat laughed. "I will, but don't lose him for the sake of a few guineas."

One of the grooms caught Roberts' attention. "Have you brought a side saddle with you, Mr Roberts? If not we can see if we've got one of the right size for Lady Wyndham's new horse."

"Yes, there is one for her. Bring her out would you."

The groom strode off and returned with a dapple grey mare that looked too tall for a lady's mount but then Lady Wyndham was a tall lady, exactly the right height to suit him. Where had that thought come from?

Bright walked forward to inspect the mare. "What a beauty, Mr Roberts."

The grooms took the horses back into the stables. Bright and Roberts followed, chatting as if they had known each other for years.

Nat laughed. "They seem to be getting on well. I'm glad I've persuaded Bright to take on the job. His father was a land agent and his skills would be wasted as a groom for all he loves horses. What a lovely mare."

"Eliza was thrilled with her. We had to retire her old horse and she's been riding Jasper but I wanted to buy her a new mount. Roberts did well to find Bella."

"Isn't Jasper the horse you lent me?"

"Yes he's a versatile old chap, quite happy with a side saddle."

"I feel guilty that I've deprived her of a horse."

"Think nothing of it. It's only been a short while. To tell you the truth she was a bit shaken up by her accident. It's only today that she would have ridden."

Nat coughed to ease the sudden tightness of his throat. "I feel awful about the accident. I wish there was some way I could make it up to her."

Max moved closer. "Perhaps you'll think of something."

Nat's collar felt too tight as Bright joined him, ready to go down to dinner. They descended the impressive staircase and a liveried footman directed them to the drawing room where the family gathered for dinner. Bright immediately spotted Roberts and went across to talk to him. It was good the two were getting on well but he could have done with some support. An older version of Lady Wyndham stepped forward to greet him. It might be easier if he pretended she was his colonel's wife.

"Delighted to meet you, Major Overton. I'm The Duchess of Cathlay, the eldest of the Lovell clan."

"Your Grace." Nat went into a deep bow.

As he straightened up, Max entered with Lady Wyndham on his arm. She looked a vision in deep blue velvet. He heard a gasp and realised it was from him. Heat flooded his cheeks when he noticed the Duchess watching him. Lord, if she thought he was interested in her sister would she take against him? He risked another glance at her but her bland expression gave nothing away. Max stopped in front of them and Nat bowed again.

"Lady Wyndham. I trust I find you fully recovered?"

Her smile didn't reach her eyes, which she quickly lowered. "I'm well thank you, Major Overton."

The Duchess led the way into the dining room and Nat found himself seated between the two sisters. The Duchess proved to be surprisingly good company. But then Uncle Henry had said she was an accomplished hostess. He found himself telling her a lot about his military career. Her interest in him seemed genuine. He turned towards Lady Wyndham and made a determined effort at conversation. Her answers were brief and she avoided any eye contact. She was determined to freeze him out it would seem. He remembered Max mentioning her love of horses.

"We had a look at the horses Mr Roberts brought with him. Your new mare is absolutely beautiful. I can see why you have called her Bella."

Her expression became more animated and she finally met his gaze. "She's lovely and seems good natured."

He laughed. "We didn't see her for long but she showed no sign of any vices. On the other hand she appeared lively."

Lady Wyndham went bright red. Oh Lord. She was remembering his ill-judged remark about her lack of driving skills. His own cheeks went hot.

"Max tells me you are an expert horsewoman. I'm sure you'll be able to handle her."

Her eyebrows shot up. "You consider me better at riding than driving then."

He opened his mouth to apologise for his boorishness on their first encounter but Max spoke before he could.

"Bella's the perfect horse for Eliza."

"Thank you, Max. She's perfect."

The Duchess finished a conversation with Mr Roberts and turned towards them. "I must remember to have a look at Bella tomorrow. She sounds wonderful. Shall we leave the gentlemen to their port, Eliza?"

Nat allowed himself a minute or two to watch them leave. Lady Wyndham was as beautiful as her new mare but his uncle's hope of a match between them was wishful thinking. She couldn't have made it plainer that she wasn't interested in him. He heard Bright ask Roberts if he had any more horses for sale.

"There are a few young riding horses. What horses do you need at Hargreaves, my lord?"

"Three riding horses for the grooms I'm told. I don't suppose any of them could be trained to pull a gig?"

Roberts pursed his lips. "There is a sturdy bay with a good temperament which might be suitable."

"Good, we'll keep that one and pick out what the grooms want. The rest are for sale, Mr Bright."

"The stables are a bit depleted at Overton Grange." Bright glanced towards Nat.

Nat grinned. "You buy whatever you think. I'll leave you to instruct my man of business as usual."

Bright nodded. "If Mr Roberts is agreeable we'll go and talk to the head groom and get it done."

Nat shook his head as the two of them left the room. "For someone who had to be persuaded to take the job as my land agent and major-domo, Bright seems enthusiastic." He laughed. "It could have waited until tomorrow but I expect he wanted to get out of tea with the ladies."

"Roberts is in awe of Augusta. I wonder if they cooked the scheme up between them. Let's go and claim our cups of tea."

Nat followed Max into a sumptuous drawing room, decorated in golden shades with a thick Aubusson carpet covering the middle of the floor.

"Are we in time for tea? Major Overton is something of a connoisseur."

The Duchess waved them to chairs near to the tea tray. "It's quite fresh."

She poured out two cups and Max brought them over. Nat thanked him. He glanced up to see Lady Wyndham studying him. She blushed and looked away. Was she quite as indifferent to him as she had appeared? Unless she was unusually bashful, unlikely from a family like this, had she been deliberately keeping him at bay? He sipped at his tea. If she had then she must think him beneath her. Something he was used to.

The Duchess smiled at him. "Have you always liked tea, Major Overton?"

"Yes, ever since I was a small boy. It was my mother's favourite drink. She died when I was ten and I find drinking tea reminds me of her."

"How sad to lose your mother so young. I understand your father is no longer with us either."

Nat sighed. "He also died when I was ten. My grandfather brought me up."

This time Lady Wyndham answered. "Oh how awful for you." She blushed. "To lose both your parents so young I mean."

He felt himself stiffen. Grandfather hadn't been perfect but he had done his best and deserved respect. "My grandfather was a good man. Of course I missed my parents but a lot of people suffer far worse."

She caught his gaze. "I know. The school Mama set up in the village has an orphanage wing. We've had children arrive in terrible states."

He relaxed. It seemed she hadn't meant any insult. "If there's time, I would like to visit the school. I have a mind to set up something of the sort in Overton."

"Didn't you say you were going to spend the morning there tomorrow to confirm the appointment of the new schoolteacher, Eliza?" The Duchess asked.

Lady Wyndham glanced towards her brother. "Don't you have rather a full schedule, Max?"

"There is a lot to get through but I need to sign some paperwork for Roberts in the morning. What are you like with a curricle, Overton?"

Nat glanced around. Lady Wyndham looked irritated but Max and The Duchess were looking at him expectantly. "I'm more used to riding in recent years but I've driven my own carriage since I was twelve."

"My greys are a bit frisky but I'm sure you can handle them. I was going to let Eliza have a go with them since she hasn't had a chance to drive since the other day. See how you go with them. Perhaps she can drive back."

Lady Wyndham looked decidedly unhappy. Was it the thought of going with him or Max's lack of tact in implying that she couldn't handle his greys when they were fresh?

"I'm entirely at your disposal, Lady Wyndham."

She gave him a ghost of a smile. "Thank you, Major Overton. The curricle will be ready for us at nine."

Chapter Seven

Eliza walked down the stairs to the hall at exactly nine o'clock. Major Overton was waiting by the door deep in conversation with Max. What a day yesterday had been. Finding out that Chesterton Court wasn't coming on the market until the autumn at the earliest had been a blow. The squire's wife was rarely wrong about such things. Then there had been Major Overton to deal with. Her body tingled in long forgotten places at the memory of his open admiration when she had walked in to the drawing room before dinner. Max and Augusta had seen for sure. Now she had ended up with Major Overton's company all morning how would she cope if he tried to fix her interest?

Both men looked up as she reached the last few stairs. She pinned a smile on her face and walked across to join them.

"Good morning. Don't expect to see us back before midday at the earliest, Max. I have a lot to do at the school and orphanage before I leave. Augusta isn't sure when we will see Cathlay. It's best I deal with everything I need to today."

Max nodded. "Take as long as you want. Once we've finished all the paperwork Mr Roberts can spend some time with Mr Bright."

Major Overton chuckled. "Bright will find it hard to get used to being called Mr Bright. He took a job as a groom rather than let his father train him as a steward. I'm not sure how he ended up in the army but I was glad he agreed to leave with me."

"Roberts is impressed with him, Nat. Right, I had better go and sign all these papers."

Major Overton offered his arm and Eliza placed her hand through it. He drew her closer to his side and the wholesome scent of soap and warm male made her catch her breath. Miles had favoured heavy cloying colognes that had lingered on her clothing. A sigh escaped her. Why was she noticing such things? She knew nothing about the man and she didn't want another marriage. He didn't appear to have heard her sigh and he led her through the door opened by the butler himself. Everyone in the house seemed to be treating him as an honoured guest, which was another reason she found him so annoying.

A groom pulled the curricle up at the bottom of the steps. The horses snorted and stamped at this restriction of their freedom. Her eyes widened. Max was right about them being frisky. Major Overton put his hands around her waist and lifted her into it. Had no one told him the polite method was to give a lady a helping hand, not manhandle her? She watched as he walked to the horses' heads and stroked their noses until they calmed down.

"Can you hold them whilst I climb up, Lady Wyndham?"

Eliza shuddered at the memory of spinning through the air into the ditch with the gig thudding into the ground behind her. She squared her shoulders.

"Of course."

Major Overton walked around to the groom's side of the curricle. "Hand the reins over and wait until the horses are settled before you jump down."

Eliza accepted the reins, determined to prove that she wasn't about to let the greys take off with her. After a brief tussle and some soothing words from her they stood reasonably still. Even so Eliza felt a stab of fear as the groom jumped down. For such a big man Major Overton proved surprisingly agile. He was in the seat beside her before her fear could communicate itself to the horses. She handed him the reins with lowered eyes, so that he wouldn't see her relief. It was the first time she had been in a carriage since the accident; she would soon regain her confidence.

When she eventually looked up he was studying her face. She stiffened waiting for him to criticise her, as Miles would have done, but he said nothing. The gateman saw them coming and had the main gate open for them. They sailed through and Eliza waved her thanks.

"The village isn't far. Turn left at the crossroads and it's about two miles. The school is near to the church."

"Thank you. It's a lovely day to be out."

Major Overton gave the greys their heads when they turned onto the road. Eliza watched his hands as he fed out some rein through long fingers. The horses settled down quickly.

"Yes it's a good day to visit the school. I'll arrange a tour for you, including the outdoor activities."

"I will enjoy that. Do you mind telling me about it?"

Eliza studied his profile. He gave every appearance of being genuinely interested.

"Mama set up the school when she first came to Hargreaves. The orphanage came later when the local blacksmith was killed, leaving four young children with no relatives. He'd lost his wife when the youngest was born." She smiled "The eldest, Tommy, now runs the blacksmiths. Mama arranged an apprenticeship for him a few miles away when he was old enough."

Major Overton slowed the horses down when a farm cart came into view. He pulled them out to overtake as soon as they came to a straight stretch of clear road. There was no denying he was an excellent whip. But then he seemed to do everything with ruthless efficiency. That included charming people wherever he went. Even Augusta had been taken with him.

"What about the other three?"

"One of the girls married a farmer. The other one worked at Hargreaves as a housemaid and is now the housekeeper. The youngest was one of Mama's triumphs. He was clever with his books and is a lawyer now."

Major Overton's face lit up. "My grandfather started out as a shipwright's apprentice and ended up as a successful business man. It's good to hear of children being given opportunities to advance. I imagine a project like this takes a lot of organising."

Eliza stared at him. He sounded so sincere. It seemed there was a lot more to him than she had thought. The church came into view.

"Turn left past the church." She found herself smiling at him. "It does but I have a good team running the school and the orphanage. All the children from the estate have to go to the school. A few of them have gone into the professions. The rest have had opportunities to train for trades."

She directed him through the gates of the school and around to the back of the building. A team of fresh faced young boys ran out, followed by an older man who raised his cap to Eliza.

"Good morning, Lady Wyndham. I see you've brought His

Lordship's greys for us to practice on."

"We certainly have, Mr Brewer. This is Major Overton, a friend of my brother."

The men exchanged greetings and Major Overton offered to help with the horses. Brewer held the horses' heads for him to climb down. He held up his hand to her and helped her down in the manner of a gentleman, almost as if he had read her earlier thoughts. Eliza kept her eyes lowered so he wouldn't see her hot cheeks.

"Perhaps you would show Major Overton the outside areas, Mr Brewer. I'll arrange for someone to show him around the school and orphanage afterwards." She glanced across at the Major and smiled. "He would like to set up something similar at Overton."

He smiled back at her. If he had invented his interest to obtain time with her, he was hiding it well.

"Thank you, Lady Wyndham."

She nodded and made her way to the school entrance. Perhaps he wasn't a fortune-hunter, she hoped not for Lord Overton's sake, but he hadn't tried to hide an interest in her despite her best efforts to put him off.

He might be a coxcomb, but Eliza, he loved that name, seemed to be showing signs of being attracted to him. She had blushed vividly when he picked her up and placed her in the curricle, so she wouldn't have time to get nervous on her first drive after her accident. He could swear she looked disappointed when he handed her down very properly in the schoolroom yard. So why was she doing her utmost to avoid spending any more time with him than she had to?

He followed Brewer around the stables, followed by the work

rooms where the older boys made furniture and the girls sewed dresses. Everything was well set out and the quality of the children's work was excellent. No one who was so involved with a project like this and spoke proudly of village children joining the professions would worry about his connections to trade would they? It seemed unlikely but then she was the daughter of a marquess. He forced his mind away from the puzzle that was Lady Eliza Wyndham and went to inspect a table and chairs more thoroughly.

"There is some excellent work going on here, Mr Brewer. What happens to the children after they leave school?"

"Some children come from the families of tenant farmers and will use the skills they've gained in their family farms. They learn how to keep accounts as well as reading and writing in the school. Others will be helped to find apprenticeships. The boy who made these has secured a place with a master carpenter who makes furniture for the gentry. A lot of the village children will find jobs in service. Lord Hargreaves's steward always looks here first when they have vacancies at the hall."

"It's impressive. Do many children go into the professions?"

Mr Brewer smiled. "We have one or two every year."

A tall young woman came up to them. "I'm Miss Pinner, one of the teachers. Are you ready for a tour of the school now, Major Overton?"

Nat thanked Mr Brewer and followed Miss Pinner across the yard to the school house. He caught a glimpse of Lady Wyndham talking to the teacher in one of the classrooms. It seemed she wasn't going to escort him personally. Miss Pinner was thorough and by the time he was taken into the staffroom and offered refreshments his head was spinning. He almost spilled his tea in surprise when Eliza joined them. He must think of her as Lady Wyndham or he would start calling her Eliza by mistake.

She gave him a tight smile. "What do you think, Major Overton?"

"I'm amazed at the opportunities you are providing for the children. I will have to start on a much smaller scale but I'm even more determined to set up a school in Overton."

Lady Wyndham accepted a cup of tea from Miss Pinner. "I'm glad to hear it. Some of the boys are asking if you could give them a talk on what it's like in the army."

"I can certainly do so. They might be disappointed though. Life in the army is much harder than most young men realise and nowhere near as exciting. I would be wrong not to explain that to them."

She nodded. "That would be wise. So often in life we go into things without thinking through potential consequences."

Her expression seemed to harden but she turned away and he couldn't get a clear look at her face. Was she talking from personal experience? Uncle Henry had said her marriage had been a bad one. When she looked at him again her smile was less forced. Perhaps he had read too much into her remark?

"I'll give them an idea of the good and bad things about army life and leave them to make up their own minds."

"Thank you. I imagine it's much harder for enlisted men than for commissioned officers."

Nat thought for a moment. "In many ways it is much harder for common soldiers. That said I found the weight of responsibility heavy at times. I don't think I could have achieved so much without the help of Bright. The best batman anyone could have. Let me have a few minutes to gather my thoughts and I'll do my best to enlighten them as to what to expect."

The talk went well. Several boys changed their mind and went out with a teacher. A handful stayed behind and Nat asked for questions. A tall, red haired boy put up his hand.

"Which regiments would you recommend and how do we enlist?"

"The best ones for you will depend on your interests. Those of you who are experienced with horses might prefer a cavalry regiment, which is what I was in. Those can be harder to get into. I'll leave a forwarding address with Lord Hargreaves. If you any of you are still determined when you've had time to think about it, I'll make enquiries for you."

A ripple of conversation went around the boys until Lady Wyndham silenced them.

"Boys where are your manners?"

The red-haired boy spoke up. "Thank you, Major Overton. We would appreciate that."

Lady Wyndham dismissed the boys after a few more general questions. They said goodbye to the staff and one of the boys was sent to the stables to arrange for the curricle to be brought around. She placed her hand through the arm he offered and gave him the most natural smile he had seen from her.

"Thank you so much, Major Overton. What a brilliant insight into army life. Jeremy Carter, the red-haired boy, seems more determined than ever. His mother is a soldier's widow. I don't suppose she will share his enthusiasm."

Nat sighed. "I'm sure she won't. How old is he?"

"Nearly eighteen. We have been paying him as an assistant teacher for the last couple of years."

"The boy seems intelligent. If he is determined to join up is there no one in his family who could buy him a commission? He would make a much better officer than some of the men who have served under me."

"I'll talk to Max about him. Mama set up a fund for boys who have the intelligence to go into a profession."

She looked so much more animated than he had seen her before. Nat smiled at her until she bit her lip and looked away. The curricle arrived and he concentrated on keeping her talking about the school. She would be able to handle the greys, now they'd had the edge taken off them, as long as she stayed relaxed. He would feel terrible if her accident put her off driving. They waved goodbye to Mr Brewer and the boys helping him. Nat carried on asking questions until he had the horses settled on a straight stretch of road.

He held the reins towards her. "I nearly forgot you were going to drive us back."

Lady Wyndham hesitated for a second but then took them from him. He caught his breath as her hands brushed his. Once he could see she was comfortable with driving he sat back in his seat.

"Thank you so much for allowing me to join you today. It's been a great pleasure."

"Thank you, Major Overton."

The drive was over far too quickly. Max was waiting for them when they arrived at the stables. A groom took the reins and another ran to their head. Max helped Lady Wyndham down. Nat jumped out and followed them to the house. Lady Wyndham disappeared at a summons from her sister and Max ushered him into the library.

"I'm glad you helped Eliza to drive again."

"It was the least I could do after causing her accident. She's an excellent whip."

"Oh, she is and quite strong for a woman, which is why I feel as much to blame as you. I'm sure she would have kept Maisie under control if she'd been concentrating. Now we have work to do. Roberts has suggested we go and spend a couple of days on the small estate I added recently. He has set up some farming experiments he wants to demonstrate."

Once Mr Roberts had finished going through new farming theory with them Nat was more than ready for his dinner. Lady Wyndham was less frosty than she had been the night before but the easy conversation of the afternoon had gone. When they went to join the ladies in the drawing room after dinner the Duchess handed a piece of paper to Max.

"A messenger delivered this earlier. Cathlay expects to be with us in the next day or so after all."

Max burst out laughing and handed the note back to his sister. "Cathlay wants me to take up my seat in the Lords. Tell him I will, but not this summer. I've a friend in Edinburgh where I'll conclude my summer travels. I've a mind to go and visit Diana before I return."

The Duchess shook her head at him. "I don't know why Cathlay keeps trying."

They fell into conversation and Nat seized the opportunity to join Lady Wyndham on a seat near to the window. He pulled up a stool so he could sit closer to her.

"Thank you for letting me accompany you today, Lady Wyndham. I'm determined to start something similar at Overton. My grandfather set up an orphanage and treated all his workers well. I'm sure he would approve."

There was no reply and he glanced across to see her looking down at her hands, clasped tightly in her lap. She had seemed so much more approachable earlier but he couldn't stop himself plunging on.

"I was hoping you would lend me a hand once you're back at Hargreaves." He smiled at her. "I enjoyed your company this afternoon. We didn't have the best of introductions but I would very much like us to be friends."

Her eyes flew to his face and there was tension in every line of her body. She would snap in two if she sat up any straighter.

"I'm sure we will find ourselves in the same company occasionally but it simply won't be possible for us to be friends, Major Overton. We would soon be the subject of ill-bred gossip if we were seen about together. Not something I would enjoy I can assure you." Her cheeks went pink and she seemed to be quivering with indignation. "I can certainly put in a word for you with Squire Meredith and his wife who live in the next village to Overton. A pleasant couple and they welcome all and sundry to call. Mrs Meredith would be delighted to help you set up a school I'm sure."

Nat caught his breath. Of all the ill-mannered, spoilt young women he had met it seemed Lady Wyndham was the worst. It was a moment before he could speak.

"I would appreciate that." He rose and gave her a stiff bow.

So that was the way of it. It must have been the mention of his grandfather in trade that had upset her. It was his age-old problem. He was neither fish nor fowl and it was always the women who were bothered by his mother's family. He schooled his features into some kind of order and went over to sit by Max. The Duchess handed them both a cup of tea with a smile.

"There you are, Major. Max tells me you are quite a tea

drinker."

Before he could answer, Lady Wyndham walked past.

"You will have to excuse me. I have developed a headache. I'll wish you all goodnight." She nodded in their direction and swept out of the room.

The Duchess sat next to him and engaged him in conversation. She seemed as friendly as her sister had been forbidding. They chatted for some time until she was ready to retire.

"It's been delightful to meet you, Major Overton. I'm sure we'll see a lot more of you in the future now you're settled at Overton."

"I hope so. Thank you for such a warm welcome to the district, Your Grace."

"My pleasure, Major Overton. Enjoy the rest of your stay with Max."

Max invited him to the library for a nightcap.

Nat settled into a leather chair and sipped at the port Max gave him. "Hm. Your father certainly knew his port."

"Yes, he did, but I'll have to start searching for more supplies soon."

"I can help you with that. I've promised to stay with an old army friend of mine for a week or two, once I've checked on Uncle Henry. He's something of an expert and between us we made some good contacts on the continent. Would you like to be included when he ships some supplies in for us?"

Max leaned back in his chair. "Now that is an offer I can't refuse. I'll take whatever he can spare, port and wine, if they are anywhere near as good as father's."

"They will be, trust me. Enstone won't buy anything substandard."

Max sat up with a snap. "Viscount Enstone? Do you mean

71

Luke Bamfield?"

"Yes, that's him. He came into the title recently and we sold out together. You know him then?"

"Not well, he's a few years older than me, but I remember him from school. Good man, he always had plenty of friends."

Nat laughed. "He's a good friend of mine. We had some adventures together in the army and not all of them bad."

"When you see him, give him my condolences for the loss of his father. I'll look him up myself later in the year."

"Of course."

"Thank you. I expect to be away for several weeks on a tour of friends, once I'm happy everything is in order with the estates. I may end with a visit to our sister Diana, so it could be months. I don't want to miss out on these wines. My secretary will sort out delivery and payment for any shipments whilst I'm away. I'll brief him."

They soon went up to bed but Nat didn't feel much like sleep. He found his dressing gown and threw a couple of logs on the remains of the fire. Lady Wyndham had put him back in his box in no uncertain terms. It was plain that the taint of trade was too much for her. He was beneath her as a potential spouse but she would mix with him as a neighbour, in the same way that she mixed with the squire and his wife. No matter what Uncle Henry and Luke said, he was never going to be fully accepted into high society. The sooner he accepted his place in the world the better.

Chapter Eight

The journey to London seemed interminable. Eliza was glad when both of the Cathlays fell into a doze after their stop for luncheon. Trying to maintain her end of conversations had left her with the beginnings of a headache. She had been so rude to Major Overton after dinner that she couldn't shake off a sense of guilt. The poor man had looked quite stricken for a moment until anger kicked in. She hardened her heart. Perhaps he was a fortune hunter like Miles and his pockets were well and truly to let. He was probably upset at losing what he might have thought of as an easy target.

A sigh escaped her. If he wasn't a fortune hunter then she had deeply offended an honest man who happened to be the nephew of a very old friend. In which case she was sorry for it but she had to make it plain she wasn't interested. Less painful to find out sooner rather than later surely? She could have been kinder but from what she had seen of him anything other than a ruthless snub might not have been enough to put him off. Better to be thought an insufferable snob than have him think he had a chance with her. It was a relief not to have to worry about fending him off.

Eliza knew the route to London well and was surprised to feel a surge of elation as they reached the outskirts. There was something exhilarating about the noise and sheer bustle of Town. The coach pulled up to wait for a wagon trying to manoeuvre out of a side street without spilling any of its tottering cargo of vegetables. The driver completely ignored all the shouts and raised fists aimed at him and set off at a steady pace as soon as he had straightened up. Two little boys ran across, to the sound of more shouts, to pick up the few items that had become dislodged.

Eliza laughed out loud at the scene. "I can never understand why people are so impatient. The poor man is only doing his job."

Augusta caught her hand. "I knew a spell in London was just what you needed. Cathlay are you dining at your club this evening? Eliza and I need a quiet night at home together to plan our campaign of amusements."

The Duke of Cathlay laid down the book he was reading. "If you wish, my dear. Far be it from me to interfere in such an important enterprise." He glanced at Eliza and smiled, taking any offence from his words.

"Thank you. It's of the utmost importance that Eliza has an enjoyable stay."

The Duke's expression became serious. "It is indeed. I hope to see her sparkle back in short order. As it happens it will suit me to visit Brooks today. There are some important bills coming up and there is bound to be someone there to discuss them with."

"Are there any I would be interested in?" Eliza asked.

"There are some you might want to follow. I could arrange for you to watch a debate or two from the Ladies' Gallery if you like."

"Yes, please. It must be fascinating to be involved with

government."

He sighed. "I wish your brother had half your interest. I've had no luck trying to persuade him to take up his seat."

"For all his outward confidence I believe the responsibility of the Hargreaves estates still weighs heavily with him."

Augusta nodded in agreement. "That's true and the business with Lavinia made things awkward for him socially. I'm glad you decided to come with us. Max wouldn't have left you had you stayed at Hargreaves and it would have been a shame for him to turn down his friends' invitations."

Eliza lay back against the squabs. Lud, she hadn't thought about what was best for Max. Augusta was right, he would have insisted on staying with her. Perhaps it was as well she had been hounded away by Major Overton's visit. It might not be so bad after all. Now she was older she might be invited to the political salons some of Cathlay's colleague's wives ran. Then there were all the theatres and museums. If she avoided the balls, she might even enjoy herself.

The butler left them to their dinner, closing the door behind him. Augusta put down her fork and smiled at Eliza.

"Now we have got rid of Cathlay we can have a proper talk."

"What is it you want to talk about?"

"I hope you will tell me what troubles you, Eliza. I know something does."

Eliza shook her head.

Augusta took one of her hands in both of hers. "I know you still miss Mama. It must have been so hard for you staying at Hargreaves with her. No one could have been a more dutiful daughter."

"I didn't only stay for Mama. After Miles it was the only place where I felt safe. I don't want to have to deal with potential fortune hunters." She hesitated. "I don't want to marry again. I absolutely don't. At Chesterton Court I would have all my friends around me and I've got plans to open another charity school. I'd be close to Max too. Moving hundreds of miles away from Hargreaves has never appealed to me.

"Overton Grange isn't too far from Hargreaves." A smile played around the corners of Augusta's mouth. "Major Overton seemed such a gentleman."

Eliza's hands went to her cheeks. "Especially not Major Overton."

"Have you taken him in aversion?"

Eliza scowled. "I don't trust him after the way he has become friends with Max so quickly."

"I can't blame him for being eager to make friends with Max. He has responsibilities to the Overton estates and all the people who rely on them for their living. Neighbours can help each other so much."

"I know but I've seen the way he looks at me sometimes when he thinks I'm not looking." Tears stung at her eyes and she lowered her head.

Augusta gasped. "Was your marriage so very bad, my darling? Are you frightened of remarrying?"

All Eliza could do was nod. Why hadn't she run home as soon as she discovered her husband's true nature? Her damned pride had kept her with Miles. She couldn't risk going through that again.

Augusta sat next to her and put an arm around her shoulders. "Most people I know are perfectly happy. You were unlucky. I'm here if you want to talk about it."

"I can't and I wish you would all leave me to make my own

decisions."

Eliza walked over to the window and peered out at the street below. If she concentrated hard enough on the people scurrying past perhaps the image of Miles's leering face would leave her.

"I'm sorry, Eliza. I don't want to upset you. I don't want you to miss out on the sort of happiness I have in my marriage, that's all."

"I know you six have all been fortunate but I don't believe many women are. You can't know what goes on behind closed doors. Besides why should I risk it? I'm rich enough to take charge of my own future."

"I think Cathlay is right. You need more time to recover from Mama's death. The distractions of London will make you feel better. Don't worry about suitors. Cathlay will send them all off until you're ready."

Eliza shook her head. "I'm not going to change my mind."

Augusta smiled. "We'll see."

They spent the next few days shopping and fitted in visits to an art gallery and a museum. Eliza was grateful to Augusta for giving her time to settle down before the inevitable rounds of socialising started. Once some of their new clothes had been delivered, Augusta declared them fit to be seen.

"That is the prettiest of your morning dresses." Augusta waved Alice away as she moved towards them at a signal from Eliza. "Leave it on, dearest. I've had a message from a dear friend. We may as well start our morning calls with her."

Eliza sighed. "If you wish. Thank you, Alice, that will be all for now."

Alice slipped out and Augusta gave Eliza a hug.

77

"Don't look so glum. You met Theodosia Grant before Mama became ill and you got on well."

Eliza wrinkled her nose. "I remember. She was great fun."

"Her sister died young and she did a lot of the raising of her nephew and niece. She is bringing her niece out this season and asks that you will meet her with a view to becoming friends. The girl is nearly twenty. Her come out was delayed because of the loss of her father. Theo says she is finding it hard to settle in London."

Eliza felt a surge of sympathy. "I can understand that. It must be difficult for her after losing her father."

"Very true. It's hard enough for us coming here for the first time without Mama. I was thinking we could call in at Hatchards afterwards. There is something so cheering about buying some new books."

Eliza gave Augusta's hand a squeeze. "I'm sorry I've been so difficult it's hard for all of us."

Augusta's expression softened. "I have Cathlay's support. If you find the girl agreeable, we could invite her to Hatchards and even back here for luncheon. I imagine she is in sore need of a friend."

"Indeed. What's her name?"

Augusta pulled a sheet of scented notepaper from her reticule. "Here we are, Grace Bamfield. Her brother is Luke Bamfield, now Viscount Enstone." Augusta smiled. "I believe he is in his late twenties."

Eliza burst out laughing. "I expect you are also going to tell me he is unmarried, rich, handsome, and looking for a wife."

"I have no idea but he certainly won't be a fortune hunter if you should take a fancy to him." Augusta smiled. "You are much more mature than you were when you met Miles. You won't be taken in by someone like him again."

"I'm not afraid of falling for a fortune hunter's schemes. It's the nuisance of keeping them at bay that bothers me. It requires a lot of mental energy." She glanced at the floor. When it was a man as attractive as Major Overton it was positively exhausting.

"I don't want you to marry just anyone but don't cut yourself off from happiness with the right man. Even if a man's fortune isn't equal to yours it doesn't always mean that is what he sees in you."

"I don't seem to attract many who aren't after my money."

"You are an attractive woman and if a genuine admirer is too timid to try his luck because he has less money than you then he doesn't deserve you. Don't freeze all men out. If it reassures you, Cathlay is happy to have any suitors you are interested in investigated."

"That's kind of him."

Augusta left to don her outdoor clothes.

Eliza dropped onto a sofa. She had every intention of freezing men out and eventually Augusta and the others would have to accept it.

Nat threw yet another neck cloth on the floor. He was no good at this fashionable gentleman business. Luke's valet, Garner, came in and sighed.

Nat grinned at him. "Go on tell me I'm doing it all wrong even after all your instruction."

"Believe it or not you're nearly there."

Garner handed him another starched cloth and this time he took it slower. Between them they achieved an effect the valet was satisfied with. He stood back and studied the end result.

"That simple style suits you, Major."

"It didn't feel simple but I'll take your word for it."

"Now for your coat." The valet picked it up and stroked the fabric. "If I may say so you have chosen well with this. Lovely bit of merino."

Nat eyed the dark grey coat. "It doesn't look big enough. The tailor suggested I was wearing my coats too loose."

It took both of them to get him into it but the valet assured him it would give with wear.

"I hope so. I'm rather fond of breathing."

He was nervous enough as it was without being trussed up like this. He walked around and shrugged his shoulders a few times. That was better, it had eased a trifle.

"You look splendid Major. Do you have a pin to decorate the neck cloth?"

Nat walked over to a side table and fished out a diamond pin. Garner's eyes opened wide.

"It's not too ostentatious is it? It's the only one I have, a present from my grandfather." From the grandfather who had wanted to turn him into a gentleman.

"No it's perfect with the plain coat and neck cloth."

He thanked the valet and ran downstairs to join Luke.

Luke whistled. "My word, you'll have all the young ladies swooning. Spare some for the rest of us won't you?"

Nat raised his eyebrows. "I thought marriage was the last thing you were interested in."

"Trust me, it is, but a fellow does need a bit of female adulation to cut a dash in Town."

Nat shook his head at him. "If this party was for anyone other than your sister you wouldn't get me there."

"There's nothing to worry about, old man. You can hide

away in the card room at the ball once you've done the pretty with Grace."

"It's the formal dinner beforehand I'm dreading."

"Aunt Theo has invited some excellent people. She does have a duke and duchess as guests of honour but they will be next to me and Aunt Theo." He grimaced. "The Duchess is a real high stickler but it's good of her to help launch Grace. The ball should be the squeeze of the season."

"You're not selling this to me, Luke. Let's go before I lose my nerve. I can't even take deep breaths in this coat."

Luke looked up at him with a gleam in his eye. "I suppose you couldn't take a fancy to Grace? Then I'd know she was in safe hands."

Nat felt himself blush. "You're a viscount. You can't have your sister marrying a man tainted by the smell of the shop."

"What nonsense is this? You'll be Lord Overton one day."

"Women are much more ambitious than men." Nat scowled. "Come on let's go before we fall out."

Luke shrugged. "I'm sorry if I've offended you but I for one would be proud to bestow my sister's hand on you. You were the finest officer I ever served under."

"Thank you, Captain. I meant no disrespect to your sister. I like her but I don't think we would suit."

He closed his eyes briefly. As pleasant as Luke's sister had seemed when he had joined her and Luke on an outing, she didn't have him lying awake thinking about her. If Eliza Wyndham was as unaffected as Grace he would risk trying to court her, despite what had passed between them on her last night at Hargreaves Hall. The realisation hit him with a thump in the chest. He glanced at Luke but he was in a reverie of his own. It must be a big responsibility having a sister.

81

Luke caught his glance. "Sorry, I was thinking. Grace is such a worry. She seems to have become interested in politics. She gets on well with the Duchess believe it or not. I find her something of a dragon but Grace is excited about attending some political salons with her." Luke pulled a face.

Nat laughed. "There's your answer then. Ask the Duchess to find her some nice, reforming peer of the realm."

"Grace has decided opinions of her own. She'll choose her own husband. I'm lucky to have Aunt Theo to guide her. I'd hate to have all the responsibility for an unwed female." He grimaced. "There are some men I'd hate to see married to my worst enemy's sister."

"That would be true if you had any enemies. Come on let's get it over with."

It was a fine evening and they decided to walk to the Cavendish Square home of Lady Theodosia Grant. Luke handed Nat a walking cane. Nat studied it with interest.

"Is this one of those canes with a hidden blade?"

"Yes." Luke showed him how it operated. "It's generally safe these days but it's as well to be prepared."

Nat laughed. "Once a soldier, always a soldier."

Lady Grant's butler signalled to a footman to take their cloaks and other outdoor things.

"Follow me gentlemen."

He led them to a receiving room where the hum of voices suggested they were some of the last to arrive. The butler announced them in a booming voice.

"Viscount Enstone and Major Overton."

Nat's neck cloth felt too tight as he followed Luke into the room. He stood back politely as Lady Grant greeted her nephew.

"Introduce me to your friend, Luke."

Nat moved forward and copied Luke in raising Lady Grant's hand for a brief touch of his lips. Oh Lord, should he have done that? He should have checked with Luke how to greet his aunt. He need not have worried. Lady Grant twinkled up at him.

"I see you're as big a rogue as my nephew, young man. I am delighted to meet you at last. Luke has told me so much about you. Thank you for agreeing to attend at such short notice. We have equal numbers now."

Nat relaxed, Luke hadn't exaggerated when he said his aunt was a darling. "The pleasure is mine, Lady Grant."

She patted his arm and tucked her hand into the crook of his elbow. "You have some acquaintances here."

A surprised Nat followed her gaze. The only society people he had met since his return were the Lovells. Sure enough, he found himself staring at Lady Eliza. Her dark blue eyes were shooting sparks at him. She wasn't pleased to see him. How could he have imagined paying court to her? He quickly suppressed a spurt of temper. He wouldn't give her the satisfaction of knowing she disconcerted him.

"Ah here is Lady Eliza." Lady Grant walked him towards her.

Chapter Nine

Eliza's heart skipped a beat at the sound of Major Overton's name. What was he doing here? She let the conversation flow around her and watched as Luke Bamfield introduced him to his aunt. Grace had mentioned Luke was expecting a visit from an old army friend, why did it have to be Major Overton of all people? He certainly seemed to charm Lady Grant. Her cheeks burned when Lady Grant led him in her direction. Her eyes narrowed as she saw the size of the diamond glittering amongst the folds of his snowy neck cloth. If that was real it would be worth a king's ransom.

She gritted her teeth. How careless of him to make such a mistake when he had arranged everything else about his attire to perfection. She ought to thank him for the warning. It saved her from wondering if she had been too quick to assume that he was a fortune hunter. There was no need to feel guilty about the brutal snub she had given him. He stepped towards her and swept a flourishing bow.

"Lady Wyndham."

A hint of his male perfume, all citrus and shaving soap and something else she couldn't quite put a name to, reached her. Her legs felt weak and she could only manage the most perfunctory of curtsies. If he noticed her rudeness in staring at his tiepin it served him right, shame on him for using his army contacts to help in his quest for advancement.

She put on her best society voice. "Good evening, Major Overton, how lovely to see you again."

Lady Grant smiled at them. "I've put you next to Lady Eliza at dinner so you won't feel completely amongst strangers, Major Overton."

The butler announced a new arrival and Lady Grant drifted off to greet them.

Eliza's face ached from the effort of smiling. She turned slightly so her back was facing the room and she could give up the pretence of being happy to see him.

"What are you doing here?"

Major Overton raised an eyebrow at her. "Isn't it obvious? I'm helping out a friend's aunt who needed an extra man to even out the numbers for dinner."

Eliza sucked in a breath. "You know what I meant."

He smiled at her. "Thank you for enquiring after my uncle's health."

Eliza resolutely resisted the urge to stamp her foot. "I wish you would play your games on someone else but, as it happens, I would like to know how Lord Overton goes on."

"He is much recovered and if you must know I am taking the opportunity to pay a promised visit to an old and much valued army friend. Since we are asking impertinent questions, what is your connection to the family?"

"You met my sister, the Duchess of Cathlay. She is an old friend of Lady Grant." Eliza saw a movement to the side and glanced around. "Here is Augusta now, bringing the Duke to meet you."

She performed the introduction and wished her sister and

brother-in-law didn't look so pleased to see him. The butler announced dinner was served and the Major held out his arm for her. She sighed inwardly watching Cathlay perform the same office for Augusta. If she refused it would cause the sort of gossip she was anxious to avoid. She placed her hand inside his elbow and shot him an angry look.

He patted her hand. "Good girl, I have no more desire to do the pretty by you than you have to accept my offer. However, I feel honour bound not to cause any comment that could detract from Grace's come out ball."

She forced herself to smile and hoped her cheeks hadn't gone too deep a shade of red. Of course she didn't want anything to mar Grace's enjoyment of the evening but he was the outside of enough. They joined the end of the line of couples making their way into Lady Grant's magnificent dining room. He must be on good terms with Luke's sister to refer to her as Grace. The thought infuriated her. She must find some way to warn Grace about him without exciting her interest. He was a handsome devil and she didn't want a lovely young woman like Grace to fall victim to his charms.

Walking by him with her hand through his arm was enough to set her nerves all on edge. No other man had ever had this effect on her. Not even Miles had given her this feeling of walking on air. Her heartbeat thundered in her ears. It must be because she didn't trust him. He stopped by her seat and pulled out her chair. As she sat, he bent over her to push it in and his breath skittered across the nape of her neck for the briefest of moments. It was enough to send waves of insistent heat shooting through her body, pooling deep in her groin. Distrust wouldn't cause a reaction like this. It was desire pure and simple. It couldn't be anything else. Lud, how was she going to cope with seeing him in town?

She was seated on the major's right hand side. Grace was to his left. She glanced to her right to see Peregrine Dempster. That was all she needed. He was the biggest gossip out of any man of her acquaintance. Even though he regularly wrote poems to her eyes when she was in London, their lukewarm friendship wouldn't be enough to spare her if she let him see the turmoil she was in. She decided to take the initiative and turned towards him.

"Good evening, Mr Dempster. Have you met my brother's new neighbour, Major Overton yet?" She nodded towards the major, who was deep in conversation with Grace.

Dempster glanced to her left. He lowered his voice so only she could hear. "Ah so the man mountain is Enstone's old army superior. The boot is somewhat on the other foot now." His lips curved into a smile. "That said he wouldn't be such a bad match for you, my dear. You could live near to your brother then, if it's true what I've heard about the Major being Lord Overton's heir."

Major Overton turned his attention her way and she introduced him to Dempster, glad to avoid having to reply to his comment. They were interrupted by the arrival of a creamy, chicken soup. Afterwards Dempster moved his attention to the lady on his other side. The Major leaned close enough to make her shiver.

He spoke softly, his mouth close to her ear. "I've never seen a waistcoat quite as fancy as that."

Eliza followed his gaze to Dempster's golden waistcoat. It was heavy with silver embroidery.

She laughed. "Peregrine does like bright clothes."

The dinner dragged on. By the time it was finished she had a headache. She begrudged the conversation the Major had with Grace and yet every time he turned to her she felt like running away. This would never do. Lady Grant finally signalled to the ladies to leave the gentlemen to their port. Eliza smiled at Major Overton and Mr Dempster as she rose from her chair. Major Overton stood to pull it back for her and it was all she could do to suppress a tremor as his fingers brushed her back.

Eliza made her way to the drawing room and accepted a cup of tea. She fell into conversation with Augusta and Lady Grant.

Lady Grant smiled at her. "I believe Major Overton is a neighbour of your brother, Lady Eliza."

"Yes he is now. He sold out of the army quite recently."

"By all accounts, since the major's return Lord Overton's health has improved markedly," Augusta said.

Eliza saw Augusta and Lady Grant exchange a quick glance. It was to be hoped they weren't speculating on a possible relationship between her and the major. If it came to that why hadn't Augusta warned her he was in Town visiting Grace's brother? Eliza changed the subject and it was a relief when it was time to move to the ballroom. Viscount Enstone led his sister out onto the floor for the first dance. Eliza found her hand claimed by Peregrine Dempster. His one saving grace was his skill at dancing and she enjoyed the dance they performed together. She watched with relief as Major Overton led Grace on to the floor for the second dance.

The Earl of Milton sauntered up. His dark hair was a little too long for fashion and his dress might have been called slovenly in someone who wasn't a peer of the realm. Despite that he appeared to be looking down his nose as if the company was beneath him. He had been popping up with annoying regularity for the past week. It was obvious he wasn't going to be denied. Eliza decided to keep him in conversation until the second dance was nearly over. Then she could take to the floor with him for the third dance and avoid any approach by Major Overton. Her plan worked and she had the satisfaction of sailing past Major Overton on the arm of the earl.

Not that her situation felt entirely comfortable. The Earl of Milton set her teeth on edge. Fortunately, it was an energetic country dance and they only came together at brief intervals. When they did his hands seemed to brush against her rather too often to be accidental. Rumour was that he was ready to settle down and she must be careful not to give him any ideas about settling on her as a potential wife. At the same time anything was better than being forced to dance with Major Overton. Or was it? She watched him dance with a cheerful brunette in the next set. He seemed perfectly at home on the dance floor and his partner appeared to be enjoying herself.

Her dance card filled up quickly and she thought she had escaped the ordeal of dancing with the Major when she turned to go in search of her next partner and came up against a solid wall of exquisitely dressed male. His diamond pin glittered under the light of the chandeliers. At close quarters the pin looked even bigger. No it could not possibly be real.

"I could be forgiven for thinking you were avoiding me, Lady Wyndham."

He gave her a lazy smile and her heart fluttered all over again. She was mesmerised and didn't think to hide her dance card. Major Overton reached for it.

"I see you are free for the supper dance."

A hand shot past him and snatched the card. The Earl of Milton wrote his name on it with a flourish.

"Too late, Overton. The lady is engaged with me for the

supper dance."

The Major lowered his eyes, but not before Eliza saw a flash of anger in them. "I'll be speedier next time." He walked away.

Eliza nodded to the earl and dredged up yet another polite society smile. He looked about to say something but Eliza's next partner came up to claim her. Normally she enjoyed dancing but tonight it was a chore. She was feeling quite breathless when the supper dance started up. If she had been engaged to anyone other than the earl she would have suggested sitting it out, but she suspected he would try and manoeuvre her outside onto the terrace for some air. She didn't trust him to keep to the line of what was acceptable.

She pretended not to see him until he was close to give herself a moment to rest. The orchestra struck up the first bars of a cotillion. At least that was less energetic than some of the country dances they had been playing. Supper was announced as the dance came to an end. She was about to excuse herself to the earl when she caught sight of Major Overton making determined progress through the crowds towards her. On impulse she gave the earl a brief smile and accepted his invitation to lead her into supper.

She caught sight of the major's face as they walked past him. He looked thunderstruck. A quick glance at the earl showed him giving the Major a smug smile. Major Overton's hands fisted at his sides and for a brief moment she held her breath, almost expecting him to throw a punch. Then he collected himself and walked past. Was there some sort of history between these two or was Major Overton furious at his prize being snatched away from him?

The earl offered to fetch her some supper but she insisted on selecting what she wanted herself. He made his own selection and found them an empty table.

"So, you are an independent sort, Lady Eliza." He smiled and studied her with a hooded gaze. "I like that in a woman."

His gaze dropped below her face and Eliza felt a blush stain her cheeks. The man was a toad. She would have to be careful in her dealings with him. She concentrated on eating until she caught sight of Augusta and gave her a slight nod. The earl was too busy staring at her bosom to notice. Augusta drifted towards her and took her away on the excuse of having someone to introduce her to. Eliza drew in a deep breath. The Earl of Milton was someone to avoid in future.

Augusta led them towards the Duke, who was standing by an open window. Eliza realised too late that he was talking to Major Overton. Was there no escaping the man?

"Eliza, my dear, I'm glad to see you enjoying yourself. I haven't seen you sit one dance out." He nodded at the major. "I must say it's a pleasure to meet Max's new neighbour here. It will be good for Max to have company of his own age when he's at Hargreaves."

Eliza smiled up at him. He could be every bit the Duke when he wanted to be but she had always had a soft spot for her eldest brother-in-law.

"Max is happy to find Lord Overton's heir so friendly."

The Major bowed and gave her a cheerful grin. "Not half as pleased as I am to find my illustrious neighbour so agreeable."

The Duke was hailed by a friend and he and Augusta drifted away.

The Major studied her face and she looked away.

"I suppose you don't have any more spaces on your dance card, do you?"

Eliza was about to deny it when she remembered she had

kept the first dance after supper free to give herself a break. "If you must know I'm not engaged for the first dance but I find myself a little fatigued."

Major Overton laughed out loud. "Aye. You've been so busy filling that card I'm afraid you're trying to avoid someone. I wonder who that might be. There's an alcove next to an open window in the ballroom. It's in full view of the dance floor. You'll be quite safe. He held out his arm. She could see people watching them and accepted it.

"That's my girl. We don't want to give the gossips any fodder, do we? As neighbours people will expect us to be friendly."

She gave him a sweet smile. "They don't know you like I do."

His expression became serious. He led her through the ballroom to the alcove and settled her on a sofa, before sitting beside her. There was just room for the two of them. His thigh was within an inch of hers and heat seemed to seep towards her.

"You don't know me at all, Lady Eliza. Are you still angry with me for spooking your horse? I wanted to apologise at Hargreaves but never found the right moment."

She glowered at him. "You had plenty of time when we drove to the school."

He shook his head. "I didn't want to upset you by reminding you of the accident. It was your first chance to drive afterwards and that can be difficult."

"You didn't show much confidence in my driving when the trip was planned."

"Ah. If you remember it was Max who was tactless, not me. I think you took an innocent remark I made the wrong way."

Her eyes flew to his face. His expression was one of concern, the irritating man. He was a good actor. "Well after calling me cow-handed how could I not?"

"That was too bad of me." He smiled at her which irritated her even more. "Although I said that either you weren't concentrating or you were cow-handed. After seeing the way you handled the ribbons of Max's curricle it must have been the first."

"Hmph! No one could have expected a horse to land in front of them like that."

"I know and I'm truly sorry."

His hand gave hers a brief squeeze. She shuddered, that had been one of Mile's tricks.

"Am I upsetting you by talking about it?"

She shook her head. His eyes narrowed but he continued.

"I should have found a spot where I could see any oncoming traffic before giving in to the temptation to let Caesar jump the hedge. I was wrapped up in the novelty of jumping him for pleasure rather than dire necessity. He's got me out of a few scrapes that horse in our time together. It doesn't excuse my actions and I apologise unreservedly."

"That's all very well but you could have apologised at the time instead of appearing to blame me. I was upset about that."

"Then I must apologise again for appearing so reluctant to take the blame." He hesitated. "Both my parents died when I was ten and it was in a carriage accident. I was riding in the carriage behind with my grandfather and saw it happen. I was shocked by what had happened to you and wasn't thinking rationally."

Eliza stared up at him. Perhaps he was telling the truth. He sounded so convincing but then she had had her fill of convincing rogues. He met her gaze with every appearance of sincerity. He was her brother's neighbour and perhaps she should try to be conciliating.

"Thank you for confiding in me, Major. Losing your parents like that must have been horrific. Since we are being honest, I confess I could have been paying closer attention to what I was doing. I suggest we forget the manner of our meeting."

A smile transformed his face. "Thank you. I have much to thank your brother for and I would prefer to be on good terms with his family."

She smiled at him. He seemed so friendly and he was certainly intriguing but she didn't feel up to taking the risk of getting to know him better. A risk she wasn't sure she was brave enough to take even if she hadn't suspected him of being a fortune hunter.

"Now that's settled we had better return to the ballroom before tongues start wagging."

He lifted a hand as if he was about to catch hold of hers and then dropped it.

"I suppose you're right but before we go I must give you a warning." His eyes narrowed to dark slits and his expression hardened. "The Earl of Milton is a dangerous man. You would oblige me by keeping away from him."

Eliza gasped and glanced at the ballroom. There was no one near to them. She jumped up and scowled at him. All feelings of charity towards him had deserted her.

"You have absolutely no right to tell me who I may and may not mix with. You would oblige me by taking yourself off and leaving me in peace."

She stalked back towards the supper room. How was she supposed to take that? The Earl of Milton was received everywhere and no one else had mentioned anything untoward about him. Lud, he was even invited to Grace Bamfield's come out ball. She could only assume Major Overton was interested in her and was trying to put her off a potential rival.

After a few steps her anger cooled and she moderated her pace. She was in time to see the Duke disappearing into one of the card rooms but there was no sign of Augusta. She made her way to the ladies retiring room. After that conversation she needed a bit of time to herself. The odious man, did he think she couldn't see what he was about. She wasn't keen on the earl herself but her preferences were no business of Major Overton. What a pity she had already stood up with the earl twice. She would have taken great pleasure in dancing with him in front of Major Overton.

After splashing cold water on her face she felt restored enough to return to the ballroom. The orchestra was tuning up and she spotted her first partner, an unexceptional friend of Max. He smiled and walked across to claim her. He looked perfectly at ease but was he one of the men who had spoken to Max about her? He had been attentive the last time she had been in London for the season. Why did life have to be so complicated?

The rest of the evening crawled by. She was engaged for all but the last two dances. Every time she glanced around the edges of the ballroom the Earl of Milton was watching her. He didn't dance with anyone else which made standing up with her twice worryingly singular. She appeared to have made another unwanted conquest. His dogged concentration on her suggested he would be harder to shake off than most.

Her last partner obligingly escorted her towards Augusta who was sitting amongst the chaperones. She could see the earl sidling in their direction. She was grateful Augusta had ignored her suggestion of leaving her to play cards on the grounds she was too old for close chaperonage. The man made her shudder. Something about the set of the lines on his face suggested he could be cruel. He was probably the sort who assaulted the maids and whipped his horses mercilessly. Now where had that thought come from? Could it be Major Overton knew something about the earl others didn't? Perhaps he was dangerous? Did she have enough grounds to suspect Major Overton of wanting her fortune? He was courteous to everyone, including Lord Overton's servants. He had treated Maisie with gentle concern, talking to her as he checked her legs.

The earl quickened his pace. Would they reach Augusta before he intercepted her? There could be no doubt his fancy had settled on her and the last thing she wanted was for him to make an offer. This was exactly the sort of situation she didn't feel ready to grapple with yet. She glanced around looking for a means of escape when it was provided by the solid form of the Major himself. He nodded to her escort who bowed and took his leave.

"Am I fortunate enough to find you without a partner at last, Lady Eliza?"

If he had been watching her he had been a lot more subtle than the earl. She inclined her head.

"In that case may I have the pleasure of this dance?"

She gave Major Overton a lazy smile. "You'll claim it anyway so I may as well say yes now and save us both some trouble."

He proffered his arm and led her back onto the dance floor. She bit her lip as she saw Cathlay join Augusta, both of them watching her on the major's arm with a smile on their faces. They had taken to him and were hoping for a match it seemed.

She wished she had never confided to Augusta her dread of moving far away from Hargreaves if she married. How could you wed a man simply because of where he lived?

She settled into the rhythm of the dance. He was a graceful dancer, particularly for a man of his size. Each time they changed partners in the set his new lady smiled up at him with admiration. He seemed to pay them little heed beyond the bounds of civility. At times she caught him watching her when he thought she wasn't looking. What if he had formed a genuine attachment for her? Would it be so bad if her money had been the first thing to attract him? He did have a respectable position to offer after all and Lord Overton would leave him comfortably provided for.

Lud, what was she thinking? Physical attraction and the chance to live near Hargreaves weren't enough. Besides he was too domineering for comfort. If she ever risked another marriage it would have to be someone with a much milder temperament. She didn't think much to the Earl of Milton but the Major had no right to tell her what to do. Could warning her off potential rivals suggest desperation? Had he got debts he didn't want Lord Overton to know about? The dance brought them back together before ending and he led her off the floor.

"I think the earl has given up and gone home. I'll take you back to your sister now."

Eliza glared up at him. "So you weren't dancing with me for the pleasure of my company then? If you want me to take your warning about the Earl of Milton seriously you will have to give me a lot better reason than your personal dislike."

Major Overton slowed their pace. He looked down at her and frowned. "I can't say any more without giving you knowledge which might put you in danger."

"That's rather melodramatic. You make me wonder if you want me for yourself and are trying to put me off a rival with more to offer."

She was surprised to see a dull red colour stain his cheeks. Either he was overcome by the heat or he wasn't a practised enough fortune hunter to hide his intent easily.

He drew to a halt by Augusta, bowed to her and walked away. Augusta gave her a quizzical look.

"What did you say to Major Overton to annoy him so? He looked furious for a moment and for a man with such natural courtesy I'm surprised he walked off without a word."

"Nothing I said should have upset him. He seems a man of strange humours to me."

Chapter Ten

N at passed an indifferent night. His warning had fallen on deaf ears. Was Lady Eliza prepared to take a man like Milton? On the other hand, why shouldn't she? That's what society women were like. All they were interested in was money and a place in society. She was bound to have money as the daughter of the Marquess of Hargreaves. Everything about the Hargreaves estate suggested wealth and careful management. She must crave a title. Perhaps Luke had a friend who was an eligible duke. His hands curled into fists under the covers. He vented his feelings by pummelling his pillows. The important thing was that she was safe.

A feather tickled his nose and he threw himself over onto his back. Much more of that and the pillows would be in shreds. He had better consult Luke. Perhaps he could get Eliza to believe she should keep away from Milton. That might serve. He owed it to Max to keep his sister safe. With a course of action decided on, he fell into a deep sleep as the dawn light fought its way around the edges of the curtains. Luke's valet woke him by drawing the curtains, allowing brilliant sunshine to flood the room. He sat up in bed with a start.

"What the devil?"

"I'm sorry, Major Overton. I forgot you slept with the bed

drapes open."

"It doesn't matter. Closing the bed drapes makes me think I'm in an army tent. What time is it?"

"Close on noon."

"What?" Nat jumped out of bed, suppressing a grin as the valet grimaced his disapproval of his habit of sleeping without a nightshirt.

Luke's valet was supremely efficient and Nat was shaved and dressed in record time. In the army Bright had looked after him as well as their horses and the thought of a smart valet had rattled him. Now he could see the benefit.

"How would I go about finding a valet?"

Garner stopped tidying his shaving things away. His mouth opened and then snapped shut.

"Out with it man."

"You could try an employment agency or ask for recommendations, sir. As it happens...."

Nat eyed him carefully. "If you know of someone suitable who you are prepared to vouch for then I'll give him a trial."

"My sister's boy is looking for a position. I've trained him myself when we've had time. He's in London at the moment working as a footman."

"Do you think he could achieve your sort of standard?"

"Oh I do indeed but it's difficult to get that first position. I was lucky as my father was valet to the old Viscount Enstone."

"I'm a hard taskmaster, but fair, and I pay well. I'll give the young man a trial."

Garner beamed at him. "He's been working for an agency which places footmen with families needing extra servants for balls and such like. He will be free by the end of the week unless he takes on anything else. As soon as His Lordship is back I'll ask him for some free time to try and find him."

Nat turned towards the window and grimaced. Luke wasn't here. Damnation.

"Will Viscount Enstone be out for long?"

"He said to tell you he would see you at dinner, Major. Estate business I believe."

"Well in that case he won't mind if I give you leave to go and find your nephew. The sooner he starts the better." He grinned at Garner. "Then you'll have more time to teach him before I leave."

"Thank you, sir. If you have everything you need I'll be on my way."

Nat wandered down to the breakfast room and Luke's well drilled servants provided him with a hearty breakfast. He found inactivity unnerving and decided to pay a visit to Lady Grant to thank her for his invitation to the ball. He wasn't sure if it was correct to visit in the early afternoon but as he was staying with her nephew he didn't think Lady Grant would mind. Luke had said she was a noted hostess so she might even have more information on the Earl of Milton.

Lady Grant and the Honourable Grace seemed pleased to see him. A family comprising two daughters and a matron were on the point of leaving. Lady Grant introduced them and he felt heat rise to his cheeks at the brazen appraisal of the matron. They said their goodbyes and he took a seat opposite to the two ladies and accepted a cup of tea.

Lady Grant's eyes twinkled. "I can see you are unused to the ways of the ton. It's not only the young ladies who come under scrutiny. Finding suitable husbands for hopeful daughters is a serious endeavour."

Nat smiled. "I can see that."

Grace gave him a saucy grin. "Several young ladies have tried to find out more about you from me. Take care or you will end up with a wife before you leave Town."

Nat burst out laughing. It was a refreshing change to meet a young woman from a noble household who treated him in a friendly manner. He felt like an honorary brother with Grace. His background hadn't bothered her in the least. He glanced at the mantelpiece clock. Now what had Luke said? Morning calls should last at least fifteen minutes and no more than half an hour. His keen ears caught the sound of a carriage drawing up, another caller perhaps? It was time to ask about the Earl of Milton.

"Luke and I came across an army acquaintance last night. He's now the Earl of Milton. He lost both his father and brother and sold out of the army a few months before I did."

Lady Grant must have caught something in his voice because she gave him a sharp look. He turned to give her a half smile Grace couldn't see.

"Ah, Luke did mention something about him last night, when he saw his name on the guest list."

Grace eyed him gravely. "Oh how awful to lose his brother. I can't tell you how much I worried when Luke was away with the army."

"It must have been difficult for you but I don't think the Earl of Milton has your finer feelings. You should have seen the way he treated his horses."

There were definite sounds of an arrival. Grace almost bounced in her seat.

"I wonder if that is Miss Hill."

"Very likely, my dear. Why don't you go and meet her."

"Thank you." Grace jumped up and strode to the door.

Lady Grant caught Nat's gaze and he decided to take her into his confidence.

"I know this will go no farther than this room but Luke and I thought the whole business was rather odd. Luke overheard him talking to his batman, giving him instructions that didn't make sense. Immediately afterwards the batman disappeared for a week or so. We were stationed in England at the time. When he came back there was an air of excitement about the pair and shortly afterwards they sold out of the army. We found out later that the old earl and his eldest son had died together in a boating accident, during the time when the batman was missing."

Lady Grant's eyebrows shot up. "Circumstantial, but worrying. Luke wasn't happy when he was announced. He told me he didn't like the man and to be wary of him. There was no chance for him to say any more."

"I heard something from my grandfather's man of business recently that seemed to confirm our suspicions. I didn't mention it to Luke until last night. It never occurred to me the earl would be in London." He grimaced. "As Luke isn't around today I felt I ought to warn you. The Earl of Milton has already run through a large chunk of his inheritance and is likely to be looking out for a well-dowered bride."

"Thank you. I am most grateful. Grace is engaged to ride in the park later with a friend, Lady Eliza Wyndham. Luke was to escort them but I've had a note from him to say he won't be back in time. You seem an eminently sensible man, Major Overton. Would you oblige me by taking Luke's place? If this Earl of Milton is on the catch for a rich wife I don't think a groom would be enough protection if he should appear."

Footsteps sounded coming towards the door. He didn't have

a choice.

"Of course I will, my lady. I've left my horse in your stables. I'll discuss times with your head groom. My man, Bright, will accompany us."

"I am in your debt. Something about Milton set me all on edge and he showed a great deal of interest in Lady Eliza last night."

The door opened and the butler announced Mrs and Miss Hill. Miss Hill and Grace walked in arm in arm. They were both attractive young women and made a pretty picture, one petite and fair and the other a willowy brunette with an engaging smile. Despite that they didn't stir his blood by even a whisper. Lady Eliza only had to walk into a room to render him spellbound. Lady Grant smiled her thanks and introduced him to the new arrivals. He took his leave as soon as there was a break in the conversation.

He made arrangements with Lady Grant's groom to collect Grace later. Lady Eliza and her groom would meet them at Hyde Park. He mounted Caesar and set off for Luke's home at a steady trot. Lady Grant didn't have to spell out what a target Lady Eliza was to a fiend like Milton but she was going to be furious when she found out he was taking Luke's place. Did she harbour suspicions that he was a fortune hunter seeing Milton as a rival? If so he wasn't the best person to protect her.

A spurt of anger went through him. How could she think that now she'd had time to get to know him? He reviewed the evidence. She had been suspicious of his motives in taking up Uncle Henry's invitation to visit when they first met. Despite her spirit there was an air of vulnerability about her at times and he'd assumed her interest in his neck cloth when they had been introduced had been the result of a sudden bashfulness. He snorted in disgust. She probably thought the diamond in his tiepin was a fake.

Eliza gasped with pleasure when she saw the red riding habit with its black collar and black beaver cap, adorned with a black feather at the front, laid out on the bed. She stroked the feather. Mama would have wanted her to wear colours again by now, but she was glad about the touches of black.

"It came in time then, Alice. It always seems strange to me that habits are made by men's tailors but this one looks lovely." She ran a finger over the soft wool fabric of the jacket. "It feels good too."

Perhaps it hadn't been such a bad idea to come to London after all. She must be a shallow creature for an orgy of shopping to raise her spirits so much. Augusta had been right in saying a change of scene would help. In fact, if it wasn't for Major Overton being in Town she would be quite content. There was no point worrying about him. Hadn't Grace said he was on a promised visit to her brother and wouldn't be in London for long? Meeting Grace was a big benefit. She was a dear girl and intent on avoiding marriage for at least a year or two. They had so much else in common and the prospect of rides and visits to bookshops and museums together to counterbalance the obligatory balls stretched before her.

Augusta's groom accompanied her to the park. The sun was out and Eliza felt her spirits soar. She patted Bella's neck. What luck the horses from Max's stud had arrived before she left for London. Bella was a joy to ride. They had picked an early time to avoid the worst of the crowds who packed the rides on fine days in the season. It would be interesting to spend time with Grace's brother. He'd seemed an energetic but pleasant sort of man when they had been introduced. The restless energy probably came from all those years spent in the army. Or perhaps it was his energetic nature that had led him to join the army? Maybe even a bit of each. People's motivations were rarely clear cut. Using herself as an example, she had no real idea what she wanted from life.

Did she want to stay unmarried and never have her own family? A year or two as her own mistress might help her decide if she could face taking a risk on another man. She sighed as they turned into the gates to the park. By then Major Overton would have taken a wife. She shivered slightly as heat pooled in her abdomen at the thought of him. Physically he was the most attractive man she had met. Why on earth did she always fall for rogues? She could have believed him to be an honest man if it hadn't been for his enormous diamond, that couldn't possibly be real, and the way he had tried to put her off the earl.

They neared the start of the ride and she busied herself looking for Grace. It wasn't long before she spotted her soft green riding habit. She had neglected to tell her about the new habit so Grace would be looking for her old blue one. She asked Bella for a trot and headed towards Grace with the groom a suitable distance behind her. Grace saw her before she reached them. My word what a beautiful chestnut her brother was riding, almost as impressive as the chestnut from Max's the stud. Her mouth dropped open as she saw the star on the horse's forehead. It was the same horse.

Her gaze drifted upwards until she met the smiling eyes of Major Overton. She snatched at the reins without thinking and Bella jinked. It took a few moments to calm her down. He really would think her cow-handed now. She tossed her head so hard she nearly dislodged the black beaver hat. She patted it back into place and gathered the shreds of her composure as best she could. Was there no rest from the man? He had dogged her footsteps at the ball and now he was intent on riding with her. How had he wangled the invitation and where was Viscount Enstone?

Grace rode towards her. "Eliza, my brother sends his apologies. He has been called away on a business matter and Major Overton has kindly agreed to deputise for him."

There was nothing for it but to thank him politely. "Thank you for stepping into the breach and rescuing our outing, Major Overton."

The words stuck in her throat. She risked another glance at him. He was perfectly dressed for the occasion as he had been the night before. A smile played about his lips. He'd known she would be cross and was enjoying her discomfiture. He did have an enticing smile. What would it be like to be kissed by a man like him? Ruthlessly, she ignored the tingling of her lips. She had to cure this obsession or she would end up walking into the kind of situation she was determined to avoid, in the power of a man who was a stranger to her. She fixed a smile on her face, despite the shiver that ran through her, and signalled to Augusta's groom to return home.

She rode alongside Grace. "How did you enjoy your ball?"

Grace's eyes shone. "It was lovely. I didn't know there were that many people in London."

Eliza laughed. "Augusta said it was the biggest crush of the season so far, so you are well and truly launched socially."

"I suppose so. I was dreading it but in the end I enjoyed myself. Now I can concentrate on enjoying my stay with Aunt

Theo. Luke says I needn't worry about finding a husband just yet, which is a big relief."

"Indeed, I know what you mean. The prospect of leaving everything and everyone you love best for life with a man whose character you can't be sure of is guaranteed to produce sleepless nights."

Grace gave her a shy smile. "Aunt Theo says when I meet the right man I won't worry about that. I've only recently got Luke back and I want to enjoy his company for a while before I find out if what she says is true."

Major Overton pulled his horse in front of them and turned it round to face them. "Shall we see if we can fit in a canter on Rotten Row before it is too busy, ladies?"

Eliza felt a blush heat up her cheeks. Major Overton might be annoying but it was no reason to treat him with discourtesy. "Of course, that would be most agreeable. I'm sorry we have excluded you from the conversation so far. We were carried away by talk of the ball."

"Think nothing of it, Lady Eliza. How do you like the horse I bought off your brother?" He gave her a smile that made the breath catch in her throat.

"I thought I recognised him. He's one of the best horses I've seen."

"Yes he's superb. I did tell your brother he was the better of the two. He still let me buy this one as the other horse is grey, like my Caesar. What should I call him, ladies? I like Pharaoh but my groom isn't convinced."

The horse pranced in protest at a leaf blowing past him on the breeze. The Major had to wheel him around to settle him.

Grace laughed. "He looks like a pharaoh to me. Come, he's losing patience with us."

They trotted along to Rotten Row and found it relatively empty. Major Overton let his horse take the lead. He had obviously been warned it wasn't done to gallop in the park and Eliza admired the way he kept the spirited animal to a steady canter. He was a consummate horseman.

When they retraced their steps they found the park much busier. Grace was hailed by the Hills who were taking the air in a majestic landau. Eliza went to follow her when she found her path blocked by a rider on a testy black stallion. Her mare backed away from him and the rider pulled hard on the stallion's reins. The man was well dressed and she realised with a start that it was the Earl of Milton. She bent forward to sooth her mare, hiding her face. With luck he wouldn't have recognised her.

"Ah, Denby." A deep voice said from beside her. "You're no better at controlling a horse than you used to be it seems. I suggest you move away from this area before he injures someone."

"You're not my superior officer now, damn you, ship-wright's boy. What right have you to stop me conversing with Lady Eliza?"

Major Overton lowered his voice so only the three of them could hear. "As her escort, I have every right."

Eliza held her breath. She had no desire to be the subject of a disagreement between gentlemen, or even worse the cause of a duel. The idea seemed far-fetched but with the enmity in both of the men's faces perhaps not.

The Earl of Milton finally got his horse under control and rode up close to her.

"Lady Eliza, would you care to ride a little way with me."

Eliza glanced at Major Overton's wooden expression. For

once she was in agreement with him. The earl should have respected the wishes of her escort but half the Ton seemed to be watching them. Heat rushed to her face. Another Lovell scandal after Max's disaster with Lavinia would do the family no good at all. Besides what harm could he do to her in Hyde Park?

"Of course, my lord. I must return to Miss Bamford shortly though."

She was watching the Major and caught a look of absolute fury, quickly suppressed. He bowed towards them.

"I will stay by Miss Bamford until you return."

He turned away and Eliza felt bereft. She should have kept Augusta's groom with her. She pinned a social smile on her face.

"Have you been in Town long, my lord?"

"Two or three weeks, I was finding it rather flat until you arrived."

He wheeled his horse around and set it to a trot. She felt obliged to follow.

"I have been occupied with estate business lately but now I am free to pursue more personal affairs, shall we say."

The sickly smile accompanying his statement made her cringe. From his greater height on the back of the rangy stallion he was looking down at her and she knew instinctively which part of her anatomy he was studying. She was glad Alice had persuaded her to wear a lady's cravat. The red habit emphasised her shapely figure but not even an inch of flesh was showing.

Bella covered the ground surprisingly quickly. She glanced around to see they were some way from where they had left Major Overton and he was making no move to follow. They were in a less popular part of the park with large bushes dotted about. The back of her neck felt rigid. The earl's leering gaze set her nerves on edge. Lud, he wasn't going to propose here and now was he? Could this day get any worse?

Her mare didn't seem to be obeying her and a quick glance confirmed the earl was pulling at Bella's head collar. She looked around for signs of other riders but no was in sight except for a workman taking a shortcut through the park. An earl was unlikely to be put off proposing by anything less than a society matron or two. She tried to pull her whip free but the hand holding it was trapped against her body. He brought their horses closer still and clamped a hand behind her neck. His wet mouth fastened on hers. A faint musty smell, as if he hadn't washed for weeks, reached her and she fought down a wave of nausea.

She sat quite still, stunned by fear. She was being irrational. Surely he was nothing more sinister than a clumsy suitor? The workman moved close to the earl's horse. Now her humiliation was being gawped at by all and sundry. The next thing she knew the earl wrenched away from her, struggling to control his horse as it reared and bucked. His face took on a mottled red colour as the stallion pulled away and refused to move back up to Eliza.

She relaxed as she spotted Grace and Major Overton riding towards her. With his stallion now calmer the earl came alongside her but it was clear he had seen them too.

"It seems we are not to be given any time alone, my dear. May I call on you tomorrow? As you must realise, I have something of a particular nature to say to you."

Eliza allowed her mare to take a few steps away from the stallion. "This is all rather sudden, my lord. Forgive me for being a little surprised. I am residing with my sister at present. Her husband, the Duke of Cathlay, is a stickler for the proprieties. I wouldn't want to abuse their hospitality by agreeing to your request without his approval."

He nodded and was about to say more but his horse reared up again. Eliza glanced towards the bush which was now behind them. A flash of grey serge disappeared from view. Was the workman spying on them? The earl yanked frantically at the reins but his horse refused to settle. What did he expect, pulling at the poor animal like that? He kicked it and her eyes narrowed as she noticed the spurs he was wearing. Red marks were clearly visible on the horse's flanks. He rode off as the others came close, calling over his shoulder.

"Until tomorrow, my dear."

Eliza watched him go and shivered violently. The red woollen habit could have been the finest gauze she was so cold. Major Overton pulled up beside her and she couldn't but notice the level of his horsemanship compared to that of the earl. She steeled herself for a telling off but apart from giving her a penetrating glance he showed no sign of reacting.

"Are you ready to depart, Lady Eliza?"

"Yes of course."

"Grace joined them. "I'm sorry you got stuck with the Earl of Milton, horrid man. At least we can have a good chat on the way home. Miss Hill had some exciting news. Her sweetheart has sold out of the army and they are to be married. They couldn't tell us this morning as he was on his way to inform his family of their betrothal."

Eliza tried to concentrate on Grace's conversation. If the earl went straight to see Cathlay would he deny him until he had spoken to her? She didn't think he would take a refusal well if Cathlay had agreed to his request to speak to her. This was the sort of situation she had been afraid would destroy her peace. Grace was saying something else.

"Are you feeling well? You have gone quite pale."

"I must own to feeling a little fatigued."

"It was probably that late night and it can't have been much fun being forced to talk to the earl."

Grace seemed disturbed by her indisposition. Eliza smiled at her. "It's nothing a good night's sleep won't cure I assure you."

They reached the door of Lady Grant's mansion. Eliza noticed another horse had joined them. Bright left his reins with Major Overton and helped Grace to alight. He waited with her until the butler had admitted her, calling her goodbyes. The door closed behind her and Bright led her horse around to the mews. She gasped as she noticed the grey serge suit Bright was wearing.

"Yes, it was Bright who rescued you from the earl's clutches, or were you relishing his embrace?" Major Overton's voice was harsh.

Eliza sat up straighter in the saddle.

"No I wasn't. I didn't want to give him any encouragement but after you squared up to him like that in front of half the Ton I had no choice."

"Of course you had a choice or do you have a fancy to be a countess?"

"Oh! You're as bad as him."

"Come let us ride on."

She saw him signal to Bright to drop back. His face looked all severe angles and disapproval in the twilight. Who was he to disapprove of her actions? She settled in to the rhythm of the mare's elegant trot.

"Do not compare me to a man like him. He's rotten through and through. If you hadn't taken matters into your own hands I would've seen him off."

He seemed to be talking through clenched teeth. Why would he think she had welcomed Milton's advances?"

"Why? So you could chase me instead?"

He was silent for a few minutes. She had a glimpse of his face in the light from an oil lamp and his chin seemed to be working with no words coming out. He was certainly angry. His voice when it came was much quieter than she expected.

"The last thing I want is to marry a woman from a noble family. As a shy young man visiting friends' houses in school holidays I had my fill of scheming aristocratic women. If it wasn't for the help I've had from your brother I'd leave you to the arms of that villain, but my conscience won't let me."

Eliza felt tired and shaken and the last bit of her composure fell away. Her voice rose to a higher pitch than normal. "If you aren't chasing me then why did you agree to accompany me today?"

Chapter Eleven

N at took a deep breath and hung on to the last shreds of his temper. "With Luke called away unexpectedly I could hardly refuse Lady Grant's request to take his place. My distrust of the Earl of Milton runs deep. After you encouraged him last night I had Bright watching out today in case he showed up."

They rode on in silence until they came to a junction.

"I'm not exactly sure where the Cathlays live."

Lady Eliza lifted her head and met his glance. "The next turning on the right and it's the second mansion along."

Nat held Bright's horse for him to show her up the steps to the Cathlay mansion. Lady Grant had a fine house but it paled into insignificance to this one. If anything underlined the impossibility of him aspiring to Lady Eliza's hand this did. Did he want to aspire to her hand? A part of him almost certainly did so this was a timely reminder. There was the lady herself to consider as well. She had clearly taken against him. One thing he was certain of was that he had to keep her safe from the earl. Tomorrow he would write to the address Max had given him and hope it found him on his travels.

Eliza ran up the stairs as fast as her pounding head would let her. If she was quick she might be able to waylay Cathlay before he set off for his club. Augusta met her in the hall.

"Eliza, what's wrong?"

"I'll explain in a minute. I must speak to Cathlay straight away."

"Go and sit in the small drawing room and I'll fetch him to you."

Augusta hurried away. Eliza went into the cosy drawing room the family used when they were alone and dropped into a seat by the fire. She bowed her head and massaged her temples. The door opened but Augusta was alone.

"I'm afraid we have missed him, he is already on his way to Brooks. What is the problem?"

What was she to do? She had to do something. She jumped up. "I'll have the carriage put to. I must talk to Cathlay before the morning."

Augusta caught her by the wrist. "Tell me what it is and I will engage to stay up until he is home to talk to him for you." Augusta gave a soft chuckle. "You will set the Ton by the ears if you turn up at Brooks."

"Lud, you are right of course." Eliza burst out laughing. "I'm so angry I'm not thinking properly. I can imagine the commotion if I knocked on their door, even in a riding habit as mannishly cut as this. It would have been better to let them fight a duel."

Eliza threw herself back onto the sofa. "Thank you. That will have to do. It will serve I suppose as long as the earl doesn't find Cathlay at Brooks."

"I think you had better start at the beginning, Eliza."

Eliza gave Augusta an account of what had happened. "With half the Ton watching I had no choice but to ride a little way with the earl but he scares me, Augusta. He forced a kiss on me with nothing but a scrawny bush to hide us." She shuddered. "If Cathlay was to agree to let him speak to me I don't think he would accept a refusal without a fight and I expect he would fight dirty."

Vague memories of remarks by Major Overton about Milton came back to her. "I should have listened to Major Overton's warnings about him, but I'm sure he is pursuing me too and I didn't trust his motives."

"The Earl of Milton did have a rather unpleasant cast of countenance. I can't say I'm surprised at his actions today. Don't worry, Cathlay won't give anyone permission to address you yet. I told him I'd promised he would fend off all your suitors and he's more than happy to do so. He said only the other day that he feels you need more time to get over Mama's death."

"That's good of him. I knew it would be like this, men chasing me for my money."

"Perhaps you had better have a quiet day at home tomorrow." Augusta took her hand and gave it a squeeze. "It's fortunate we have no engagements we must be keep tonight. Tomorrow we are dining at home. Cathlay said he would invite one or two of his friends to join us."

"As long as they are married I won't mind. I mean to stay away from all bachelors for now."

"I am sure Major Overton is a gentleman, whatever his eventual intentions towards you. You will be quite safe to go about in company with him and the Bamfords. The alternative is to turn into a recluse."

Eliza sniffed. "At this moment the prospect of becoming a recluse has a great deal of appeal."

Bright waited until the door closed behind Lady Wyndham. He walked down the steps and reclaimed his horse. As Nat waited for him to mount he spotted a male figure slipping silently out of the front door. It looked like the Duke of Cathlay. On an impulse he jumped down and threw his reins to Bright.

"I'll walk home from here."

He waited until Bright had disappeared from view and then set off in pursuit of the figure. From the direction he had taken he was probably on his way to his club. With his long legged stride he soon caught up with the Duke. The dilemma of how to approach him was solved by the Duke himself. He stopped on a dark stretch of road and turned to face him. Nat noticed him take a tighter grip on his cane. No fool the Duke of Cathlay, it looked like the ones Luke had with the hidden blades.

"I mean you no harm, Your Grace."

"Ah, Overton. I thought it might be you from your height. Walk with me and tell me what it is you want."

"I'll happily walk with you but what I have to say needs to be said in private."

"Good Lord, is it my permission to offer for Lady Eliza you want? I expected to be showered with requests but not this quickly. Let me tell you now, I intend to shield her from hopeful suitors until she is in a better frame of mind."

Nat felt the blood rush to his cheeks. What sort of a savage did the man think he was?

"I can assure you nothing was further from my mind."

The Duke gave a soft laugh. "I can hear offence in your voice. I'm sorry for it but you must realise this is a rather unconventional meeting."

Nat struggled to contain his temper. "Of course I do. My grandfather may have started life as a shipwright but I have been brought up as a gentleman."

"There is no need to poker up, young man. I apologise unreservedly for offending you. It seems I am to understand your business with me is extremely urgent. What are your politics?"

"Politics? That isn't something I've given much thought to." Nat was so mystified he relaxed.

"I am dining at Brooks tonight. I would hesitate to invite a committed Tory to join me there."

"I'm still in my riding gear."

"I have friends to talk to first but I could meet you for dinner later, if you are happy to be seen there."

"That's kind of you but what I have to say has to stay private. I followed you on a whim as I consider it something you need to know urgently."

"My friends are all discreet but I'm sure I can arrange some private conversation. Brooks in an hour?"

Nat sensed the Duke was losing patience. Could he risk having his say here? The sounds of someone walking past decided him.

"I will see you at Brooks in an hour."

"Excellent. Tell them you're my guest and they will bring you up to me. Now if you will excuse me." He walked on, swinging his cane.

Nat turned on his heel and set off for Luke's house at a trot. If Garner wasn't back he was in trouble. Five minutes later he ran up the stairs to Luke's townhouse. One of the footmen opened the door immediately.

"Is Garner back yet?"

"Yes, Major. I'll send him up to you. I believe he has brought his nephew with him."

Nat ran up the stairs and was tearing off his clothes when there was a knock at his bedroom door.

"Come in."

Garner entered, followed by a gangly but pleasant faced young man.

"This is the nephew I told you about, Major."

The young man raced across to help him pull off his boots. "I'm Jones, sir."

A quick witted young valet was exactly what he needed. "I'm pleased you're here Jones. I need to be at Brooks in three quarters of an hour, dressed for dinner."

Garner pulled out a selection of evening clothes. "You help him into those, Rhys. He's not good with cravats. I'll fetch a selection and order a carriage sent round at the same time."

"It might be quicker to walk, Garner."

"They will drop you as close as possible without slowing too much for traffic."

"An excellent suggestion. Thank you."

By the time Garner came back with an armful of cravats he was fully dressed apart from his coat and Jones was helping him into his evening shoes.

"If you don't mind me helping, sir, I have a quick way of tying a reasonable cravat for you. I've mostly been working as a footman but I did have a couple of weeks with a sociable old gentlemen who was generally too far to the wind to manage to do it for himself."

Nat laughed. "I'm perfectly sober but I still haven't mastered the art of tying a good cravat for civilian wear, so yes please."

An anxious looking Jones picked up a well starched neck cloth. "I didn't mean to imply you were foxed, sir."

"I perfectly understand, Jones. When can you start working

for me?"

Jones fumbled with the neck cloth. He dropped it and picked up a fresh one. "Thank you, sir." He smiled happily. "I can start straight away. I was engaged for a month at the Earl of Milton's establishment but most of us have been let go, with no pay."

Nat went still. "Why was that?"

"Oh it was nothing to do with our work, sir." Jones looked worried. "I shouldn't say this but I believe the earl has serious money problems."

"The earl was my captain in the army for a brief time period. I soon had him replaced. I can believe he could have run through his inheritance so quickly. He loved to gamble but he's the worst card player I've seen, too reckless by half."

Jones nodded as he finished tying the cravat. "How is that, sir?"

Nat smiled at the eagerness in his voice. "It will be better than anything I could do. Thank you. I'm pleased you're able to join me straight away. I believe I shall be socialising rather a lot for the next few weeks."

Jones's information magnified what he had already heard. If Milton's money troubles were so pressing he would stay by Eliza's side until Max was able to return. Jones beamed at him and held out his evening coat. With Garner's help it was the work of a few moments to ease him into it.

"We mustn't forget your diamond pin, major." Garner showed Jones where Nat kept his personal items and handed him the pin.

Jones held up the pin. "What a fine piece, Major. It will be a pleasure to dress you."

Nat moved to a looking glass and placed the pin in the snowy folds of his neck cloth.

"It was a coming of age present from my grandfather but I find it a little too ostentatious for everyday use. Tomorrow I'll have you help me decide on something a little plainer."

Nat ran down the stairs with the hall clock showing he still had fifteen minutes. The coach was waiting for him outside. It dropped him around the corner from Brooks and he walked the rest of the way. His pace slowed as he neared the elegant building made largely of a warm coloured, almost yellow, stone. He wished Jones hadn't tied his neck cloth quite so tight. He gave the Duke's name at the door and was shown up to a large dining room. The Duke stood to greet him.

"Overton. I'm glad you were able to join us at such short notice." The Duke's glance swept over him and he seemed to approve of what he saw.

"Gentlemen, allow me to introduce Major Overton. He is the nephew of Lord Overton of Overton Grange, a neighbour of my wife's brother."

Introductions were made and Nat realised he was to join all of them for dinner. His mouth felt dry at the prospect but surely it could be little different to a regimental dinner. Except of course he would be on show to a group of distinguished Whig politicians. He knew a moment's panic, quickly damped down. He owed it to himself and his family to give a good account of himself.

He was careful to drink little of the excellent wine on offer during the meal. He needed a clear head. Cathlay's friends proved to be much more welcoming than he had expected and he was soon enjoying himself. The talk moved to politics and most of what was said made sense to him.

"I can see you nodding agreement there, Overton," the Duke

said. "Do you see yourself as a Whig now we have introduced you to politics?"

Nat considered for a moment. "I think I may well be, Your Grace."

The man sitting next to him clapped him on the back. "You're Overton's heir, aren't you?"

Nat felt a blush flood his cheeks. "Yes I am."

"Excellent. We'll have you on the Whig benches in the house one of these days. You had better put him up for the club, Cathlay."

To Nat's surprise, there was a general murmur of agreement. What a shame his grandfather wasn't alive. He would have relished his success tonight, but this wasn't getting him any closer to warning the Duke of the danger Eliza stood in. The meal came to a close and Cathlay invited him to join him in a glass of brandy. The rest of the party went off to the gaming room. They adjourned to a quiet alcove and once they had been served the Duke picked up his glass and stared at the amber liquid.

"You did well there, Overton. I would certainly be happy to put you forward for Brooks if you like, but that's not what you came here for."

Nat glanced around. There was no one near. "I believe your sister-in-law is in danger. The Marquess of Hargreaves has given me a lot of assistance and I feel honour bound to protect her."

The Duke's eyes narrowed and he studied Nat intently. "What exactly is the nature of the threat? I have made sure we won't be disturbed."

Nat nodded but still had another glance around. "The lady in question is being pursued by an individual who Viscount

Enstone and I believe to be a murderer."

The Duke's eyebrows shot up. "What?"

"I know it sounds improbable but it's true. We believe the Earl of Milton, Captain Denby when we knew him, arranged for the murder of his father and older brother. I have information from a reliable source, corroborated by something else I heard only today, that he is now in considerable debt."

"Even if all this is true how can she be in danger with her family to protect her?"

"A desperate man is a dangerous man. I stood in for Luke today to escort his sister and Lady Eliza on a ride in the park. The earl appeared and separated her from the group. After his particular attention to her at Miss Bamfield's come out ball last night I was ready for his possible appearance. My groom, formerly my batman, spared Lady Eliza from a most uncomfortable experience when the earl tried to force his attentions on to her."

"What were you doing letting him take her away from your party if you suspect his motives?"

Nat flushed. "I was much at fault. Captain Denby was under my command for a brief period. I allowed a comment from him about my grandfather to overturn my good sense and I lost my temper. Lady Eliza felt she had to agree to ride with him to avoid a scene. She seems to mistrust me more than she is wary of the earl."

The Duke shook his head. "I'm not sure my wife did the right thing in encouraging Eliza to come to Town. She is still not over the death of her mother and she is wary of any young man who could potentially be a suitor. Hargreaves Hall is her last link with the past."

A flash of hope hit Nat. Could there be a chance for him once

Eliza was more settled? "She has certainly taken against me but then it was partially my fault that she overturned her gig and she hasn't forgiven me. I have an address for her brother but he told me he will be touring Scotland and it may be some time before a letter reaches him. I decided I should extend the warning to you as her nearest male relative in London."

"Thank you. I intend to have any suitors investigated but, echoing what I said earlier, I didn't expect that to be needed quite so soon. Do you have any proof of your suspicions about the earl?"

Nat pulled piece of paper out of his pocket. "This is the address of my grandfather's man of business in Manchester. The Milton estates are near to Manchester. He will tell you what he told me. The financial side is proven I think. When he mentioned it I asked him to employ someone discreet to investigate the circumstances of the late earl's death. What he came up with is interesting but not enough to go to the authorities with."

"Thank you. I am grateful to you for your assistance. Do you have a personal interest in the case? It seems a lot of trouble to go to out of idle curiosity."

"Self-preservation. I thought the more information I had the safer I would be. Denby never forgave me for having him removed from my command. If it had been up to me I would have had him court martialled."

The Duke's eyebrows shot up. "Would you care to share what happened with me?"

"We were on the continent. He went out one night and brought a local girl back to camp. Luke and I heard screams and went to investigate. We were too late to save her." Nat paused and took a deep breath. "The woman was expecting a child and he was so rough with her she lost the baby a few hours later and bled to death. Her face was beaten black and blue and there were bruises on her neck." He shuddered. "I wouldn't want to see any woman married to him and particularly not the sister of a man who has been so kind to me."

The Duke stared at him. "I'm surprised the story never got out."

Nat felt his colour rising. Did his word not count as the grandson of a shipwright? He started to rise but was stopped by a hand on his shoulder.

"No need to look angry, I believe you. You may safely leave it with me to find out if anything can be done. I can't see a peer being tried but if I can find enough clear cut evidence we might be able to force him to flee the country."

Nat leaned back in his chair. "Thank you. I'm surprised at how relieved I am to share this with someone like you. It's been weighing on my mind. It was a shock to see him at the Bamford's ball hanging around Lady Eliza, I can tell you. I tried to warn her about him but...."

The Duke's eyes twinkled. "You could hardly tell her the whole story and without that she wouldn't believe you I suspect."

Nat nodded. "I think she saw the blood on his horse's flanks today. If I had been quicker witted I could have told her about the way he treated his horses, but she may not have believed me even then."

"Eliza won't be interested in a fellow who spurs his horse. I thank you once again for watching over her. I would be delighted if you would dine with the family tomorrow. We have a quiet night at home for once." The earl smiled but the invitation felt like a summons.

"Thank you, Your Grace. What time should I arrive?"

Chapter Twelve

Eliza refused an offer of tea and went back to her room. Alice helped her out of her habit.

"I think I'll take to my bed for a bit, Alice. I have the most dreadful headache."

"I'll have cook make up a tisane for you, my lady."

Alice helped her out of the rest of her clothes and into a fresh nightdress. She crawled into bed with a sigh of relief. The tisane took the edge off the headache and she managed to eat most of the light supper Alice brought up to her. She drifted off into an uneasy sleep and eventually woke up early the next morning with her sheets in a tangle. She sat up in bed as the last mists of sleep lifted. Her dreams had been full of a tall, dark haired military man with grey eyes that missed nothing. In her dreams she had enjoyed kissing him.

A maid came in to light her fire and went down to the kitchens afterwards to order hot chocolate for her. She read for a while but had to keep going back over each page before anything sank in. Eventually she rang the bell for Alice. She hardly noticed the pretty soft green morning dress Alice laid out for her. Once she was dressed she ran down the stairs and poked her head around the door of the breakfast room. There was no sign of Cathlay. A glance at the clock in the hall showed it to be nearly nine o'clock. He must have stayed out late last night if he wasn't at breakfast yet.

With nothing better to do she wandered in and found a seat near to the window. The breakfast room faced east and the sun shining through lifted her spirits. The butler came in and laid the morning newspapers at the head of the table.

"What can I get you, Lady Eliza?"

"Some coffee would be lovely, thank you."

She was on her second cup of the hot liquid when the door opened to admit Cathlay. A sigh escaped her.

"Eliza you look troubled." The Duke sat next to her and took her hand. "Augusta has told me about your unwanted suitor. Don't worry I won't give any man permission to address you without checking with you first."

Eliza let out a trembling breath. "Thank you. I can handle most men but the Earl of Milton frightens me. He had spurred his horse unmercifully. The poor animal had blood all over his flanks."

"I have heard some rather unsavoury tales about the man. If you would feel safer away from London we can always take you to stay with one of your sisters for a while. We could even travel up to Scotland and find Max if it would make you feel better."

Eliza stared at her brother-in-law. Rather than brushing aside her fears, as she had been afraid he would, he was taking it seriously.

"So you don't think I'm worrying unnecessarily?"

Cathlay hesitated. "No. I don't think you are. I'm going out later to check some facts. I'll know more after that. Try not to worry too much today but I will specify to all the staff the only callers who are to be admitted."

129

The muscles at the back of her neck tightened and she shivered. "I have a bad feeling about this. Can't you tell me what you have heard?"

"Not until I have found out more. A quiet day at home will be good for you. I have told Sayers we are not at home for the rest of the day." He stood up. "Come. Let's see you eat some of this breakfast or my chef will feel under-appreciated."

Nat woke up much later than he usually did and with a head that suggested he had drunk a little too much the night before. A few hours in the gaming room at Brooks with such congenial company as the Duke of Cathlay and his friends had been more fun than he could have imagined. Perhaps he should take up the offer of sponsorship to join Brooks.

He rang the bell for Garner and he arrived with Jones in tow.

"If you are agreeable, Major, I could start teaching Jones how you need to be looked after. With the viscount still out of Town I have plenty of time on my hands."

Nat nodded absently. Strange Luke hadn't mentioned a trip away before, what could be keeping him? "Thank you, Garner. That would be a great help."

Garner was a good teacher and Jones was quick-witted. He was soon made ready to face the day.

"I have no engagements until dinner. After breakfast would you two make me a list of everything I need to buy in the event of a prolonged stay in London?"

Garner answered for them. "We'll be delighted. Jones and I could purchase most of the items on your behalf."

"What about evening wear? Have I got anything suitable for an informal dinner party with a small group of friends in a private house?"

"I think we can manage that," Garner said. "However, now they have your measurements, the tailors should be able to make you some more coats with one fitting when they are ready."

Garner studied him, hopefully. Nat smiled. "Order everything you think I will need. I trust your judgement and it will help Jones to accompany you. I'll buy some more tie pins myself. Where would you recommend?"

"Rundell and Bridges, sir, without a doubt. They are at 32 Ludgate Hill."

After a hearty breakfast, Nat's niggly headache had lifted and he found he was looking forward to dinner with the Cathlays and Lady Eliza. He borrowed one of Luke's canes and walked around to the mews to find Bright. He should have sent a footman to order a carriage but he was so used to doing most things for himself in the army he couldn't get used to Luke's army of servants. Besides which he needed to speak to Bright in private. Bright must have spotted him because he was waiting for him when he reached the mews.

"Can you borrow one of Luke's carriages to take me to Rundell and Bridges on Ludgate Hill? I shan't need you after that, but have a nose around wherever you think you might find news of our friend the earl."

Bright grunted. "He's no friend of mine."

"Indeed not." Nat pulled out a roll of notes. "Buy whatever items you want as disguises. We may have to stay in London longer than I had expected. Garner and Jones are off to buy me some more clothes. If you need any advice I expect they will be back in a few hours."

"Yes, Major. Are you sure you don't want me to stay by you? Denby will be as mad as fire at you getting in his way with the lady."

"He will be occupying himself trying to speak to the Duke of Cathlay today so I should be safe. I'll be back by late afternoon I expect."

Nat waited by the mews, enjoying the unseasonably warm day. His mind kept drifting to the prospect of spending more time with Eliza. He fingered the cane. He must stay alert. Perhaps he should take Bright with him but he was too short to pass as a footman.

Bright walked towards him, followed by the coach. "I'll come with you as far as Ludgate Hill, Major. It's as good a place as any to start a search." He jumped up beside the coachman.

Nat agreed to have his purchases sent around to Luke's house, as long as they arrived before the evening. With the amount of money he had spent he couldn't blame Mr Rundell for wanting time to check if he was genuine. They parted on excellent terms with Nat accepting an offer to call him a hackney coach.

He stopped the Hackney before they reached Luke's house. A walk would help to clear his head. As luck would have it, he bumped into a couple of old army friends and spent a pleasant few hours with them. His stomach flipped when they parted company. It was time to go back and prepare himself for dinner with the Cathlays, a daunting prospect. The Duke appeared genial on the surface but he couldn't entirely hide his sharp intellect. Then there was the Duchess. Even Max spoke of her with awestruck affection. She was a formidable woman and if she guessed he was attracted to Eliza would she think he wasn't good enough for her? Heat swept through him at the memory of a spiteful girl giving away his secrets, and her equally spiteful mother. The mother had made it plain she had only allowed her son to invite him because of his grandfather's money. A shipwright's boy would never be good enough for one of her daughters.

He stopped abruptly and had to apologise to a gentleman who nearly fell over him. Denby had called him a shipwright's boy. The story of him being sent home in disgrace in an outside seat on the stagecoach must be common knowledge. The memory of his humiliation was still enough to make him want to curl up and hide. The object of his ardour had laughed at him and called him a silly boy for thinking there was anything between them. He had always hoped that had been for her mother's benefit.

He must think rationally. He was nearly twelve years older and the army had taught him a lot about people. Lady Eliza's family seemed much more sensible than most of the families he had stayed with. He would find out later if his instincts about them were true. A small part of him was daring to hope he might have a chance of wooing Eliza but the most important thing was that he wanted to be allowed to protect her. He kept his head down as he walked but stole a glance around. No one was near to him but he would have to take Bright with him next time with so much to distract him. Denby was a real threat to all of them but especially Eliza.

He turned into Grosvenor Street and reached Luke's house without incident. He ran up to his room, eager to see what Garner and Jones had unearthed for him. At least now he had the means to make sure he was well dressed. Not like the time his then best friend's sister had laughed at his outmoded evening wear. A footman let him in and he went straight up to his room. An excited Jones held up an exquisite waistcoat. It was plain enough to look manly but delicately embroidered in a shiny golden thread barely a shade darker than the colour of the material.

"The tailor had this almost made when the order was cancelled." Jones held up the waistcoat. "He added a bit of decoration to make it a little different to the order and we bought it for you. They've finished it off to your size. What do you think?"

"It's elegant. You're not trying to turn me into an over-dressed fop are you?"

"Of course not, Major." Jones dropped the waistcoat back on the bed with a look of horror on his face. He glanced up and saw Nat's grin. He grinned back.

"I like it very much. Will it be suitable to wear tonight?"

"I think so." Jones looked at his uncle.

Garner nodded. "With one of your plainly cut coats it will be perfect, Major Overton."

They set about preparing him and two hours later Garner declared him to be as fine as five pence.

"That's all down to you two, thank you. I like this cologne you found for me. What is it?"

"It's a mixture of lavender and lemon from Harris and Company. Jones will make a note of it and keep you stocked up."

"Do that but I will still try the other ones you bought."

Jones nodded. "Yes, Major. A package was delivered from Rundle and Bridges earlier."

"Good. My new tiepins."

Jones fetched the package. Nat opened it and laid the pins out on a side table for Garner to study.

"What do you think?"

"A good selection, if I may say so, sir. For a visit to a duke's establishment I think the ruby or even your diamond. The horse is perfect for a bachelor party and the pearl pin is more for day wear."

Nat hesitated and then plumped for the ruby. The diamond was too showy for his taste. He smiled to himself. His grandfather had been so ambitious for him. He settled the pin in the folds of the cravat he had managed to tie for himself. He walked across to the looking glass and a stranger stared back at him.

"I don't know how you have made a big fellow like me appear so elegant but thank you both. At least I don't have to worry about my appearance letting me down tonight."

Garner stared at him. "You have a natural elegance, Major Overton. If I wasn't already working for a splendid gentleman I would be jealous of my own nephew."

Garner seemed perfectly sincere and Nat's tight muscles relaxed out of their knots. He must remember he was an elegant gentleman now and not a scrubby schoolboy.

Eliza joined Augusta in the small drawing room. "How many friends has Cathlay invited?"

Augusta looked up from the letter she was reading. "Didn't he say? He has only invited Major Overton."

Eliza straightened her spine until it hurt. "Why invite him?"

"He met him at Brooks last night and thought to show civility to Max's neighbour. From the little I've seen of Major Overton, he seems a personable young man. Cathlay is quite taken with him, even though he lost some money to him, playing piquet of all things." Augusta laughed.

Eliza felt the blood drain from her face. Cathlay hardly ever lost at piquet. Could Major Overton be a card sharp? Surely not or he would have been drummed out of the army wouldn't he?

"Are you quite well, Eliza? You look horribly pale."

Eliza forced a smile. "It must be a trick of the light. I had better go and dress for dinner. Alice wants to try out a new style for my hair."

Augusta missed nothing and she was glad of the excuse to avoid more of her company. Alice was waiting for her. She helped her into a deep red dress which had just been delivered.

"There, I knew that dress would look well on you." Alice stood back studying her. "What about your pearl necklace with this?"

Eliza studied her reflection. The dress was fairly low cut but perfectly acceptable. "Yes that would be best. This dress is quite dramatic and needs something to soften it."

Alice piled her dark, silky hair high on her head and threaded a string of tiny pearls and rubies through the whole arrangement. At last she was satisfied. Eliza joined the Cathlays in the formal drawing room they used to greet dinner guests. Cathlay rose as she entered and led her to a chair. He sat next to Augusta on the sofa opposite.

"It was Major Overton who provided me with worrying information about the Earl of Milton."

Eliza glared at him. "When did he have the opportunity?"

"He sought me out last night." Cathlay smiled. "He has annoyed you, hasn't he? He said as much."

"It sounds like he said rather too much altogether." Eliza gritted her teeth. "I'm sure there is some sort of personal battle going on between him and the earl."

Cathlay's expression hardened. "You are correct. He told me about that too." He hesitated. "As Captain Denby the earl served under Major Overton. Overton tried to have him court martialled but Denby had powerful friends. He was removed from Overton's command but, from what I can find out, he received no other punishment."

He looked uncomfortable, what wasn't he telling her? She glanced at Augusta. Cathlay nodded and Augusta continued.

"Major Overton and Captain Bamford, now Viscount Enstone, found Captain Denby ravishing a local woman. They were too late to save her from her ordeal and she died."

Eliza gasped. "Is there proof of this?"

Cathlay nodded. "I've spoken to someone from the regiment. Overton's account was accurate. Going out so early I avoided the earl this morning but I expect he will keep trying."

Eliza jumped up and strode about the room. She had been a fool to ignore Major Overton's warnings.

"I had a feeling the wretched man was trying to fix his interest with me at the Bamford's Ball. Major Overton stayed near me and he couldn't. Then his groom rescued me from what I'm sure was an attempt to force me into marriage, after the earl separated me from the rest of my party in the park."

"I expect so. The word is he is completely done up." Cathlay looked from one to the other. "I don't think you should go out without a bodyguard and an escort."

Eliza resumed her pacing. She reached the window overlooking the front of the house.

"Lud. I'm sure that's the earl running up the front steps now." She stepped back from the window and shuddered.

There was a loud knock followed by angry words interspersed with Sayers's calm responses. It was some minutes until Eliza saw the earl run down the steps and stalk away.

"I knew my money would attract fortune hunters. I didn't expect to have problems like this. I had better go back to

Hargreaves."

Cathlay joined her and put a hand on her shoulder. "I'm not sure that would be safe. I found out today that, if anything, Milton is worse than Overton said and he is correct that the man is desperately short of money." He smiled. "I wondered last night if Overton had a fancy for you himself and was exaggerating to see off a rival."

Scalding heat ran through her and settled in her face. She strode over to Augusta and sank onto the sofa beside her.

"Augusta, what shall I do?"

Augusta gathered her into an embrace. "Hush now. We'll keep you safe. I wish I hadn't persuaded you to leave Hargreaves in the first place."

"I don't blame you. I was enjoying the change of scene as you said I would. No one could have anticipated me attracting a rogue like the Earl of Milton. He makes me shudder whenever I see him."

Cathlay took the seat opposite. "So many people know your godmother left you everything that Milton may well have decided to target you even before you came to London. As I see it we have two alternatives. We could send you to Diana with an armed guard. Their castle is well-nigh impregnable. The other option is to stay here. I've got people investigating the Earl of Milton over another matter Overton brought to my attention. If he disappears before there is enough proof to accuse him you won't have any peace of mind for fear of him tracking you down."

Augusta gasped and Eliza stared at her brother-in-law.

"You mean I would be the bait to keep him in London?"

Chapter Thirteen

Nat ran lightly up the stairs and lifted the heavy knocker. The door was opened almost immediately and his heart hammered in his chest. He was ushered inside by a tall footman who helped him out of his greatcoat as the brass-faced, longcase clock in the hall chimed seven o'clock. With Luke not around to ask, punctuality seemed best and as an ex-military man perhaps he would be forgiven if the custom was to arrive late, as so many did to evening functions.

The butler appeared. "Major Overton?"

Nat nodded. "I am indeed."

"I believe you are the only guest tonight. Follow me if you would."

Nat lowered his gaze to hide his surprise. Why would the Duke only invite him?

The butler opened the door of a well-appointed drawing room.

"Major Overton, Your Grace."

Nat was barely aware of the exquisite décor and sumptuous carpets. He clenched his fists to stop himself from tugging at his suddenly too tight neck cloth. The three people in the room stood up to greet him as he entered. He almost took a step back as his eyes found Eliza. Her expression seemed much softer than he was used to. The deep red dress she was wearing emphasised every womanly curve. He longed to bury his face in her glossy hair. Somehow he must find the courage to court her. How could he ever settle for anyone else?

The Duchess stepped forward. She appeared surprisingly friendly for a matron with such a fearsome reputation. He grasped the hand she held out and bowed low over it.

"A pleasure to see you again, Your Grace."

"Indeed, Major Overton. From what my husband tells me we are much in your debt."

He glanced at the Duke who smiled.

"I've told them the whole story, Overton. We want to ask your advice after dinner but let's enjoy ourselves first."

Dinner was announced and the Duke held out an arm for Augusta and led the way into the dining room. Nat found his voice when Eliza stared up at him.

"You look quite delightful, Lady Eliza."

She gave him an appraising glance before accepting his arm. "Thank you. You are very fine yourself."

She tucked her hand around his elbow, bringing her much closer. He caught his breath as he savoured the scent of a rose garden in summer with a hint of something spicier.

"Augusta told me you beat Cathlay at piquet. No mean feat."

Nat stiffened. Was there an accusation in that comment? He followed the Cathlays into an intimate family dining room.

"I was fortunate in the cards. We were well matched in our first two games. I would say His Grace is slightly the better player."

Cathlay laughed. "Don't listen to him, Eliza. I believe I have found my master." He handed Augusta to a chair. "We don't stand on ceremony here for small parties, Overton. If you sit opposite we can share the conversation between all of us."

Nat pulled out Lady Eliza's chair for her and settled into the chair opposite Augusta, who smiled at him. The tension between his shoulders eased.

"How are you enjoying London so far?" The Duchess asked.

A chuckle escaped him. "It is certainly interesting but I suspect I'm more of a country man at heart."

Lady Eliza frowned. He longed to reach out and rub the lines from her brow.

"Don't you know?"

He sipped at his wine. Not even Luke had so far served a better one. The Cathlays certainly lived in style. "No I don't believe I do yet. I went into the army at eighteen. I was abroad a lot and have never spent much time in London."

"What made you sell out?" the Duke asked.

"My grandfather's failing health. I'm glad I was able to spend his last months with him." Nat forced a smile as he waited for a probe into his background that didn't come.

Lady Eliza touched his sleeve. "How sad for you. Our mother died a year ago." Her voice tailed off and she looked away from everyone.

Was that a tear on her cheek? "I was sad I hadn't been in England to spend much time with him during my army days but it was wonderful to get to know him all over again as an adult." He took a deep breath. "He achieved a lot in his life and I feel privileged to have been his grandson."

Again he waited for questions that didn't come. A snuffling sound had everyone turn to Lady Eliza. Nat controlled the impulse to take her in his arms when he saw the tears staining her cheeks. He contented himself with offering her a silk handkerchief. Eliza buried her face in it for a moment.

"I'm so sorry but that's how I feel about Mama."

Nat gently squeezed her hand before he realised what he was doing. "You have no need to apologise. I still feel sad about my grandfather and it must have been worse for you as you were used to living with your mother."

Lady Eliza nodded. "Thank you. I do miss her dreadfully. At least at Hargreaves Hall I still felt close to her." She blew her nose and smiled up at him.

The forced smile and slight flush in her cheeks told their own story but she had herself back in hand. He searched, unsuccessfully, for something to say to ease the tension.

"It was hard for you seeing Mama through her last few months," The Duchess said. "It will be a while before you are more settled."

The meal lived up to the wine and Nat sat back with anticipation when the ladies left them to their port. He savoured his first sip.

"This is an excellent port, Your Grace."

"Thank you. We Whigs like our port." The Duke sat back in his chair. "Now there is something I want to ask of you."

Eliza sat with her hands around a dish of tea, savouring the warmth. She studied the shadows cast by the fire crackling merrily in front of her. Perhaps she should stay in London and face up to the problem of the Earl of Milton? She shivered. Running away from Hargreaves to avoid Major Overton hadn't exactly worked out well. Something about the Major irked her but at least she didn't feel she was in physical danger when she was with him. Augusta sat beside her.

"You seem pre-occupied. Are you still worrying about the

earl?"

"I'm thinking about what Cathlay said. He's right. I won't have any peace of mind with the earl on the loose, now I know what he's capable of. Alice heard he tried three times today to speak to Cathlay."

"He is certainly persistent for a man who has only recently met you. Suspicious in itself, given your fortune." Augusta smiled. "Not that I'm suggesting for a moment he couldn't have succumbed to your charms. Major Overton struggled to take his eyes off you when he arrived."

Eliza scowled. Overton was at least a gentleman, even if he had made her ride astride his horse, but she wanted some time to herself. "I wish men wouldn't do that."

"Do what?" Augusta wrinkled her nose.

"Assume any unmarried woman is fair game for their fantasies."

Augusta laughed out loud. "You can't blame a man for looking. Where would we be if they weren't interested in us?"

"Enjoying some blissful peace and quiet."

The door opened and Eliza glanced up to see Major Overton walking towards her. Augusta rose and offered the men tea. Eliza saw her point to her vacated seat and smile at the major. He hesitated but sank down next to her. His thigh brushed hers briefly and she gasped. He pulled apart quickly but he seemed to radiate heat. A shudder ran through her. Augusta and Cathlay were talking on the other side of the room and after a quick glance their way he caught her hand.

"I've agreed to help with the Duke's plan but only if you are happy to go ahead." He squeezed her hand gently.

The concern in his voice was nearly her undoing. Lud, what was the matter with her? She was a Lovell for heaven's sake.

"It's not only me is it? I would hate any other woman to become his prey after what you told His Grace about him. This is something I have to do."

"As long as you're sure about it. I will do everything in my power to keep you safe. Bright was my batman in the army. There isn't a better bodyguard the length and breadth of England. I'll have him follow you everywhere. He's a master of disguise."

A grin escaped her. "He did a marvellous job getting me out of the earl's clutches yesterday."

"That's my girl. You'll do."

Eliza felt a warm glow at his words. She could imagine following him into perilous situations without a second thought. He must have been a good commanding officer.

"I hope so."

She smiled at him. Her attention was caught by the quality of his clothes. He was beautifully turned out. The golden embroidered waistcoat revealed by his cut away jacket was a masterpiece. He looked as if he had been dressed by an expert. There was no sign of the diamond pin but the ruby one that had taken its place looked almost as fine. Perhaps he had been left money by one of the Overtons?

"Where did you go to school?" she found herself asking."

He raised a quizzical eyebrow at her. "Rugby. My grandfather insisted. I would have rather stopped at home but I got used to it in the end. I'm grateful to him. I wouldn't have found my way into the army without that education."

Augusta handed the Major a dish of tea and Eliza noticed her exchange a smile with Cathlay. Her eyes narrowed as she looked from them to the major.

"The earl said your mother was a shipwright's daughter.

How would your grandfather have been able to afford a school like that?"

The words were out before she could stop them. She looked away from him and fanned her suddenly hot face. Lud, how could she be so impertinent? His reply was surprisingly gentle.

"My grandfather started life as a shipwright but by the time he died he had many business interests."

Eliza kept her head bowed. "I'm sorry, that was so rude of me."

He put his tea dish down on a side table and rested a hand on her arm. "I've had worse, especially from aristocratic girls."

A shadow passed across his face but she was prevented from replying by Cathlay's voice.

"I expect Major Overton has told you he is prepared to help protect you whilst my investigators search for the evidence to rid us of the Earl of Milton. The final decision on whether to go ahead with the plan is yours, Eliza. Do you want some time to consider?"

Eliza shook her head. "What is there to think about? It needs to be done. Major Overton says his man, Bright, is an expert bodyguard." She squared her shoulders. "How are we going to use me as bait?"

"First of all, I will have to talk to Milton if he calls tomorrow. I'll tell him I'm not turning him down but I've promised you I won't give permission to any man to address you until you have known them for a while." He glanced across at the major. "Major Overton, will escort you somewhere of your choosing tomorrow so you won't have to face the earl."

Eliza stiffened. She hadn't thought how much time she was likely to spend in Major Overton's company.

"Can we invite Grace to accompany us?"

Cathlay glanced at Major Overton. "What do you think?"

"I consider Milton so dangerous I couldn't countenance including Grace without Luke's express permission, given with full understanding of the situation. He's expected back tomorrow. If he shares the escort of Lady Eliza no one will think anything of it, since she and Miss Bamford are good friends."

He studied all three of them one by one before laying a hand on Eliza's arm. "Are you absolutely sure you want to go through with this?"

Eliza shivered, despite the warmth of his hand. "I've made my decision. I would never forgive myself if some other woman suffered as a result of my cowardice. Besides I trust you to keep me safe."

A furious rush of heat swept over her but yes she did trust him.

"Thank you. Of course the obvious thing is to take you to Lady Grant and Grace for the day." He looked across at Cathlay. "I have already warned Lady Grant to avoid Milton coming into contact with Grace. I believe it would be safe to take her into our confidence."

It was Augusta who answered. "I've known Lady Grant for a long time. We can trust her discretion. So unless she and Miss Bamford have unbreakable engagements tomorrow, Eliza could spend the day with them."

Cathlay nodded. "Agreed."

Augusta rang for a footman. "I'll write a note for Lady Grant and have it sent straight round. I believe they are having a quiet night at home like us."

Cathlay followed Augusta to a side table and they set about composing the note. The Major sat back and Eliza jumped

146

when his thigh touched hers again. The sofa was a tight fit with his large frame taking up so much of the space. This time he left his thigh pressed up against her. She risked a glance at him and he looked down with a smile playing at the corners of his mouth. Heat pooled deep in her abdomen. She fidgeted, trying to find a comfortable position. He pulled away and she noticed spots of dull red colouring his cheeks. Was he feeling the tug of physical attraction too?

He inched away from her and sat up straight. "What about tomorrow evening? Do you have an invitation to the Gilbert's ball?"

Cathlay turned to Augusta. "I believe we do?"

"Yes I'm sure of it."

"You can safely attend that one as Colonel Gilbert had no more time for Milton, Denby as he was then, than me or Luke. I know he hasn't been invited."

A smile spread across Augusta's face. "Splendid, Major Overton. It will be good to have an enjoyable evening without worrying."

Eliza groaned. "Couldn't we simply stay at home?"

Augusta shook her head. "I'm afraid that won't serve. We have to appear as normal as possible. If people notice changes in our behaviour Milton may get to hear of it. Cathlay is engaged with friend's tomorrow night but that is no reason for us not to go."

"You make an excellent conspirator, Your Grace. I am happy to escort Lady Eliza to Cavendish Square tomorrow and both of you to the Gilbert's ball later."

"Thank you. I'll ask Lady Grant if they are attending."

Augusta blotted her note and Cathlay folded it and secured the folds with one of his seals. The footman who answered

Augusta's summons was despatched to Cavendish Square to deliver it. The Duke suggested a few hands of whist. Eliza was no mean card player herself, but she had to acknowledge Major Overton as a master. Relief flooded her at the realisation he could easily have beaten Cathlay without cheating. They knew so little about him but everything they did know was positive. Why did it matter so much to her? She only just stopped herself in time from playing the wrong card as the truth hit her. She was attracted to him as a potential husband and the prospect scared her.

There was a knock and a servant entered with a note on a silver salver. Augusta accepted the note and placed it on the table.

"I recognise Lady Grant's handwriting. Shall we make this the last game now we have our reply?"

Cathlay gathered up the cards when they finished. "I'm glad we aren't playing for money. I would have been trounced again."

"We had the run of the cards and Lady Eliza must take much of the credit."

Augusta laughed. "Eliza always was a much better player than me." She scanned the note. "Lady Grant is engaged with friends tomorrow but she is quite happy for Grace and Eliza to entertain each other. She says for Eliza to join them as early in the morning as she likes. They have a soiree they can't miss in the evening, unfortunately."

Major Overton rubbed his chin. He smiled at Eliza. "Much as I would like to escort you myself in the morning I think we will have to be content with Bright riding with the driver. Milton will probably have a lookout stationed in the area. Bright will be armed. I'll send him around early so you can leave when

148

you want, Lady Eliza."

His eyes sought hers. There was a pause before Eliza was able to reply. "Thank you."

She lowered her gaze. It wouldn't do for him to see the disappointment she felt at not spending time with him.

"I'll have a couple of Luke's men join the Grant household for the day. In the evening I'll borrow one of his coaches with Bright sitting up with the coachman and escort you both." Again his gaze sought hers. "I'm sure we can guarantee you an enjoyable evening."

Eliza looked away quickly. A warm current ran through her and settled into an ache between her thighs. Cathlay's voice seemed distant. She forced herself to concentrate.

"I expect results in a few days from my investigators, Overton. Tomorrow will give Eliza a breathing space but there will be a few days where we can't avoid her meeting the earl in company. I'll do what I can to hint I don't want her rushed but we'll have to plan our campaign carefully."

"With your permission, I'll call here fairly early the day after tomorrow. Bright will bring me via your mews."

"Good. Now would you excuse me for a moment? I need to check something with Her Grace."

He led Augusta out of the room. Eliza felt a blush start in her toes and finish in her face. Cathlay wasn't matchmaking was he? Augusta would perhaps, but surely not Cathlay? The Major jumped out of his chair and moved around the table to stand behind her. He caught her hand in his. Her blush deepened as he gently traced her palm with the forefinger of his other hand. He leaned over and lowered his mouth to her ear.

"I shouldn't be doing this." His breath tickled her ear and he carried on caressing her hand. "Do you want me to stop?"

"No, I like it." The words were out almost before she realised she had said them.

"Good, so do I but my back is starting to ache from bending over."

She stood and would have overbalanced if he hadn't caught her wrist. What was the matter with her legs? They felt so heavy. He put his other arm behind her waist and pulled her towards him. She gasped as their bodies came together.

"Am I going too fast for you?"

Speech wouldn't come so she shook her head. The sensations shooting through her blocked everything else out of her mind. Now she knew how even sensible women allowed themselves to be seduced. He dipped his head and put his lips over hers. Shock made her open her mouth. Gently his tongue entered and she copied his movements. Loud voices in the hall brought them to their senses. He pulled away and after planting a quick kiss on her lips tucked her hand in his arm. He seemed much less affected than her.

"Come let's take a turn about the room." He walked her towards the fire. "I'll keep you safe. You don't have to worry."

She smiled at him. "Thank you. I know I have nothing to fear from the Earl of Milton with you to protect me." It was her attraction to Major Overton she feared.

It was cold outside but Nat was glad he had opted to walk home. Heaven knew he needed to cool down. What had possessed him to seduce her like that? A sound at the side of the road had him looking around, simultaneously unleashing the sword from Luke's stick. He stopped before he reached the corner so he wouldn't be too visible in the light from an oil lamp fixed there. A soft chuckle came to his ears and he sheathed the blade. Bright came up beside him.

"I see you haven't lost your touch, Major. Good, you'll need all of your skill before this adventure is through I'll be bound."

They fell into step together.

"You may be right. I hope we're not taking too much of a risk with the lady's safety."

"As to that, I had a drink with m'sister's husband tonight. He's in that Bow Street Group. Runners to you or me but he gets mighty offended at the term. Word is a duke has hired every one of them not already on a case."

"That must be Cathlay. I know he has instructed investigators."

"Not just investigators, he's had people posted all over the place. Taking no chances like. Can't say I blame him."

Nat considered. "Will it make our job difficult do you think?"

"They've been told to keep watch over the lady and only step in if needed. I'm not complaining about extra pairs of eyes. Denby is a devious bastard."

Nat shuddered. "That's what's worrying me. If he realises he's being watched it might push him into desperate measures."

"With so many men working on it, it shouldn't be long before the Duke has him. Can't see them hanging a peer though." Bright fingered a knife tucked inside his waistcoat. "Anyways, even hanging is too good for the likes of him."

Nat gave a grim laugh. "Tempting as it is, the thought of tearing him limb from limb, let's leave retribution to the Duke. He's not a man to be squeamish when his family's safety is at stake and I don't want to lose you to a prison cell."

Bright sighed. "If you say so, Major."

They reached Luke's house. "I do. Here's the plan for

tomorrow."

After giving Bright his instructions Nat let himself into the house and found his way to the library. He sat sipping some of Luke's excellent brandy. He would be glad to see Luke back. Leaving town so suddenly seemed odd in the circumstances. No he was seeing shadows where there were none. This business with Denby had got him rattled. Not to mention his surge of attraction to Lady Eliza, the daughter of a marquess no less.

No wonder he felt unsettled, when she had so obviously felt the same attraction to him. He remembered her hand fluttering in his, her startled reaction when his thigh touched hers and her luscious lips opening to deepen their kiss. Enough of this torture, he must stop thinking about her. Better to concentrate on keeping her safe and worry about the attraction afterwards. He needed to keep a clear head, which was going to be one of the most difficult things he had ever had to do.

Chapter Fourteen

Eliza doused her face in cold water. Her sleep had been broken by images of a handsome face and the feel of warm lips on hers. What would have happened if they had been on their own? Heat flooded though her at the thought. The sound of a firm rap on the door knocker jolted her out of her daydream.

Alice ran in and confirmed it was the Earl of Milton. "He's with His Grace now, Lady Eliza. Another conquest for you." Alice peered at her with a knowing smile. "He's nowhere near as handsome as a certain military gentlemen is he?"

Lud, had even the servants noticed her infatuation with Major Overton. Best to ignore her.

"I'd like a hot bath, Alice."

"Yes, my lady." Alice looked away but not in time to hide her grin. "I'll organise it immediately."

"Thank you. Also arrange to have a message sent up when the earl has gone."

Alice bobbed a curtsy and slipped out of the room. She had always been a level headed girl. What on earth had got into her? The same could be said of herself of course. Alice came back followed by a succession of footmen. The last one emptied his can of hot water into the bath. Red-faced he hesitated in front of her. Eliza smiled at him.

"Do you have a message for me? Jamie isn't it?"

"Yes, my lady. That is yes twice. Mr Sayers said to tell you the Earl of Milton was with His Grace for twenty minutes but he's gone now."

"Thank you, Jamie."

What a relief. Alice shut the door behind him and dropped one of the little bags of dried flowers Eliza had been given at Overton Grange into the bath. Eliza sank into the hot water. She squeezed and shook the bag until she was enveloped in the smell of summer roses.

Major Overton could be annoying but she had never been frightened by him, unlike the earl who had terrified her in the park. And yet she was afraid of marrying the major. Everything she had seen of him suggested he would be kind, not cruel as Miles had been. She shuddered so violently at memories of forced lovemaking that waves of water lapped at the side of the bath, threatening to spill over. Would she want to dwindle into an old unmarried aunt, as Max had suggested? After the warm feelings the Major had stirred in her the night before perhaps she owed it to herself to find out if she could be intimate with him without fear taking over?

Eliza sat patiently as Alice put the finishing touches to her hair. An uneventful day in Grace's company had left her feeling much more relaxed. They had decided on a more subdued dress in deep blue silk for the Gilberts' ball. Coupled with a simple string of pearls it would have been almost prudish if it hadn't been cut so low. Eliza studied her reflection in the glass.

"I'm not sure about the neckline. What about adding a

fichu?"

"Oh no, my lady. That would spoil the line of it. It's the height of fashion and besides the Major will be here soon. He won't want to keep the horses waiting."

"Never the less I want to add a fichu."

There was a tap at the door and Augusta entered.

"You look quite charming, Eliza."

"Hmph. The dress is far too low cut. I could either add a fichu or change it."

"Nonsense. You are out of mourning now and half the ladies there will be wearing something similar."

She pointed to her own dress. "Even we matrons are wearing lower necklines these days."

Eliza gave in and allowed Alice to drape a silk evening shawl around her shoulders. They reached the entrance hall at the same moment that Sayers opened the front door to Major Overton. Eliza's eyes opened wide. He had picked a plain black coat and a dark coloured waistcoat. The large diamond pin glinted from the folds of his snowy white cravat. She bit back a gasp. She glanced at the open, honest seeming face above it. The diamond must be real. He'd said his grandfather had done well in business.

Greetings made, he escorted them to the waiting coach. Eliza glimpsed the solid and reassuring presence of Bright sitting up with the driver. Major Overton handed Augusta into the coach and turned back to her. He raised her hand to his lips for the briefest of moments but it was enough to set her pulses racing.

"There's no need to look worried. Tonight is for enjoyment. The Earl of Milton definitely isn't invited."

"That's as may be but he doesn't seem the sort of man to let a minor detail like that get in his way."

Major Overton let out a chuckle. "I'm sure you're right, which is why there are men posted at all the entrances to make sure he doesn't get in. You would have made a good soldier. Come we mustn't keep the Duchess waiting."

He handed her into the coach and jumped up behind her. Eliza lowered her eyes, not that he could see her expression in the gloomy interior. She settled in to her seat. Even the sight of his athletic body was doing uncomfortable things to her. He turned around to knock on the front wall of the coach and his knee brushed hers. The sudden movement of the horses jolted her backwards and broke the contact. She took a deep breath. She was going to enjoy his company tonight and worry about where it might lead afterwards.

It was a short ride to the Gilberts' mansion. Major Overton kept them in the coach until it could drop them right by the front door. Here great wall sconces lit up the pavement and four footmen stood to attention. Even so he appeared to search the gloom all around before he helped them down. Somehow Bright appeared at her elbow and the two men flanked them both until they reached the steps up to the door, when Bright merged into the shadows and slipped around the side of the mansion towards the gardens. Major Overton was taking his protective role seriously, which gave her a warm glow.

He offered an arm to both of them. Augusta initially accepted but, when they joined the back of the receiving line, she excused herself to join a friend in front of them. They made slow progress up the stairs. The Major was such a restful companion. She didn't feel the need to cast around for conversation as she did with so many people. He squeezed her hand.

"It won't be long now. I served under Colonel Gilbert for the first few years I was in the army. I was lucky. He helped to set me on course for rapid promotion. You will love Mrs Gilbert, such a sensible woman. They always did like to entertain but I didn't realise they lived in quite this style in England."

Eliza laughed. "This is a rather splendid house and I think the crush even eclipses Grace Bamford's come out ball."

"It does. I keep nodding to military men I know. The Gilberts have a lot of friends from the army."

Eliza spotted a couple turn around. "There is a lady on the arm of a military looking gentleman trying to catch your attention above us."

He followed her gaze and gave a short wave of acknowledgement. "The Mastertons. I served with John for several years."

"Oh you mean the Earl of Hatton?"

"Yes but he was plain Johnny Masterton then." He sighed. "Life was much more egalitarian in the army. I never worried about my friends antecedents and they didn't worry about mine."

The wistful note in his voice made her study him.

He caught her glance and smiled. "I must remember I am the heir to a baron now and stop feeling inferior."

Eliza suppressed a grin. He certainly didn't look inferior and there were plenty of ladies sending him interested glances from behind their fans. A man like him would have plenty of friends but more than his fair share of enemies. Shipwright's boy, the Earl of Milton had called him and it had sounded like a practised insult.

At last they came before Colonel and Mrs Gilbert and were announced. The Gilberts beaming smiles suggested they were firm friends with Major Overton. Mrs Gilbert darted a quick glance in her direction as Major Overton bowed low over her hand. She laughed and rapped his knuckles playfully with her fan.

"I see you have the most beautiful woman in London this season on your arm. I remember when Augusta came out. There was no one to compare to her either. Watch you don't get cut out by a handsome duke, young man."

He blushed slightly. Eliza's heart leapt. He must be interested in her beyond a flirtation. The two men fell into a discussion of men they had served with. Major Overton was clearly well respected. How could she have thought him a fortune hunter? Mrs Gilbert gave her another appraising glance and drew her to one side.

"Let's leave the men to their reminiscences. I hope you don't mind me teasing but you would be perfect for Major Overton. He's always lacked confidence around eligible young women but he seems quite comfortable with you. We have no children of our own and he was a bit of a protégé of ours. We missed him when he got his promotion to Captain and was sent elsewhere." She patted Eliza's hand. "I would love to see him happily settled."

Eliza felt herself blushing. Colonel Gilbert saved her from searching for an answer.

"Now then, my dear, we mustn't detain these young people any longer. Go and enjoy yourselves."

"We certainly intend to, Colonel." Major Overton held out his arm for her and led her into the ballroom.

He covered the hand resting on his sleeve with one of his own and led her into a quiet corner. "I intend to claim two dances this evening in payment for my escort services. I choose the supper dance. Which other one would you prefer?"

The orchestra were tuning their instruments. If she opted for the first dance she could legitimately stay with him until it started.

"The first dance I think. I know less people here than I usually do."

"The first it is then. Let's stroll around the room and I'll introduce you to some of my friends. You won't lack partners for long."

They moved out into the open and were soon surrounded by groups of young people. A few Eliza knew but most were seeking out Major Overton. Her head was soon spinning with introductions and her dance card was gratifyingly full within minutes. The orchestra struck up the first few chords of a country dance. They took their places in a set.

The Major squeezed her hand. "I'm happy to report that all your partners are sensible men who you can trust, so as the Colonel said, enjoy yourself."

"I'll do my best." Even if she did feel strangely breathless before the dance had even started.

Every time they came into contact he had the same effect on her. She was almost glad of a reprieve when he delivered her to Augusta to wait to be claimed by her next partner.

Nat glanced around looking for old army friends. He skilfully avoided eye contact with any matron who looked to have a young charge with no partner for the next dance. A bead of moisture trickled down the back of his neck. He couldn't remember the last time contact with a young woman had such an effect on him. He was in danger of losing his head. Although would that be such a bad thing? Her family seemed to approve of him, largely because he was the heir to Overton

Grange perhaps? Would their approval still hold if he aspired to Lady Eliza's hand? That was the question. His thoughts were interrupted by a hand landing on his shoulder.

"Luke. Where have you been or shouldn't I ask?"

"Some business connected to one of my northern estates. It's in hand for now but I fully expect to have to post up there for a week or two once the season is over. You were looking pensive then. Problems?"

"You could say that." Nat checked no one was within earshot. "Connected to our friend the Earl of Milton."

"You look hot. Let's go and get you a drink. I came past the refreshment room and it's nearly empty. We'll find a quiet corner so you can tell me what's been happening."

"It sounds like I came back at the right time. I've promised to escort Grace to the British Museum tomorrow afternoon. She's keen to see the Greek and Roman antiquities." Luke grimaced. "If you and Lady Eliza join us, Milton will be kept in check for another day."

Nat laughed. "I'm not sure about antiquities."

"I don't see why I should suffer alone and it gives Lady Eliza the plausible excuse of a prior engagement. It's going to be tricky protecting her without alerting him to something being afoot."

"Don't I know it?" Nat rubbed the back of his neck. "I hope the Duke's people get what they need quickly. I don't trust Milton to toe the line if he's thwarted for long. His financial situation is so bad he's got rid of most of his servants. Come on, I don't want to think about him tonight. Let's go and find some partners."

At last it was time for the supper dance and Nat went in

search of Lady Eliza. He found her sitting with the Duchess at the far side of the room. He was hailed on all sides as he weaved his way across. He pasted on his friendliest smile and hoped no one noticed his impatience. At last he reached her. She looked up and gave him a smile that took his breath away. She was lovely. The orchestra struck the first chords of a cotillion.

The Duchess waved them onto the dance floor. "Quickly or you will miss it. I'll find you in the refreshment room later."

Nat bowed. "Thank you, Your Grace."

Eliza, he preferred to think of her as Eliza rather than Lady Eliza, placed her hand on his proffered arm and he led her onto the dance floor. She was a graceful dancer and a picture in a deep blue silk evening gown that enhanced the colour of her eyes. He couldn't help but notice admiring glances from several other men. She could have her pick. Was there any chance she would choose him? The dance brought them together briefly. He bent and whispered in her ear.

"You look quite glorious tonight, Lady Eliza."

They were separated before she could respond but the pink glow in her cheeks at his words gave him cause to hope. Cowardice wasn't an option. He had to put it to the test once Milton was out of the way or he would never forgive himself. At last the dance came to an end. He put a possessive hand on the small of her back.

"We've finished by the door to the refreshment room. Let's make our way straight there before it gets too crowded."

Her musical laugh rang out. "Yes please. I feel in need of a drink after that dance." Her cheeks became redder than before.

The hand she placed on his arm trembled slightly. He hid a smile. Surely she wasn't indifferent to him? They selected drinks and refreshments and sat at a table near to an open window. Eliza fanned herself.

"The breeze is wonderful. Even at this time of year these packed ballrooms can be unbearably hot."

"I know what you mean and of course dancing makes it worse."

He reached for his drink at the same time as Eliza reached for hers. Their hands brushed and a flash of awareness travelled from his hand all the way through his body. He tried to steady his breathing but his efforts were hampered by the sight of her luscious lips as she put her drink down. Her tongue flicked out to mop up a stray bead of moisture and he almost groaned aloud.

"Did you learn to dance so beautifully in the army?"

"Mostly but I had learned the basics at school and at friends' houses in the holidays." Holidays he preferred to forget.

"Didn't you go home?"

"Only at Christmas, apart from the odd week here and there. Grandpa worked long hours building up his businesses. I would have been in the way."

"Oh!" Eliza looked at him with concern shining out of her eyes. "How lonely for you."

"Sometimes, but we corresponded regularly. He loved to know what I was doing. I suppose it seems strange to you. Coming from such a large family you must be used to plenty of company."

"Not entirely. Max is the younger by a year but as he matured he was often away and of course he went to school and university. When I was small I was surrounded by family but gradually my sisters married and spread out all over. Two of them have their main home in Scotland, although the Cathlays spend a large part of the year in London."

There was an air of wistfulness about her that wrenched at his heart. People were joining them at the table.

"Have you had sufficient?"

Eliza nodded. "Yes, thank you."

"Let's have a walk around for a bit. It's heating up in here now."

He led her towards the open window behind them. It appeared to lead onto a small balcony partially shielded from the room by a brocade curtain. He pulled the curtain back and sure enough there was room for both of them to stand, suspended over the garden. They stepped out and he let the curtain drop behind them. They were partially in view so there could be no impropriety. Or to be more accurate, he was fully in view but Eliza was largely obscured. He watched the play of emotions on her face, illuminated by a full moon.

"What a beautiful spot. We must be over the gardens. I imagine the smell of roses is wonderful in the summer. Assuming there is a rose garden."

She leant over the balcony in an effort to see, giving him a wonderful glimpse of her shapely derriere. He grinned to himself.

"Very true and there are lovely views too."

"In the summer you mean?"

"No now. Look above you. There's a whole tapestry of stars up there. I can tell you what most of them are. We used to navigate by them more often than not."

She leaned back so her body was resting against him. Lord. It was to be hoped she couldn't feel the evidence of the effect she was having on him.

"Tell me about the stars." Her voice was a throaty whisper.

He pointed out all the main constellations and told her a bit about each one and the history of their names. "It's strange but when we were abroad it never felt like it at night because we saw all the same stars."

Eliza leaned back even harder and twisted her shoulders around so he could see her face.

"Oh, what a beautiful concept. Have you ever tried writing poetry?"

Nat couldn't answer. Poetry was the farthest thing from his mind, all he wanted to do was drink in every detail of her face. He shifted so they were both partly behind the curtain and then he bent down and placed his lips on hers. He could resist no longer. Joy surged through him as her lips moved against him. His mouth dropped open and her tongue teased his. The noise of conversation from the room behind them faded. The world consisted of them and the stars. He drank in every moment of the kiss, trying to store up every detail in his memory.

He came to with a jolt as the hands resting on the front of his shoulders moved as if she was going to throw them around his neck. He caught them quickly and pulled away from the kiss.

"We had better stop there, my sweet. This is far too public a place."

Eliza sighed. "You're right."

The sounds of the orchestra warming up drifted out to them.

She laughed. "Let's stay for a while longer. I own I'm hotter than when we came out."

"Tempted as I am by that invitation, we had better make our way back. We don't have to walk too quickly mind."

They found Augusta sitting with some other matrons in the ballroom and agreed a meeting place for the end of the evening. Nat went off to find his partner. If only he could dance with

Eliza all evening he would be a happy man. It took all his military discipline not to keep searching for her as he twirled around with partner after partner. At least in this environment, where the vast majority of guests had links with the army, he felt comfortable in a way he hadn't at Grace's ball.

Chapter Fifteen

E arly the next morning Nat waited in the shadow of a tall hedge as Bright tapped at the partially concealed door behind the mews. It was opened by Sayers himself. He beckoned to Nat to follow him. Once inside he secured the door with several locks and bolts.

"I'll take you up to the library, Major Overton. His Grace is waiting for you."

Sayers opened the library door and ushered him in before slipping away. The Duke occupied a leather chair in front of a large table, strewn with documents.

"Do please take a seat, Overton." He indicated a chair on the other side of the table. "I'm sorry to see Eliza far from herself over this business of the earl. I was surprised she gave in to my wife's persuasion to come to London in the first place."

The Duke sat back and studied him. Nat took a deep breath. Someone as astute as him would see his admiration for Eliza. Was he about to be told he wasn't worthy of her? The muscles at the back of his neck twitched.

"When I set enquiries in train about Milton I took the opportunity to find out more about you. I like what I heard."

Nat's head shot up. "Really?"

"Yes, it confirmed my own impression of you as a man.

I must confess I also found out more about your financial position." The Duke smiled at him. "I merely wanted to confirm you hadn't run up huge debts or anything of that nature. You have to understand that the Lovells have been plagued by fortune hunters in the past. Miles Wyndham proved to be a scoundrel. One of our children was ill the summer Eliza met him and we stayed in Scotland. Augusta always felt guilty as she's sure Eliza wouldn't have married him if she had been around to advise her."

"I see. That explains a lot." If Eliza had been taken in by a fortune hunter it wasn't surprising that she was wary of being tricked again.

"I was pleased to hear you honour your grandfather when you came to dinner. There is nothing in your background to exclude you from becoming part of this family, if that's what you want."

Nat let out a long breath. He seemed perfectly sincere. Perhaps Luke was correct in telling him his mother's parentage wouldn't matter?

"I'm honoured to have your approval but I doubt the lady in question will soften towards me enough to consider marriage."

"My advice is not to rush her. She may simply not be ready to face up to the future." The Duke's lips twitched. "Although my wife tells me the two of you pushed the bounds of propriety last night on a certain balcony. Fortunately, she is sure she was the only person to notice."

"Oh Lord. I thought no one would see us. Eliza was hot and we went out onto the balcony to cool down." Nat ran a hand across his brow to stop beads of sweat trickling down into his eyes. "I was pointing out some of the constellations of stars to her."

The Duke held up a hand. A soft chuckle escaped him. "There is no need to explain, Overton. Augusta was pleased to see you making some progress with Eliza. She is afraid Eliza is too trapped in the past to ever find a future outside the family. Before we worry about that, we have to sort out this wretched business with Milton."

Nat nodded. "Viscount Enstone is back and he has invited both of us to join him and Grace on an outing this morning. Grace will send a note around to Lady Eliza as soon as she is up. That will take her out of the house for most of the day. How quickly do you expect to have enough information to remove Milton?"

"As I believe you have heard, I have half the Bow Street Runners working for me as well as some of my servants. Even so it will be some days."

Nat's eyebrows shot up. He must have informants all over the place. "Milton's financial position sounds pressing. My new valet was working in his household until recently. I'm glad you are taking this so seriously. We need to have Lady Eliza guarded night and day."

"Agreed. I'll have people following you today. One of them will be in the mews soon hoping to talk to Bright. Milton has someone posted further up the street watching for Eliza's movements and is bound to show up during the day. Bright can have overall control of my men. They will have to be careful not to alert Milton to the fact he is being watched."

"Thank you. Bright is excellent at this sort of thing."

The Duke laughed. "I know. I spoke to a general you both worked for once on a special operation."

"Are you sure it wouldn't be better to take Lady Eliza somewhere safe? Bright has been asking around in the taverns my valet said the earl's servants use. If the Earl of Milton wasn't a peer he would be in a debtor's prison by now by all accounts. From things Bright has heard I have a feeling the earl may be planning something desperate."

"It's tempting, but between us we have enough men to guard her and it will be safer in the long run to have him out of the way."

The menace in the Duke's voice had Nat's head shooting up. The earl laughed.

"Don't worry, Overton. I'm not about to have him murdered. I was thinking more along the lines of shipping him off to the West Indies. All I need is enough proof of wrong doing to persuade the right people to make it official. Well semi-official shall we say."

Eliza sipped the last of her tea and opened the message.

"It seems Viscount Enstone is home and Grace invites me to make up a party to visit the British Museum with them today." Eliza looked down as if rereading the note so Augusta wouldn't see her hot cheeks.

True to his promise to guard her, Major Overton would be joining them. How did she feel about that? After her reaction to him on the balcony she could be in no doubt she was strongly attracted to him as a man but was she brave enough to take it any farther?

"I shall accept, of course. Anything is better than sitting at home waiting for the Earl of Milton to try and accost me."

Augusta laughed. "You always enjoy time spent with Grace. Cathlay has people watching over you, so you can enjoy yourself and not worry about Milton. I have some letters to write, if you will excuse me."

Augusta rose and dropped a kiss on her cheek. "I'll see you at home for dinner and then it's a musical soiree at Lady Crane's this evening."

Eliza asked Sayers to send a footman to accept the invitation for her and ran upstairs to change. It wasn't until she had tried on a third outfit that she was satisfied with her appearance. Poor Alice looked exhausted. For someone who wasn't sure if she wanted to take her relationship with Major Overton any farther she was going to rather a lot of trouble. She pushed the thought to one side, determined to enjoy the day. The British Museum was somewhere she loved to visit. It would be good fun to share it with Grace and she wasn't going to let the memory of a pair of intelligent grey eyes locking with hers under a starry sky intrude.

She jumped when a footman arrived to announce that Major Overton was waiting for her downstairs. How on earth was she going to act normally around him? She sent Alice to go and have her breakfast and sat down at her dressing table. After checking her appearance in the looking glass, she squared her shoulders and took a deep breath. Alice had turned her out immaculately, as usual. It was time to face the man who had taken over her dreams.

She found him in the drawing room talking to Augusta. He appeared perfectly composed but spots of red, high on his cheekbones, suggested he wasn't entirely comfortable. He stood as she entered and bowed low.

"Good morning, Lady Eliza. The others are waiting for us outside." He grinned. "Viscount Enstone is particularly looking forward to seeing the Greek antiquities."

Eliza burst out laughing. "What a bouncer. Grace said her brother has been putting her off for ever over his promise to take her to the museum, specifically because he can't stand antiquities."

His grey eyes twinkled down at her and Eliza's heart thumped for a second. "I know and Grace is grateful to you. He admitted he thought the museum was such an unlikely place to chance upon the Earl of Milton, he was prepared to put up with them."

Eliza smiled back at him. Lud, when he looked at her like that she was lost. She placed her hand on the arm he held out and they said their goodbyes to Augusta. Warmth shot up her arm, from where her hand rested on him, and through her body. It pooled deep inside her core. Fear and excitement duelled for supremacy. A wave of dizziness hit her and she missed her step.

Major Overton tucked her hand deeper into the crook of his arm. "All will be well, my sweet. I promise you. There is nothing to be afraid of."

Eliza lowered her eyes, she was afraid of what he might see in them. How could she cope with so much troublesome emotion? Perhaps she should beg the Cathlays to take her to stay with Diana in her Scottish castle after all? All she wanted was a quiet, peaceful life not this perpetual state of painful excitement. Major Overton glanced around the street and then lifted her bodily into the coach. The warmth of his hands enveloped her waist. The spicy, musky smell of his cologne invaded her nostrils. Nothing else in the world seemed to matter except him. Surely a feeling as uncomfortable as this couldn't be love? He jumped in beside her, so they were sitting opposite to Grace and her brother. The coach moved forward. His thigh rested so close to hers she could feel its warmth. She tried to block the sensation from her mind as Grace addressed her.

"Hello, dear friend. I've wanted to visit the British Museum for an age."

Grace looked up at her brother and Eliza couldn't help but smile at the mischievous grin she gave him.

"I'm sure Viscount Enstone is happy to be of service."

Viscount Enstone brushed an invisible speck of dust from his coat sleeve. "It's fortunate I've managed to contain my enthusiasm for the project up until now. It's the ideal place if we wish to avoid a certain earl."

Eliza laughed out loud. "I think brothers are best ignored when they are in a teasing mood, Grace."

Major Overton stiffened beside her. Was she so attuned to him that she noticed his every reaction?

"What's wrong?"

"I think Luke's sacrifice might prove to be in vain. I'm sure I've just seen Milton turn out of a side road and follow us on horseback."

Viscount Enstone smothered an oath. "What bad luck, him spotting us!"

"I expect he has someone watching the Cathlay residence." He captured her hand. "Don't worry, Lady Eliza. There is nothing he can do whilst we are with you."

Eliza chewed at her lip. "He might try and prise me away from you in front of others, as he did in the park."

"I'll be ready for that tactic this time, with my temper firmly under control."

His body jerked, pushing his thigh even more firmly against hers. Heat flooded through her. She must concentrate and his nearness was making that difficult. Grace leaned forward and tapped her on the knee.

"I have an idea. We are much of a height and we both have

dark hair. We are also wearing similar coloured pelisses. Why don't we swap bonnets to draw him towards me?"

Eliza shook her head. "He's only just started following us so he won't know what I'm wearing."

"If he was tipped off by one of his spies he will have a description, surely. Luke and I stayed in the carriage the whole time we were waiting for you." Grace exchanged glances with her brother.

"She's right. It might well serve to give you some peace for a while."

Grace nodded and removed her bonnet. "Luke and I will be set down alone. You two drive around the block a few times and don't come in until you are sure he has followed us. We'll lead him a merry dance and then hide amongst the Greek antiquities."

Luke groaned. "I can't fault your logic but does it have to be the Greek section?"

"Yes, because it's always busy in there. Much easier to hide in a crowd. With the earl following us Eliza and Nat can enjoy the rest of the rooms. Arrange to have the coach come back in about two hours. That should give us plenty of time."

Eliza handed over her bonnet and placed Grace's on the seat next to her. The coach pulled up and the Bamfords jumped down quickly. The Major tapped the front of the coach to tell the coachman to drive on and then flattened himself back against the squabs. Eliza did the same. Viscount Enstone must have spoken to the coachman because they turned off the main thoroughfare almost immediately. Eliza closed her eyes and tried to relax. She shouldn't be alone with Major Overton in a closed coach but that seemed insignificant against avoiding the earl. A tremor shook her.

"Are you cold?"

"No, but I'm wishing I'd stayed at Hargreaves Hall. The Earl of Milton terrified me the other day."

A strong arm pulled her close against the major's solid body. "He is a scoundrel but there's no need to be frightened."

He kissed her forehead and she trembled again, this time from excitement. He was wearing different cologne. It had a similar citrus tang to it but there was a hint of mint mixed with musk underneath. She buried her face in his chest and his arm tightened around her. His other hand stroked her hair. His touch was surprisingly gentle. What would it feel like to have those hands stroking her body? Miles had never bothered to consider her pleasure. He had forced himself on her whenever he felt like it without considering her wishes. Major Overton seemed a much kinder man. Perhaps it would be different with him?

Shouts came from outside. The coach lurched to a halt and she jolted upright. Major Overton pulled what appeared to be a small pistol from his coat pocket. He leaned towards the door and lowered the window.

"There's a cart what's dropped some of its wares blocking the way. Here."

He extracted another pistol and passed it to her. "Can you use one of these?"

"Yes." Eliza accepted the weapon. "Is it an ambush?"

"I don't think so but it's as well to be prepared. We'll cover a door each. Bright is on the roof. Try not to shoot him if he comes to your door."

As he said it, they heard Bright shouting instructions to the carter.

"We ain't got all day. Here's a shilling, leave the rest and let's be on our way."

"Ah. He sounds annoyed rather than worried. I think all is well."

Eliza risked a glance out of her window. A grimy urchin was gathering vegetables from under the wheels of a cart and throwing them into a sack.

"Come on you stupid ox or I'll have my shilling back." Bright shouted.

Bright's face appeared at the window on the major's side. "We'll be off in a moment, Major. It's too risky around these streets. We'll get you somewhere safer. Cover up your windows."

The coach moved forwards and picked up speed.

Major Overton pulled his window up. "Well done, Eliza. Many a female would have been in hysterics there. I can put my pistols back now but we had better do what Bright said."

She pulled the leather curtain across her window and passed his pistol over.

"It was worrying. I can't imagine how soldiers cope with constant fear for their lives."

He put a pistol into each pocket and covered his window, leaving them in semi-darkness. A large hand surrounded hers.

Chapter Sixteen

Nat felt a tremor as he reached for Eliza's hand. He almost drew his away before she gripped it. Bright would want to get well away in case the delay had been arranged by the earl's men. He wouldn't want to risk being followed. They had some time alone and didn't his body know it. He shifted on the seat. Could he risk stealing a kiss? Not unless he wanted to be as bad as the earl.

"Eliza, what would you say if I told you I had an urge to kiss you?"

"Yes please, Major Overton."

"I'm not sure I can kiss someone who calls me Major Overton. My friends call me Nat."

"Yes please, Nat."

He could just about make out the shape of her face in the gloom. He put a finger under her chin and gently lifted it up. His lips found hers and waited to see how she would react. He let out a sigh as she pressed her lips against his. When he eased them open with his tongue she angled her head to make it easier for him. She was hesitant at first but soon gained confidence.

She tasted so sweet and the scent of roses and lavender enveloped him. He ached to explore the rest of her body but now wasn't the time. What had he been thinking of? He hadn't been thinking, which was the problem. She groaned and pulled him closer. He should stop now but he couldn't resist the invitation in the little cries she made as he picked up the pace with his tongue. His hands around her waist seemed to move higher without being asked until his thumbs were caressing the edges of her breasts. He held his breath but she pressed down on to his hands with her bosom until the underside was resting on them.

He sensed the coach was slowing down and wrenched his lips from hers. He forced his hands to return to her waist. His heart was beating so hard he could hear its rhythm thundering in his ears. His body yearned for so much more than kisses. It was time to stop whilst he still could. His breath came in shallow gasps. The coach was definitely slowing now.

"I think the coach will stop in a moment. How do you feel?"

She gave a shaky laugh. "I'm not sure. I've never been kissed like that before."

"I'm glad." He touched his lips to her forehead. "Your brother-in-law warned me to give you plenty of time and yet here I am demonstrating why a young lady should never be alone in a closed carriage with a man. I don't think I can call myself a gentleman."

She pulled away. He wished there was enough light to see her face.

"You've spoken to Cathlay?"

"It was a case of him speaking to me. He guessed I was interested in you." He smiled to himself. Better not to tell her they had been seen out on the balcony by her sister. "Any red-blooded bachelor would be interested in a beautiful woman like you."

"Oh."

She was about to say more, he was sure of it, but the coach pulled up and there was a rap at the door. Lord, was his cravat messed up? He fumbled at it in the darkness. It would have to do. He was dimly aware of Eliza patting her hair and donning Grace's bonnet. He slid across the seat and moved the curtain back with one hand. Bright was outside. A quick glance confirmed Eliza looked presentable. He pulled the curtain across and wound the window down.

"No sign of anyone following us, Major. What do you want to do?"

"We had better go back to the museum."

Bright saluted and moved away from the window. Nat left it open. He needed some air. He heard Bright talk to the coachman before they set off.

Eliza tapped his arm. "Why did it matter if we were followed? I don't understand."

Nat sighed. "Bright and I are worried the earl will do something outrageous like try to kidnap you."

"Oh heavens." Wide blue eyes stared at him. "Do you think he might?"

"It's hard to say. I mentioned it to His Grace but he still wants to have Milton removed from the country semi-officially." He stroked her cheek with a finger. "Would you rather leave London? If so, say the word and I'll go with you to talk to the Duke."

"Cathlay would move me in a heartbeat if I told him that was what I wanted but it's not." She glanced up at his face. "I want to stay here with you."

Nat caught his breath. He hated the Earl of Milton with a vengeance but he couldn't help being grateful to him for throwing Eliza into his orbit. His early anger had been a clumsy attempt to deflect himself from his admiration of her, admiration that had terrified him because of her status. He was a grown man now and he wasn't about to lose her because of some boyish humiliation, bad as it had been at the time.

He squeezed her hand. "I'm glad. With any luck he will have given up and gone home by the time we get back to the museum."

The carriage pulled up and Nat spotted a party about to enter the museum. He jumped down and handed Eliza out in time to walk immediately behind them. To a casual observer they would appear to be a part of the group. He bent so his mouth was close to her ear.

"We'll stay with these and it will make us less obvious to anyone looking for a couple."

Nat tried to appear interested in the exhibits even as he scanned each room they entered for signs of the earl. One of the people in the group in front was particularly knowledgeable and he found himself listening to their commentary. Once this was all over he would have to bring Eliza again so they could enjoy the place properly. He could feel the tension in Eliza's arm where it wound through his. He patted her hand and nearly stopped walking when they moved into another room to find the Earl of Milton inside.

He didn't spot them immediately and Nat considered trying to double back. Eliza's step faltered and the moment was lost as the earl glanced in their direction. The man had a smile plastered from ear to ear, no doubt for Eliza's benefit. Eliza's hand tightened painfully on his arm, but outwardly she appeared perfectly serene. The Earl of Milton stepped forward and bowed low.

"What a surprise seeing you here, dear Lady Eliza. Such an amazing place, don't you think? I always try and visit when I am in London. Would you care to take a turn about the room with me? I am reckoned to be something of an expert on antiquities."

Eliza inclined her head. Despite watching the earl's face, Nat couldn't help but notice how regal she looked. She was like a younger version of the Duchess of Cathlay.

"How kind of you, Lord Milton. Another time perhaps? I am engaged to join Miss Bamford shortly."

The earl pursed his lips, his cheeks gleaming bright red, and tried again. "I saw her only a moment ago. I would be delighted to escort you to her." He held out his arm.

Eliza smiled at him. "Another time, my lord. As you can see, I am promised to Major Overton this morning."

The earl threw a glance at him, his face screwed up with anger. "I'm sure Major Overton will make away for a peer of the realm, Lady Eliza."

Eliza put her free hand over the one wound around his arm. "As a Lovell, I would be loath to drop a man because of his rank, my lord."

Nat's breath caught in his throat. Did that comment have a double meaning for him? Was she trying to reassure him? He looked up to see a small crowd of interested observers hovering in the room, seemingly reluctant to move on until their little drama had played out.

The earl followed his gaze. "You are causing quite a scene as always, shipwright's boy."

His voice was little more than a hiss. Had even Eliza heard him? At quick glance at the spots of angry red on her cheeks suggested she had. She nodded her head and produced a gracious smile.

"It was lovely to see again, my lord. I trust we will meet again soon."

The earl pursed his lips and seemed about to argue. Nat watched him, taking care to keep his own face expressionless as the crowd pressed a little closer. Milton didn't like to be crossed. He fought the urge to plant the facer the scoundrel so richly deserved. He took a deep breath. Now was not the time to lose his temper, but from the hold Eliza had on his arm there was no way she was going to accept Milton's escort. It was to be hoped the Duke of Cathlay hadn't misplayed his hand keeping Eliza in London. This confrontation would do her reputation no good at all. A tawny head appeared through the crowd and Nat relaxed.

Luke manoeuvred Grace through the throng. "Ah there you are. Grace has been telling me all about the Greek artefacts further along. She will appreciate a more interested audience than me, I'm sure."

Grace laughed. "I certainly will. Eliza, would you care to take my arm and let me share my enthusiasm with you. Luke has been doing his best to dampen it."

Nat kept his body between Eliza and Milton so he couldn't step into Grace's place as the two ladies linked arms. Grace turned them away from the taut figure of the earl and went into the next room. That was well done. Grace would have made a good military tactician had she been male. The earl turned on his heel and marched after them. He didn't seem to care about the press of people watching him. Nat signalled to Luke and they followed behind.

"We had better stay close, Luke. I don't trust him around Eliza."

"Eliza? So that's the way of it?" Luke whispered.

Nat grimaced. "It's too soon to say but whatever happens I'm determined to keep her safe. Why the wretch doesn't go after a less well-guarded victim I don't know."

"That's easy. The Lovells are all well off, even Lord Hargreaves had a famous escape from a fortune hunter, but Lady Eliza is fabulously wealthy. Her godmother left her a huge sum, on top of what was left of her substantial dowry after Wyndham got his hands on it."

Eliza kept a firm hold on Grace's arm. She was damned if she was going to let the Earl of Milton outmanoeuvre her and she could sense he wasn't far away. The desperation gleaming in his eyes as he had tried to displace Nat at her side was frightening. The last thing she wanted was to spend any time in his company. What she did want was time to consider how she felt about the change in her relationship with Nat.

Grace patted her hand. "Don't worry, if that loathsome man tries to walk off with you again I'll stab him with the extra-long hatpin I carry in my reticule to ward off toads like him."

Eliza laughed. "I do believe you would. Why carry something so fierce?"

"No particular reason but it's always as well to be prepared. Luke and Nat won't be far away so I doubt I'll need to use it."

"I don't suppose you've got any spares have you?"

"I'll find you one."

They heard the sound of masculine voices behind them and Luke moved up to join them.

"I'm sure this is a quite wonderful place, but don't you think it's time to leave, Grace?"

Grace raised an eyebrow at Eliza and she nodded. It was

indeed a wonderful place but she had too much on her mind to enjoy it. Luke's coach swept up as they came out onto the pavement. Grace stamped a foot.

"I don't know. My brother will use any excuse to avoid being educated. He must have had the coach circling to arrive this quickly."

Luke laughed. "Once the Earl of Milton is out of the way you and Lady Eliza can spend as much time here as you like but you're not getting me inside its walls again."

Eliza glanced across at Nat. His eyes roamed all around. At last he seemed satisfied and he moved forward to assist her into the coach. She caught a reassuring glimpse of Bright climbing back up on the box beside the coachman. Bright looked relaxed but one hand rested inside his jacket pocket and the hilt of a pistol was visible. The sight did nothing to ease the knot of tension at the back of her neck that had started when the earl tried to get her away from Nat. Perhaps she should get Cathlay to send her up to Diana and yet it was true she didn't want to leave Nat. Her heart raced. He was the most exciting man she had ever met.

Luke handed Grace up and jumped in beside her. "I've told the coachman to take us back to Aunt Theo's. Milton might have look-outs there as well but I suspect not. I'm not sure his funds would run to it."

Nat took the seat next to Eliza. She settled back against the squabs. His large frame pressed against her as they rounded a bend and her heart raced. What would have happened if the coach hadn't started slowing down when they were alone earlier? A flush of heat shot through her. She looked down to hide her face from the two opposite.

Nat's hand caught hers under the cover of his coat tails. A

glance towards him had her staring at his strong legs. He braced himself as they turned another corner and she could see his thigh muscles tighten through the material of his breeches. She swallowed hard and forced her gaze to the floor. What was she doing imagining his legs unclothed? Nat's grip on her hand tightened. A wave of panic hit her. He fascinated her but she was still terrified of committing to anyone after her experiences at Miles's hands. Could she even be sure Nat felt as deeply as she did? What was it he had said?

"Any red-blooded bachelor would be interested."

That sounded more like lust than anything else. There had been no mention of love. The possessive hand holding hers, delightful as it felt, was no proof of anything else. Was what she felt anything more than desire? Her body thrummed with excitement but what did she know of him as a person? Viscount Enstone obviously thought a lot of him and he had been horrified by the Earl of Milton's mistreatment of a woman. He would probably be much kinder to her in the marital bed. That didn't mean he would be an amiable husband in other things. A man with a military background like his would very likely expect obedience in a wife. She was a weak-willed fool to act as she had and give him cause to anticipate a marriage between them. What was she going to do now?

The coach came to a halt. Eliza felt as if she was in a dream. She was dimly aware of Nat helping her down. The butler showed them into Lady Grant's informal rose coloured drawing room. Lady Grant stood up to greet them.

"Do come and sit down. Did you have an enjoyable morning?" She took Eliza's hand and led her to a chair.

"You look worried, my dear. Did the Earl of Milton waylay you?"

Eliza sighed. "I'm afraid so. We drove around in the carriage for ages hoping to shake him off but he still found us once we were back at the museum."

"What a shame you had your morning ruined. You'll feel better after some tea and cake." Lady Grant nodded to her butler. He scurried off.

"Thank you. I shall be glad when everything is resolved and I can go back home to Hargreaves Hall."

Nat raised his eyebrows at her and frowned. Lud, he did think she was his for the taking if he didn't like the thought of her going back to Hargreaves. He turned towards Lady Grant and she couldn't resist studying him from head to toe. Her eyes were drawn to his shapely calves as he crossed them over. Despite his height everything about him was elegant. She wrenched her eyes away from him and tried to concentrate on what Lady Grant was saying.

"I saw Lady Crane this morning and she would be delighted to welcome you gentlemen at her soiree this evening. I believe that's where you're going with Augusta, Eliza."

"Yes we are."

Luke groaned. "A soiree now. Is there no end to the dizzying round of entertainment you ladies have lined up for me?"

Nat laughed out loud and caught her eye. "There is no need to look guilty, Lady Eliza. It's about time Luke came under a civilising influence."

"I do feel guilty though. I'm sorry to put you both to so much trouble."

Nat smiled at her and it felt like they were the only people there. The room seemed to circle around her. Why was life so confusing?

He held her gaze. "Trust me. We will both be much happier

if the Earl of Milton can be brought to book. When he got away without being court martialled, Luke had to almost tie me down until he'd been removed to another location."

"I was only returning the favour. I would have throttled him the night we caught him without you holding me back. He was a disgrace to the uniform. The people who used their influence to get him off so lightly ought to be ashamed."

A shudder ran through Eliza. If only she had listened to Nat at the beginning. "I should have had the sense to keep well away from him."

Grace shook her head. "You did nothing to encourage him."

Lady Grant caught her hand. "Grace is right my dear. He would have known you were wealthy simply because you are one of the Lovell clan. I would have been surprised if he hadn't targeted you. Let's forget about him for a while. You'll be well guarded tonight. We'll make sure you are never alone."

Chapter Seventeen

Nat put the finishing touches to his cravat. "This is so much easier after your training, Jones."

Jones handed him the diamond pin.

Nat grimaced. "You don't think this one is too showy?"

"It's perfect with a plain cut jacket like yours and the diamond sets off any colour scheme."

Nat considered his reflection in the looking glass. "You're right about a diamond going with any outfit but this one is too large for every day events. I'll go back to Rundell and Bridges for something more modest. Anything on our friend the earl?"

"Nothing new but I bumped into one of the footmen I got on well with and he's the only footman now." Jones grinned. "I told him I had fallen into a well-paid post and have an evening off tonight. I said if he could sneak away I would treat him to a few tankards of ale in the Cross and Keys Inn he likes."

Nat laughed. "Good work. You are duly granted the evening off. I can manage perfectly well without you to undress me, so don't worry about getting back. If you are home before me then have an early night. I'll pay you an advance on your salary plus a bonus to cover the cost of the hospitality."

Nat had one last look at his appearance. He smiled at himself. He was becoming worse than any woman but he wanted to look his best for Eliza.

He ran downstairs. Luke was already waiting for him in the library.

Luke held up a decanter containing a warm brown liquid. "Would you like a brandy before we go to numb the pain of this soiree?"

Nat burst out laughing. "You'll love it, Luke. I've been told the soprano is superb."

Luke groaned. "Can this evening get any worse? The last soprano I heard gave me a headache for a week. I haven't been to anything musical since."

Nat slapped him on the shoulder. "You'll love this one. Come on we haven't got time to waste drinking."

"Why so keen Nat? I'm convinced you're out to court Lady Eliza." Luke grinned at him.

"I told you, it's too early to say if there's a chance for me. I want to try and get to the soiree before Eliza to see if the earl is there and keep watch on her if he is." He felt his cheeks burn as he realised he had said Eliza rather than Lady Eliza once again. "Besides which I want a good seat."

Luke jumped up. "Lead on then. The coach should be around from the mews at any minute."

"Who's the one in a rush now?"

"Whilst you were making up to Eliza I asked Aunt Theo to send a message around to Lady Crane asking if we could have access early to have a look around. Permission has been granted."

"What if I hadn't been ready early?"

Luke raised his eyebrows. "You're always ready early when you're meeting Lady Eliza."

The coach pulled up as they walked through the front door.

Nat rolled his shoulders to ease the tension in them. When would he get used to attending society parties?

"Have you ever met Lady Crane?"

Luke laughed gently. "You're the most sought after bachelor in town this season and you're still worried about being accepted aren't you? Lady Crane is one of Aunt Theo's oldest friends and an absolute darling so stop worrying. If all goes to plan Milton shouldn't be able to get into the soiree even if he knows that's where Lady Eliza is going. So you can enjoy yourself this evening."

"I suppose so."

"You don't sound enthusiastic. Don't tell me you don't like music any more than I do?"

"My mother had a lovely voice and I am truly looking forward to the soprano. Although I won't be able to enjoy anything until that man is languishing in the West Indies."

They pulled up at yet another large mansion. Nat followed Luke out of the coach and squared his shoulders. Their coach appeared to be the only one around.

"I'm surprised there aren't more people about?"

"We're early. Aunt Theo arranged it so we could smuggle Bright in with us. Insurance in case Milton was to get past the staff somehow. Which is why we didn't call in for her and Grace."

They heard the soft thud of someone jumping down from the coach and Bright joined them.

"Good thinking, Luke. If any of the earl's men are about they might be keeping an eye out for him going in by a staff entrance. Bright, you had best walk between us. Come on let's not stand about waiting for someone else to arrive."

They strolled up the stairs. It opened before they could knock and they were greeted by a stately butler.

"Good evening gentlemen. Now you have arrived I'll have the front doors opened and the wall sconces lit." He shut the door behind them and signalled to a footman. "Show Major Overton's man around and do everything he asks of you."

Bright grinned as he saluted them and went off with the footman.

"This way gentlemen."

They were shown into a drawing room near to the back of the main rooms. A tall elegant lady rose to greet them.

"Luke. What a delight to see you again. I suppose I ought to call you Lord Enstone now."

"Devil a bit, not when we're private." Luke bowed over her hand. "Allow me to introduce my good friend Major Overton. Nat, this of course is the infamous Lady Crane."

She laughed. "Take no notice of him, Major Overton, he always was a rogue. I'm delighted to meet you. Do please be seated."

Nat bowed low. "Thank you." His cheeks burned as she subjected him to a careful scrutiny.

"You're like your father. He was a head taller than all the other men in the Ton too."

Nat gasped. "You knew him?"

"Yes, quite well. He and your Uncle Henry were friendly with my brother at one time. I never understood why your grandfather cut him out of the family. I suspect your Uncle Charles was behind it. He always was a nasty boy. Now Henry was a different matter altogether and I'm pleased to hear you and he are reconciled."

"He wrote to my man of business and I agreed to go and see him. We get on well and I'm happy to have a link to the past.

Forgive me if I seem a little stunned. For some reason it never occurred to me I might meet people who had known my father as a young man. Once we've resolved our current problem I would enjoy a conversation about him."

"I shall look forward to that. I checked the guest list for Lady Grant. The Earl of Milton wasn't invited. I've told the servants to admit no one who's not on the list, no matter who brings them."

Nat slumped in his chair. "I'm glad to hear it. Lady Eliza hid it well but I believe she was seriously upset when the earl tried to disengage her from me when he found us at the British Museum this morning. I don't know how much Lady Grant told you but we would appreciate your discretion."

Luke burst out laughing. "Have no fear, Nat. Aunt Theo and her friends are a tight knit group and completely reliable. Don't mind him, Lady Crane, he was the best officer I ever served under and his natural caution saved us more than once."

"I understand. Don't worry. It will go no further than my husband and I. Now I had better join him to receive our guests. Feel free to roam wherever you want. I've told the staff to expect two military friends of mine checking for weak points, because of all the burglaries happening at these types of event."

They stood as she left the room. Nat shrugged his shoulders and stretched his neck backwards but it wasn't enough to release the knot of tension at the top of his back.

"Clever of her. At the same time I'm uneasy about more people knowing what we're doing."

"There is no way we could have kept it from Aunt Theo and she wouldn't have taken Lady Crane into her confidence if she wasn't sure she would keep it to herself. Besides it's only for a few days at most isn't it?"

"I suppose so and the Cranes are two more people to keep an eye on Eliza. I keep getting the feeling we need to be extra vigilant."

Luke frowned. "I'm always worried when your instincts are stirred. It generally means trouble."

"It's not just me. Bright is feeling edgy too. Do you know the layout of the house, Luke?"

"I have a good idea. I came here a lot as a child."

"Good. We had better take Lady Crane at her word and explore. Come on let's put my mind at rest for this evening at any rate."

They did a quick tour of the main rooms and ducked through a partially concealed door as they nearly walked into the first of the other guests to arrive. It led to a set of servants' stairs.

"Let's follow this down to the kitchens, or wherever it comes out, and find someone to show us where the outside access for the servants is," Nat said.

They ran down the stairs and came out opposite what looked like the door to the housekeeper's room. Nat rapped on it and a pleasant looking woman answered.

"Ah, are you the two military gentlemen Lady Crane was expecting?"

"Yes, this is Viscount Enstone and I'm Major Overton."

"It will be a relief to have you check our security, what with all these burglaries in the area she was telling me about." She ran a hand through her hair and repositioned some of the pins securing it in a bun at the nape of her neck.

Nat smiled. "I can see you're busy. A maid will suffice to show us around."

"The worst of it is over now, sir. All the refreshments and

so on are in hand. I'll show you myself."

She led the way through a busy kitchen. They dodged scurrying servants as best they could and took a detour to avoid the area French curses were emanating from. The housekeeper laughed.

"Antoine is rather temperamental but his cooking is wonderful."

They came out into an outer lobby, manned by two sturdy looking footmen. "This is the main servants' door."

"I can see it's well protected," Nat said. "It would be best to make sure there is at least one footman there all evening. These sorts of event are proving a real draw to thieves hoping to take advantage of everyone being busy."

"I can show you the side door but it's locked and bolted at the moment."

"We had best check it anyway."

They retraced their steps through the kitchen and veered off towards an empty room. Nat and Luke checked all the windows, high up on the walls as they were partially underground.

The housekeeper followed his gaze. "The only other windows on this floor are in the kitchen and there are always people in there."

Nat stroked his chin. "This all seems well secured. Are there any windows on the next floor that could be climbed through?"

They went up a floor and they walked around every window at the front of the house. The windows at the back were much higher up as the building was cut into a slope.

"Are there any trees at the back near to windows?" Nat asked.

The housekeeper took them into a side room where they could see the garden. There was one tree by the house. Its branches came within touching distance of the house a floor higher."

Nat looked at Luke. "We had better check the room near the tree as well."

"It's next to a corridor. The main reception rooms are off it."

They followed the housekeeper up yet another flight of the servants' stairs. She peered through the door and beckoned them to follow her. The tree had branches against two windows near to the centre of the corridor. They could hear musicians tuning their instruments in a nearby room.

"Can you spare a footman to patrol the corridor?" Nat asked.

"If you say so, sir, I'll find one."

"Thank you. Then we have done all we can. Tell me, where is the ladies' withdrawing room?"

The housekeeper's mouth dropped open.

"I'm sorry to say that jewellery is one of the thieves' chief targets. Is it anywhere near the tree?"

"Wait here, sir."

She strode down the corridor before opening a door. She waved them forwards.

"It's empty. I'll stay on the door so you can have a quick look around."

They both checked the windows.

Luke put his head out of the one nearest to the tree. "This is too far from the tree to worry."

"Perhaps. Come on. Let's hope there is no one outside when we go out."

They were in luck. There was no one but the housekeeper. Nat pointed to the door to the staircase. Once they were through it he turned to the housekeeper.

"We think the tree is too far away to be a possible route in. Could you have a maid stationed in there to be on the safe side?"

She nodded. "Yes of course. I'll put one of my most reliable girls in there."

"Thank you. Tell me. Do you have any new staff?"

"Only a kitchen maid but she's the daughter of our coachman and I've known her all her life."

Nat nodded. "What about the musicians?"

"We use them regularly and the butler is keeping a close eye on them."

"Excellent. I don't think we'll have any trouble here." Nat smiled his thanks. "Now would you be so kind as to direct us to the bottom of the receiving line. If you're worried about anything at all we won't mind being called out." He ignored Luke's grin. "We'll sit on the end of a row in case we're needed."

Chapter Eighteen

The sound of Alice in her dressing room woke Eliza from her nap. She stretched and sat up. She'd had the bed curtains left open but it hadn't been enough to stop her drifting into a deep sleep and her head felt muzzy. Nat had seemed completely unaffected by their kisses and yet she had been worn out by trying to act normally so Lady Grant wouldn't notice anything amiss. Of course it was different for men. They were allowed to have adventures before they settled down. Why should he be affected when he had probably kissed dozens of women before? With more intimate experience of men she might have been more skilled at pleasing Miles. If she married Nat would things work out any better?

Alice put her head around the door. "Good, you're awake. I thought I heard you stirring. I'll go and fetch you some tea shall I?"

"Yes please. That would be lovely."

Eliza barely noticed Alice leave the room. She would have to slow things down with Nat to give her time to think. Marriage was always a gamble and surely marriage must be his intention. She was far too well protected to trifle with. Lud, was that the answer. Miles had lied to her about so much, had he lied about her deficiency as a lover? If she seduced Nat at least she would find out if she was capable of responding properly to a man. Her body trembled at memories of intimacy with Miles. Her hands touched her cheeks and she could almost feel bruises there like the ones Miles had given her.

If Nat loved her would he be able to help her overcome her difficulties? Augusta was correct to say that her sisters were all happy in their marriages. They all had husbands who couldn't hide how much they loved them. Not every woman was so lucky. She had expected to be happy with Miles but had soon found out he didn't love her. Of course she had been young then and perhaps had only fancied herself in love. She had never had the same intensity of feeling about him as she had for Nat.

A wave of longing for the security of Hargreaves Hall washed over her. Her sisters had all left home and now both her parents had died but the Hall was always there. Overton Grange wasn't far away but if she married Nat and found he didn't love her wouldn't its proximity mock her? When she was with him her doubts seemed to disappear but as soon as she had time to think they came tumbling back. How could she be sure of his true feelings when he was impossible to read? He was the most guarded individual she had ever met.

She agreed to all of Alice's suggestions about what to wear and then panicked that the blue silk dress Alice had put her in was too daring.

"Alice, I'm not sure about this dress now it's on. It's low cut."

Alice smiled serenely. "It's perfect, my lady. I've found out your sapphires to go with it."

"I'm not sure that doesn't make it worse. Pearls would be

better."

"The sapphires go beautifully with the dress." Alice fastened the shimmering necklace around her neck.

"I'm not sure."

There was a knock at the door and Augusta entered.

"We're ready to leave, Eliza. My word you look charming."

Eliza grimaced. "This dress seems far too … Oh I don't know…"

"The word you are searching for is alluring, my dear."

"Oh no. I'll have to change it."

Augusta smiled at her. "There isn't time. The outfit might be alluring but it is perfectly acceptable."

"It won't take a moment to change the sapphires for my pearls."

Augusta caught her hand. "The sapphires are perfect, it's a simple arrangement. If you were a young debutante I might agree but then you wouldn't be wearing a deeper coloured dress. The pearls would look insipid with it. Come, let's go. You know how tetchy Cathlay gets when he's kept waiting."

Eliza sighed but followed Augusta as she swept out of the room. Hadn't Lady Grant said she didn't think the Earl of Milton had an invitation to the soiree? The last thing she wanted was to attract any more attention from him. It sounded like his interest in her was largely monetary but her person was an added bonus from the way he had slobbered over her in the park. Her heart lurched. Could that be Nat's position as well even though it seemed he was comfortably off?

Cathlay was waiting for them at the foot of the stairs. "What a charming sight you ladies make. Tonight we are going to enjoy ourselves. Lady Crane's gatherings are always select and I would be surprised if Milton has been invited."

He offered an arm to each of them and led the way to the waiting coach. Eliza settled into her seat. Her mind might be unsure of Nat but her body thrummed with suppressed excitement at the thought of seeing him again. Lud, what was the matter with her? She couldn't drag her thoughts away from the interlude in the coach. Would Nat find any opportunity to be alone with her tonight? He had even kissed her on the balcony at the Gilbert's ball. Perhaps he was a practised flirt who knew all the tricks of dalliance?

They turned a corner and the blaze of light coming from one of the mansions marked the home of Lord and Lady Crane. They joined a slow moving line of carriages waiting to drop their passengers at the door. Eventually it was their turn and Eliza half expected Nat to be waiting to lift her down. There was no sign of him and Cathlay handed them down and proceeded up the stairs with a lady on each arm.

"It will be interesting to see if the soprano is as good as everyone says she is," Cathlay said.

"I don't think we will be disappointed," Augusta said. "Several of my friends have heard her sing."

Eliza felt a rush of anticipation that had nothing to do with the annoying Major Overton. "I'm looking forward to this. It's an age since I have been to one of Lady Crane's soirees. They're always good."

They reached the head of the receiving line and Eliza's hand was caught by Lady Crane.

"My dear, I am delighted to welcome you."

"Thank you. I'm always happy to attend one of your events."

Lady Crane inclined her head. "I'm sure you will be pleased to hear that your brother's new neighbour, Major Overton, is here tonight. I knew his father, you know, as well as his Uncle

Henry. Both delightful men and the Major seems to be from the same mould don't you think?"

Was it her imagination or was Lady Crane watching her carefully?

"Indeed, he seems to be a most charming gentleman."

Lady Crane smiled and Eliza heard Cathlay laugh at something Lord Crane said. They moved on into the first of the reception rooms. Eliza lowered her eyes. She didn't want to be seen to be searching for Nat, especially not by him. They milled around, chatting to friends and acquaintances. Eventually she heard the deep tones she had been waiting for and her heart skipped a beat.

She couldn't help but study his tall figure as he moved towards them. Even at a social occasion like this he couldn't hide his strength. It was evident in the width of his shoulders, which set off the military cut of his jacket so well, and his purposeful stride. He was every inch the man of action. Nat greeted the Cathlays and moved to her side, offering his arm. She tucked her hand under his elbow. The warmth from his body sent shivers of delight through her.

"You look lovely tonight, Lady Eliza." He laughed and lowered his voice so only she could hear. "Not that I'm implying you don't always look beautiful."

His eyes sought hers and when they found them they were the only people in the room. It was a few moments before she lowered her gaze. This wasn't the way to cool the heat between them.

He patted her hand where it rested on his arm. "You look rather hot. Shall we go and stand by a window?"

A nod was all she could manage. He led her towards a window and she risked a glance up at his face. There was no hint of shadow on his cheeks. He must be freshly shaven and the scent of his cologne enveloped her. She could smell lavender, bergamot and the tang of orange in this one. They stopped at a window at the far edge of the room with no one near them. The cool breeze felt wonderful on her hot cheeks. Had he guessed it was his nearness causing her to overheat? She had to think about something else.

"Cathlay says the soprano we are to hear tonight is excellent."

"I've heard the same thing. I'm looking forward to her performance. My mother had a wonderful soprano voice. She played the piano beautifully as well."

A wistful look danced across his face. It was gone in an instant, he was so good at hiding his feelings, but she was sure she hadn't imagined it.

"We're quite a musical family. Augusta plays the piano wonderfully well."

Cathlay joined them. "She does but then so do you, Eliza."

He looked around. "No one is near enough to hear us here. I'm hoping we will be able to enjoy this evening without any distraction from our friend the Earl of Milton. What's the situation on that, Overton?"

"No one who's not on the guest list will be admitted and he definitely isn't on it, Your Grace." Nat laughed. "Bright is behind the scenes and I'm sure I saw some of your men out in the street earlier. Luke and I have been over every inch of the house checking all windows and doors. Everywhere is well protected. So yes, I'm confident we will have a good evening."

Nat swept a glance around the room. "We're still private. How near are your men to getting the evidence you need? My impression is that the earl's financial situation is becoming desperate. He only has one footman left to his name."

"I'm hopeful of having the business concluded in a day or two."

Nat lowered his voice so Eliza could barely hear. "The sooner the better. I don't think Milton will stop at anything to get what he wants. He never did when he was in the army."

Cathlay stroked his chin. "I'm hoping for enough within two days. I'll have an invitation for dinner at Cathlay House for the evening after tomorrow sent around to the earl. He's unlikely to consider such a desperate course if he thinks I'm keen on the match. That should keep him in check until then."

The room was filling up, with other people coming closer. They turned the conversation to general things until the Duke moved off to talk to some friends. Eliza spotted Grace with Lady Grant.

"I ought to go and talk to Grace."

Anything to get away from Nat's unsettling presence and it would cause gossip if they stayed together all evening. It would be awful if people realised she had developed a tendre for him. She wouldn't give in to her feelings for Nat unless she was sure he loved her. They moved towards Grace and Lady Grant. By now the room was quite full and their progress was slow. Nat stiffened and stopped momentarily, before leading her on a slightly different path. Who was it he wanted to avoid?

She glanced back as the press of people closed behind two unfamiliar women. Perhaps it wasn't them who had affected Nat? Possibly not but they were the ones he had veered away from. She memorised as much of their appearance as she could. Two short women overburdened with so many frills and furbelows shouldn't be difficult to find later. One appeared to have blonde hair and what was visible of her dress under all that decoration was blue. A quick glance at Nat's face revealed a wooden countenance, except for the twitch of an eyelid, rather than his normal relaxed expression. Whoever he was avoiding, seeing them had shaken him.

She risked another glance. His mask of masculine charm was firmly back in place but there was a tension in his posture that hadn't been there before. They reached Grace and Lady Grant. Nat greeted them and then excused himself to join Viscount Enstone, who was behind them. She turned back to find Grace looking at her with one eyebrow raised. Was Grace the only one to notice her interest in Nat? She spent the next few minutes chatting determinedly. A pair of large doors was flung open and the butler invited them to take their seats in the ballroom. Eliza linked arms with Grace and they followed a stream of people into the ballroom, where the musicians were tuning their instruments and practising a few bars of various tunes. She paused by a large vase of petunias and camellias mixed with sprays of evergreen leaves.

"My word, the flower arrangements are wonderful for so early in the year."

"Aunt Theo said Lord Crane is a noted horticulturist. They have an estate not far from London with extensive hothouses. I expect they shipped the flowers in from there. Where would you like to sit?"

Eliza was trying to decide when Nat and Viscount Enstone appeared on either side of them. She saw the siblings share a quick glance and Grace let go of her arm and went to her brother. What was going on here? Were they trying to push her towards Nat? Sure enough he moved closer to her. He lowered his head towards her ear.

"We're not expecting any problems this evening but Luke

203

and I have promised to sit on the ends of rows so the servants can reach us if they're worried about anything."

She stood silently by him trying to control a spurt of anger. Viscount Enstone was a particular friend of Nat's. If Cathlay hadn't made his own enquiries she would be wondering if Nat had exaggerated the stories about the Earl of Milton to give himself an excuse to stay close to her. Had he simply seized on the situation and could the Bamfords be helping him in a quest to fix his interest with her? Grace was her friend but she seemed a biddable sort of girl and she and her brother were close. They'd let him drive off alone with her after dropping them outside the museum, after all.

She only had Nat's word for it that his and Bright's worries of a kidnap threat to her had necessitated them driving around for quite some while. He had certainly made good use of the time. Her cheeks flamed at the thought of her enthusiastic response to him. Oh he must consider her a complete fool. To think she had been on the brink of dismissing all her worries about marriage and taking a risk on accepting an offer from him, if he made one.

A hand took her arm and guided her to a seat. She watched as if in a dream as Nat lowered himself into the seat next to her, at the end of the row. He bent over her poised to say something but Lady Crane mounted the large dais, which was occupied by a good sized group of musicians, to welcome them all to the event. Nat sat back in his chair. Eliza hid her hands under her reticule so he couldn't claim the one nearest to him. He glanced at her with knitted brows but she kept her gaze firmly forwards. They hadn't discussed anything in words, all the exploration had been done physically. He couldn't complain if she extricated herself from any commitment.

At the interval she pretended not to see Nat's outstretched arm and positioned herself next to Grace.

"Will you accompany me to the ladies withdrawing room?"

"Of course." Grace looked at her brother. "Perhaps the gentlemen will save seats for us."

Viscount Enstone nodded.

Eliza took Grace's arm and led her away. There was a queue already forming when they reached the ladies' room. Good, she needed some time away from Nat to gather her scattered thoughts. Grace kept shooting little glances at her. Had Nat said anything in front of her? She had the same air of suppressed excitement she'd had when her friend had become engaged. Well if Major Overton thought he could bounce her into anything he would soon find out his error.

They reached the private areas and she took advantage of the facilities. Before she went out she gave her hair a tug so part of it was hanging loose. Outside she found a place in front of a looking glass. A young maid offered to help her repair her hairstyle. Grace stood to one side waiting.

"I thought I could feel my hair moving. What do you think of the music so far?"

"Quite excellent, but like most people I'm waiting for the soprano."

The maid put the final pin into her upswept style. Eliza studied it in the glass and caught sight of the women with the frilly dresses coming in. She took her time, pretending to check all around her head. She was rewarded with a snippet of conversation from the woman in the blue dress.

"Fancy seeing Nathaniel Overton here, Mama. My goodness, he has matured well."

Eliza took her time searching in her reticule for a coin for

205

the maid, but she couldn't hear the reply. They did know Nat, so her instinct that they were the cause of his shock was right. The maid thanked her prettily for the coin and she followed Grace outside. There was no one near them as they walked along the corridor. Perhaps Grace would know who they were.

"Did you see those two with their dresses smothered in frills and lace?"

Grace kept her voice low. "The Countess of Bidford and her mother, Mrs Rees. Aunt Theo said they would probably be invited as Mrs Rees is a first cousin of Lord Crane. She meant to warn Luke."

Why would Lady Grant want to warn Viscount Enstone? Grace looked as if she was holding something back but there was no time to question her further before they reached the refreshment room.

"Oh there they are. See, Luke is waving at us."

Both men rose as they reached their table at the back of the room.

Nat pulled out a chair for her. "The refreshments are excellent. I wish all Ton parties were like this one. What would you like? Lemonade or something stronger?"

"Lemonade please."

Nat nodded. "I'll bring a selection of what's left of the food as well."

She didn't feel hungry but he was gone before she could stop him. She spotted the woman in blue sitting at a table where Nat would have to pass her. Now this could be interesting.

Chapter Nineteen

Nat strode across the room, head down. Eliza seemed out of sorts this evening. Was she regretting the interlude in the coach? She had seemed almost frightened initially but then her responses had become enthusiastic. Perhaps he had rushed her. He should have held back but the temptation had been too strong. A female voice hailed him. Fiend seize it. He had forgotten about the Rees. He trailed to a halt and concentrated on keeping his breathing steady. There were other people nearby and he couldn't risk ignoring Anna. At least her harpy of a mother didn't seem to be with her.

"Good evening, Miss Rees."

Anna pouted. "You didn't used to be so formal, Nat."

He pinned a smile to his face and refused to respond.

"Didn't you know I'm the Countess of Bidford now?"

Nat bowed. "Indeed I didn't. My apologies, Lady Bidford. I congratulate you on your advantageous marriage."

"Aren't you even the tiniest bit jealous, Nat?" She lowered her voice to a whisper. "I've produced two fine sons and it's time for me to enjoy myself, if you take my meaning."

Nat gritted his teeth. Lord, how had he ever found Anna attractive? "I hope you are enjoying the soiree. I hear the soprano is excellent. Now if you will excuse me?"

He turned to move on but his way was blocked by Mrs Rees.

"What do you think you're about, Nat Overton? You've caused our family enough trouble."

He caught the glare Anna threw at her mother and the belligerent stare she got back. Anna still had an eye for the men did she? Why wasn't he surprised? How many other young fools had she tried to seduce before her mother had married her off? A sudden stab of amusement eased his temper.

"Good evening, Mrs Rees. What a pleasure it is to pick up the threads of old friendships."

Mrs Rees turned her back on him and sat down next to her daughter. He walked past them and caught a speculative gleam in Anna's eyes. What had possessed him to torment Mrs Rees? Now Anna would be thinking he was ready to cuckold the Earl of Bidford. Something else to watch out for.

He avoided conversation at the supper buffet by dint of keeping his eyes lowered. On his way back to Eliza he overheard Mrs Rees talking to a lady who had joined them.

"A major is he. I grant you he's a fine figure of a man but my goodness is he prepared to use that to his advantage. He's paying court to Lady Eliza Wyndham, daughter of a marquess no less. He always was a social climber that lad."

The temptation to throttle her on the spot was so great he nearly dropped the tray he was carrying. She could insult him all she liked. She could hardly do him any more damage than she had when he was a boy. But to mention Eliza's name like that was unpardonable. He forced himself to keep walking. From what he had seen of Anna her actions had already proclaimed to the world what manner of woman she was. Anyone who knew of the old scandal about him would surely work out what had truly happened. A young man flattered and seduced and then used as a shield when her mother found out. He could see that clearly now. It was time to forgive himself and put it behind him. At least he'd had the sense to stop and refuse to take the virginity of the daughter of his hosts.

He arrived at their table and put the tray down in front of Eliza. She picked up the lemonade.

"Thank you. I'm in sore need of this."

She did look rather hot. Something was bothering her too. He longed to trace a finger over her brow and smooth out the creases. Luke joined them.

"Sorry I've been so long. I came across someone I know." He set his tray down by Grace and took the seat next to Nat.

The butler announced the start of the second half before Nat had a chance to talk to Eliza. She seemed to draw back at his touch but then accepted his proffered arm. He was getting jumpy. Seeing Anna and her mother had unnerved him. They settled in their seats. Nat made no attempt to take Eliza's hand after her rebuff in the first half. Perhaps she was too nervous of being seen? He must be a little more circumspect in company.

The music wrapped him up in a blanket of pleasure. The orchestra were the best he had heard for a long time. The opening piece drew to a close and there was a buzz of anticipation as the soprano was introduced. He caught his breath as she broke into one of the haunting ballads his mother had loved to sing. He had never heard a voice to match his mother's but this lady came close. Suddenly he was ten again and listening to the mother he had been about to lose. The song came to an end and he lowered his head to hide the tears he could feel sliding down his cheeks.

He carefully extracted his handkerchief and blew his nose, blotting the tears at the same time. It was time for him to settle down and start a family of his own. The problem was if Eliza wouldn't have him how could he settle for anyone else. He risked a glance at her face. She seemed to be engrossed in the music. He let the sounds wash over him and felt more relaxed than he had done for some time, since he had met Eliza if he was honest with himself.

The performance came to an end. Nat rose and escorted Eliza out into the hallway. She still seemed quiet and a little distant.

"Did you enjoy that, Lady Eliza?"

"Yes I did. It was a fabulous performance."

Nat smiled. "It was wonderful. I think I will have to go to more soirees."

They were joined by Luke and Grace.

"Good Lord, Nat. Did you just say what I thought you said?"

Grace dug her brother in the ribs. "I can't believe you're as bad as you make out. You can't hate museums and musical events."

Nat laughed out loud. "Oh he is, and he can, believe me. Let's get out of this crush and find somewhere quieter to wait for the Cathlays."

They drifted into the edge of the supper room where they could see through to the hall and the queue to take leave of Lady Crane.

Nat glanced around. "We're alone here. What are your plans for tomorrow Lady Eliza?"

"Grace has invited me to spend the afternoon with them but I'm not sure about the evening."

"Milton seems to know where we are whatever we do. I'll borrow a carriage from Luke, if he doesn't mind, and escort you to Lady Grant's house myself."

Luke nodded. "Order one sent round whenever you want. If I've finished my estate business I'll come with you."

Nat watched Eliza's face. She looked relieved at the prospect of Luke being with them. "I'll wait for you, Luke. We need to stay vigilant."

The Cathlays appeared to be the last people talking to Lady Crane. Nat caught Luke's eye. "Would you go and check our carriages are waiting. I'll ask the Cathlays their plans for tomorrow evening."

Luke slipped out and the rest of them walked across the hall to the Duke and Duchess and Lady Crane. Nat swept a deep bow.

"Thank you for a wonderful evening, Lady Crane."

"It was delightful to meet you, Major Overton. I hope you will attend more of my musical entertainments."

"I shall look forward to that."

Luke came back with the news that their carriages were outside. Nat kept Eliza's arm tucked through his elbow and followed the Cathlays to their coach. He handed her in and turned to the Duke.

"I'll escort Lady Eliza to Lady Grant's house tomorrow afternoon. Are you going out in the evening?"

"I think we're going to the Comerfords' Ball. I'll check with Augusta. We can let you know when you call for Eliza." The Duke glanced around and nodded at the silhouette of Bright up with the Cathlay coachman. "Well done, Overton. Your man is a reassuring presence."

Nat watched them drive off and then jumped into Luke's coach. Luke seemed inclined to talk but he wanted time alone to think. When they arrived at Enstone House he pleaded fatigue and went straight up to bed where Jones was waiting for him.

"I thought I gave you the evening off."

"William turned up at the Cross and Keys, had one drink from me and then left. He said he had an important job to do but he didn't say what and he was off before I could press him."

"Disappointing. I was hoping you'd get some information from him."

"He did mention he might be there tomorrow afternoon. Would you like me to try again?"

Nat stroked his chin. "We've nothing to lose. Let me give you the extra money I promised you."

Nat handed him all his loose change and a couple of guineas. Jones gasped.

"That's generous of you, Major."

"I think you've earned it. There is one thing Jones. I hope I haven't given you the impression that I intend to live in Town?"

"I hadn't thought about it, Major. I'm happy to have a good job with the chance to learn from my uncle first. I don't mind where it is."

"That's good because, when this episode is over, I've a fancy to settle down to a quiet life in the country. I've agreed to move in with my uncle and manage the estates. I'm his heir. Overton Grange is in Kent."

"I shall look forward to it."

The door closed behind Jones. Nat sat and stared at the fire until a shiver made him notice it had nearly died down. He climbed into bed and drew the covers over his head. He was no nearer to working out how best to approach Eliza. He had

212

never met a woman who had intrigued and challenged him as she did. She had been quite subdued at the soiree. Had he read too much into her actions? Did she have no more than a passing fancy for him? If so what could he do? No matter what the risk to his pride he had to try and win her somehow.

Chapter Twenty

Nat was up late the next morning. He stepped off the last step into the hall to see Luke coming out of the library.

"Have you had breakfast yet, Luke?" He stretched to ease the tension at the back of his neck.

Luke looked at his watch. "Not yet. We've got time before we need to collect Lady Eliza."

They filled their plates and sat down opposite each other. A footman brought in a fresh pot of coffee and put it down by Luke.

"Thank you. Have a carriage sent round in about half an hour would you. Oh, and close the door when you go out. We don't want to be disturbed."

Nat leaned back and glanced across at Luke, eyes wide.

The door closed and Luke pursed his lips. "What is it old chap? You look quite dejected."

"I'm worried about what our friend the earl will do next."

"We all are but that's not all of it, is it? Out with it man."

Nat sighed. "If you must know, last night I had the feeling Eliza isn't as interested in me as I thought she was."

"You may not be sure about the lady's feelings but from what I've seen of them I'm sure her relatives are rooting for you. I told you there was no reason to expect that the Ton wouldn't accept you."

"I'm not worried about what the Ton thinks of me anymore. I'm glad if the Cathlays approve but it's Eliza's approval I need and I'm not at all sure how she's feeling."

"She did seem rather quiet last night but Grace said she was shaken by the incident in the park. I expect she will be fine when it's all sorted. You don't need to worry. If you ask me she's seriously enamoured of you."

"We'll see."

Luke smiled. "I hope we do. Don't take any notice of Anna Rees and her mother. I'm sure Lady Eliza would sympathise with you if she knew the whole story."

Nat stared at him. "How do you know about that?"

"I've always known. You've nothing to fear. Anyone who has ever met Anna Rees won't blame you at all."

Nat stared out of the window. Could someone have told Eliza about the incident with Anna Rees? Could that be why she seemed to have cooled towards him so suddenly? No matter what Luke said, it was an episode of which he was deeply ashamed. Could Eliza be having second thoughts about allying herself to a man like him with a mixed pedigree? Surely she was too straightforward a personality for that. He would feel much happier with permission from Cathlay to court Eliza openly, as long as he could be sure he wouldn't mention it to Eliza straight away. She might take fright if he did. The vulnerability he sensed in her was puzzling given her normal confident manner. She was intelligent enough to realise the seriousness of the threat from Milton but there was something else troubling her.

Nat accepted another cup of coffee. "The Cathlays and Lady

Eliza will all be at the Comerford Ball this evening. Are you invited?"

Luke grinned at him. "I'll fetch my invitations."

He came back with a pile of gilt edged cards. "Let's have a look."

After a few minutes of rummaging he pulled a card out with a cry of triumph. "Here it is. We can go around to my club once we've greeted Aunt Theo. I expect old Comerford is holed up there out of the way. He has three unmarried daughters so he will be delighted to entertain you but it would be best to make sure."

Nat laughed. "I'm getting used to be eyed up by matrons looking for a husband for their daughters."

Luke shuddered. "I know. I suppose I'll have to negotiate my way around them one of these days. You're lucky to have chanced upon someone without having to bother about all that nonsense."

"I wish I had your confidence in my ability to fix my interest with Eliza. Come on, the carriage will be ready soon."

Sayers opened the door to them at Cathlay House. "Follow me, gentlemen. His Grace has already gone out. Her Grace and Lady Eliza are in the morning room."

Nat squared his shoulders and followed Sayers. His hope of a quick word with Cathlay was dashed. Should he see if he was at his club later, using the information from Jones as a way to ease him into a conversation about Eliza? He might have a problem gaining admittance. What a pity he hadn't taken up Cathlay's offer to sponsor him as a member. It was too late now. If Mrs Rees got word of it she would more than likely arrange for him to be blackballed. That was a humiliation he could do without.

His mouth felt suddenly dry when Sayers introduced them. How would Eliza receive him? She kept her eyes lowered as she greeted him. The Duchess waved them to seats opposite to the sofa she was sharing with Eliza.

"Did you enjoy the soiree, gentlemen?"

Nat grinned at Luke's grimace. "I enjoyed it very much, Your Grace. Before my parents died our house was filled with music." He sighed as long buried memories surfaced. "My mother loved to play the piano and sing and my father often sang with her. As soon as I was old enough she gave me lessons at the piano. Sadly, I haven't played for years."

She laughed. "I don't suppose pianos were much of a priority for the army. I'm glad you're musical. Remind me to invite you around to a family supper once this business with Milton is over. We often finish with some music."

So, the Duchess expected they would carry on entertaining him then. That must be a good sign surely? Nat stole a glance at Eliza. Her countenance gave nothing away.

"Thank you. I would enjoy that. Before I forget, are you going to the Comerfords' Ball this evening? Viscount Enstone has an invitation and we will be happy to keep watch again."

"We are invited to the Comerfords' ball. Cathlay means to go. We can stay at home if you prefer."

Eliza sighed. "We had best go or all our efforts to date will be for naught if the Earl of Milton gives up on me and disappears. It will be such a big affair I expect he is invited."

The Duchess laughed. "With three unmarried daughters and two already out, I doubt Lady Comerford has left out any unmarried man with a title. Her ambition is a title for all of them, awful woman. Viscount Enstone should be able to get you in, Major Overton."

"He's going to introduce me to Lord Comerford if he's at his club."

"Good, but even if you can't find him I can't see them turning you away."

A wave of longing shot through Eliza as Nat handed her into the coach. She shivered as she settled onto the seat. She returned Lord Enstone's smile with an effort as he sat opposite to her. Nat climbed in and folded his long frame onto the seat next to her. The coach swung around a corner throwing them closer together. The heat from his thigh pressed against hers did nothing to still the tremors going through her. Lud, what should she do? What she felt had to be love. Nat filled her every waking moment.

She could start by trying to find out all she could about Nat from Grace. Her friend would surely guess why she wanted to know about him but it couldn't be helped. It might be best to be honest with Grace about her predicament, at least some of it. She would be more likely to tell her all she knew. The more she knew about Nat the easier it would be to understand how he felt about her. If she could be sure he loved her she would have to confide in him.

Both men were quiet, each looking out of a different window. How long would it take to resolve the problem of the Earl of Milton? Bright opened the door of the coach when they arrived in Grosvenor Square.

"All clear, Major."

Nat jumped out and Lord Enstone followed him. Nat helped her down. Lord Enstone stood one side of them and Bright the other. They were taking the whole thing so seriously it was unnerving. Lady Grant and Grace were waiting for them in the hall. Lady Grant asked the two men to join her in the formal drawing room leaving Grace to take her into a small sitting room, which had a window ideally placed to capture the afternoon sun. Her heart thumped as she engaged in small talk until the maid with the tea tray had left them. Grace handed her a cup with a smile.

"Forgive me, Eliza, but you seem a little distracted."

"I am. Major Overton is paying me a lot of attention. I know so little about him."

"Will it help if I tell you everything I know?"

Eliza leaned forward slightly. "It might."

"Luke said he was the finest officer he ever served under in the army and a man of great integrity. I honestly believe that he was hoping Nat would take a liking to me but although I like him as a friend he doesn't set my pulses racing. Aunt Theo assured me I should never settle for anything less."

Eliza couldn't help but smile. It confirmed her impression of Lady Grant as being an incurable romantic. She would certainly recommend she marry Nat given the effect he had on her.

"Your brother's regard is a strong point in his favour but how men deal with each other isn't always how they treat women."

Grace screwed up her face. "He loves his horses and he's popular with the servants. The female servants are besotted with him but there has been no hint of him taking advantage of that. He seems a fair minded sort but there's not much more I can tell you."

Eliza took a deep breath. "I'm sure he knows the Countess of Bidford and her mother. I saw them talking at the soiree. He looked annoyed to see them there but then he appeared friendly when he spoke to them."

Grace stroked her chin. "I'm not sure what, but he had some

sort of problem with Anna Rees, as she was then, when he was young. I overheard Luke tell Aunt Theo that in his opinion she was the reason Nat went into the army."

"That seems an extreme reaction. I wonder what the problem was."

"I couldn't hear that bit but it must have been bad. Luke told me once that Nat's grandfather wanted him to go to university but he insisted on joining the army so he could get away from society. Luke says even now he finds it difficult going to society balls and suchlike, but you would never know it." Grace laughed. "He's far too clever to give away what he must have been feeling when he came across Anna and her mother. Luke said he's the cleverest man he's ever known."

Eliza slumped in her seat. That confirmed her impression of Nat as a man who could hide his feelings.

Grace smiled at her. "So you see Major Overton is a thoroughly admirable character. When shall I wish you happy?"

Eliza stared at the floor to hide her consternation. With luck Grace would think it was a show of modesty. What if Nat wanted to marry her to improve his status? It was all too possible. If his experiences, whatever they were, had left him unsure of himself in society he might consider that a bigger prize than any amount of money. He had suggested he was comfortably off after all. Her head ached. She couldn't admit her suspicions to Grace. She fixed a smile in place and looked up.

"It wouldn't do to read too much into his actions, Grace. He's determined to protect me from the Earl of Milton because he feels beholden to my brother for all the help he has given him."

Grace put her head on one side and studied her. "It seems

like more than that to me. You like him don't you?"

"I admit I find him attractive and that's why I wanted to know more about him. I don't think he's seriously interested in me. We shall see."

Grace laughed. "Methinks the lady doth protest too much."

Eliza tried to smile. If only it was that simple. "I wish I could have a chance to talk to him alone."

Voices came from the hall. "Grace, do you think we could persuade them to take a turn about the garden with us before they leave."

"Leave it to me." Grace grinned at her and ran out.

She threw her arms around her brother. "Luke you're not going to escape without a proper talk with me. I've hardly seen you lately. It's a warm day. Why don't we all take a turn about the garden before you go? I want to know what this trip up north was all about."

Lord Enstone looked about to refuse but changed his mind at the wink Grace gave him.

"I might as well give in, you minx. I'll have no peace unless I do."

Eliza held her breath in case Nat declined to join them.

Lord Enstone laughed. "It looks like we're caught, Nat."

"Thank you." Grace signalled to a footman. "Can you fetch Lady Eliza's pelisse and ask my maid to bring me one down, please?"

Grace chatted away to her brother. Nat seemed content to listen. Grace liked him and he appeared to be a good natured man. Could she trust him to be truthful with her? It was obvious Nat desired her but did he love her? Even if he did that was the least of her problems. She craved him physically but what if her old fears came back and stopped her being fully intimate with him?

Augusta couldn't have made it plainer that Nat would be welcome as a brother-in-law, pressure she could do without. Augusta had a way of spotting people to be avoided. She'd always wondered if Augusta would have seen through Miles if they had been in London that fateful season. So why didn't she trust Augusta's judgement now? She smiled at the memory of Augusta's talk on relationships given before her London debut. Without Augusta's explanation of how a marriage was consummated her wedding night would have been even more hideous. Perhaps she didn't trust Augusta's judgement any more than her own because part of her didn't want to.

She would be the untruthful one if she didn't tell Nat of her fear of intimacy after her problems with Miles, but it was too shameful to talk about. If she couldn't even talk to Augusta about it how could she broach the subject with Nat? Lud, what a mess she was in. Grace's maid arrived with their pelisses. Grace grabbed her brother's arm and led them out into the garden. Eliza placed her hand on the arm Nat proffered and they followed several steps behind them. Now she had her chance Eliza couldn't think of what to say.

Nat patted her hand and smiled down at her. "I'm glad of this chance to talk privately. I owe you an apology for letting my enthusiasm get the better of me in the carriage yesterday."

Eliza's eyes flew to his face. "That's plain speaking. I must accept some of the blame."

"There is no need to look so guilty. I promise you my intentions are honourable."

"Are they? I only have your word for it that our detour in the coach was necessary."

"The plan was to drive around the block so any lookouts

would believe the Bamfords were on their own. I hope you don't think I'd told Bright to give us plenty of time together. The incident with the cart made him extra cautious, knowing what the Earl of Milton is capable of."

Eliza tilted her head and studied him. "I did wonder. We were held up by a cart on our journey into London, it happens a lot."

Nat glanced at the floor and then at her. "I let my feelings for you get the better of me in the coach. I shouldn't have rushed you. My intention was to give you an enjoyable time away from the earl."

"You certainly did that." She gasped and her free hand flew to her cheek. "Oh, you detestable man. Now look what you made me say."

He couldn't hold back a grin. "So you enjoyed my advances then, even if you're feeling guilty now?"

She looked away from him. He stayed silent, giving her time to compose herself. Her family didn't seem the sort to burden their females with over many strictures like some he had come across. Surely at her age they wouldn't be worried about a few stolen kisses as long as they were discreet? Ice flooded his veins. Could she be afraid she had given him the impression of being open to a courtship with him when she wasn't? Women must have urges too. He saw her wipe away a tear with a handkerchief.

"I'm sorry to be guilty of upsetting you. Are you trying to tell me you have no interest in furthering our acquaintance in the future?"

She turned to face him. "I don't know."

A wave of anger threatened to overwhelm him but the sight

of her woebegone face made it fade. He hated to see her unhappy. They came to a clump of bushes, tall enough to shield them from view. He led her behind them and put a hand on her shoulder.

"I'm sorry. I won't press you to decide until a better time."

"That would be best. I'm so confused. Part of me longs to get to know you better and another part...." She chewed at her lip.

Before he could stop himself he folded her into an embrace and dropped a kiss on her forehead. He lifted her face up with a finger under her chin until their eyes met.

"You can trust me. I would never knowingly do anything to hurt you."

Her arms found their way around his neck and her nearness sent the blood rushing to his groin. His own face grew hot. They were so close she must be able to feel the evidence of the effect she was having on him. He tried to pull away. She gave a little cry and pressed her soft body closer to him. His back arched as passion threatened to overwhelm him. He closed his eyes and drank in the smell of her. All floral scents mixed with a tantalising essence of woman. No other woman had ever affected him beyond reason like this. The pressure of her arms around his neck increased. Her lips found his and he fought for control. The kiss deepened. He let it consume him for a few moments and then pulled back.

He smiled down at her. "Is this some sort of test of my trustworthiness? If it is I've failed miserably."

She shook her head. "No that was the part of me that longs to get to know you better."

"What about the other part?"

"The other part is a problem."

"If you tell me what your problem is perhaps I can help."

She shook her head and pulled away from him, red-faced. With her arms crossed in front and a wide stance she looked almost angry. He was reminded of their first meeting when she was furious with him. She seemed quick to think the worst of him but then he had been the same with her to start with. Was he fooling himself that she was different to the young misses he had known in his youth? Perhaps it was time to tell her more about his past, including the incident with Anna Rees. The voices of the other two came closer. He spotted a stone bench in the corner of the garden.

"Let's go and sit on that bench for a minute."

She followed him but she had a distant expression on her face. If only he knew what she was thinking. He whipped out his handkerchief and wiped the bench over.

"There, I think that's clean enough to sit on now." He held up the green-stained handkerchief. "I'll be in trouble with my valet though."

His sally drew a faint smile and she perched on the cleanest part of the bench. He sat beside her but resisted the urge to take her hand.

"Are you wondering how I know Mrs Rees and the Countess of Bidford?"

Hers eyes flew to his face. "I am puzzled. You seemed angry to see them but when you couldn't avoid talking to them you looked extremely friendly."

He laughed. "The army was the making of me. I learned how to appear friendly with people I couldn't stand and how to appear brave when I was terrified. Something I'm doing now. The second part that is. I might not show it but I'm terrified you will turn me away."

She looked down and he couldn't see her expression. He sighed. Whatever was troubling her, it was going to be the devil of a job to get it out of her.

"Anyway, back to the Rees. My grandfather was ambitious for me. He was also angry because the Overtons wouldn't acknowledge me. He was determined to prove to them that his grandson was as good as they were. He got me into Rugby school. I'm sure money changed hands; he had a lot of that. He insisted I get myself invited to friends' houses in the holidays as much as I could."

He looked across at her. He had her attention now and she seemed to relax. Perhaps she was upset because she had read too much into the incident with the Rees.

"Peter Rees was one of those friends. I was just seventeen. His sister, Anna, showed a lot of interest in me and I fell for her. I thought I was in love." He felt a blush heat his cheeks but carried on.

"Anna wanted me to take her virginity but I had the sense to refuse. Her mother got wind of our relationship, such as it was. Anna told Mrs Rees I had tried to seduce her to deflect any blame from herself and Mrs Rees had me thrown onto the roof of the next stagecoach home."

"Oh how awful for you."

"It was. I was mortified and my grandfather was furious. After that I endured a lot of ill-natured teasing. My so-called friends' sisters enjoyed tormenting me when the incident became common knowledge. A favourite taunt was to call me a shipwright's boy."

"Ah. I'm sure I've heard the Earl of Milton call you that."

"Yes he has but he didn't go to the same school. It must have been even more common knowledge than I had realised. All in all I think I made the right decision to enter the army at eighteen. I found my place in the world there and no longer worried about society." He laughed. "Well not so much anyway. What's the worst thing that's ever happened to you?"

She blinked rapidly and looked near to tears. This time he did take her hand and he gave it a squeeze. She flinched and pulled it away. Grace and Luke came into view. Damn. A few more minutes and he might have got her to open up on what was bothering her.

Luke grinned at him. "Sorry to intrude but we must go now if we're to have any chance of finding Comerford."

Chapter Twenty One

There was no sign of Comerford when they arrived at Luke's club. Luke introduced Nat to some friends and they chatted for a while. Eventually they got up to leave. Luke stopped at the sound of a loud voice in the hallway.

"That could be Comerford. Man is a touch on the deaf side." Luke smiled as a portly gentleman came in to the lounge. He motioned to Nat to move beside him.

"Comerford. Just the man. This is my friend, Major Overton, who is staying with me at present. How would it be if I brought him along tonight?"

Comerford stared at him until Nat felt a blush colouring his face.

"You must be one of the Kent Overtons from the looks of you."

Nat stiffened. "Yes, I've moved in with my uncle at Overton Grange."

Comerford beamed at him. "So you're the heir. Excellent. By all means bring him along, Lord Enstone. My wife will be pleased."

"Thank you, Lord Comerford." Luke bowed. "Until this evening."

Nat had an uneasy feeling of being watched as they walked back from Luke's club. He kept checking but could see no one. If they were being followed it was by someone good.

Luke put a hand on his arm. "What's troubling you?"

"I keep thinking we're being followed but there's no sign of anyone. Bright is even more jumpy than I am. It's making me nervous, that's all."

Luke quickened the pace. "I'm getting worried. You and Bright both have a nose for trouble."

It wasn't long before they were home.

"May I borrow Garner? I think I'll take my new horse out for a ride to get the fidgets out of both of us and Jones is off trying to get information out of one of Milton's servants he knows."

Garner helped him change into riding gear and he went down to the mews to find that Bright had already exercised Pharaoh.

"Caesar is fully recovered now if you want to take him out for a good ride. I'll come with you."

"That won't be necessary."

Bright shook his head. "I can see there's no moving you but take care."

He helped Bright saddle Caesar up and headed for the park at a steady trot. Caesar seemed to be going well, with no traces of the muscle pull that had dogged him for weeks. It suited his mood to be on his old campaign horse. His current problems had the feel of a military campaign. He turned in at the park gates and a sudden tension at the back of his neck made him glance over his shoulder. Yet again his instincts insisted that someone was watching him but he could see nothing. His imagination must be overactive, what with Bright's unusual edginess and being on the alert to protect Eliza.

They cantered around for a while. Nat was careful to avoid

other park users. Near to where Eliza had been mauled by Milton, Nat's instincts hit him as surely as if he had been thumped between the shoulder blades. He whistled at Caesar who whipped around in a tight circle. At the same moment he ducked low over the horse's neck a shot rang out. It passed so close to him he could smell the gunpowder.

He whistled Caesar around again and galloped him towards the busier part of the park, taking care to stay in the open. He slowed down as he reached the throngs of riders and carriages out to see and be seen. Several frosty looks were thrown his way after his mad gallop. He ignored them and rode around looking for anything that might be a clue as to who had meant to kill him. Could it have been Milton himself? As Captain Denby he had been a noted marksman.

It would be foolhardy for whoever the marksman was to make another attempt to kill him in this well-populated area. He steered Caesar towards the main entrance and made for Enstone House at a steady trot. It had been lucky he had been riding him and not Pharaoh. Once they were back at Overton Grange they would have to set about training the chestnut to work to whistles. Bright was waiting for him when he rode into the mews before dismounting. There was no hiding his lucky escape from Bright. He would know from the exhausted condition of Caesar that they had met with trouble.

Bright came up and held the reins as he dismounted. "What happened?"

"Someone tried to shoot me in Hyde Park of all places."

He helped Bright give a shivering Caesar a good rub down and filled in the details.

"I hope I haven't done Caesar any harm."

"He's had worse on the battlefield. He's just tired because

he's not fully fit." He threw a rug over the horse and tied him up to a large iron ring. "There's a good few years in you yet, old fellow."

Nat stroked Caesar's ear. "I was lying when I promised you a quiet life back home in England."

"He likes a bit of adventure. I'll escort you up to the house through the garden."

Bright produced a key for the locked door to the gardens. "Denby is the most vicious man I've ever met. I knew there would be trouble when he appeared on the scene. Perhaps you should try and stop Lady Eliza going to the Comerford ball tonight."

Nat stroked his chin. "I'm not sure it would help. This is bound to come to a head eventually. I'll be glad to get it over with. On the other hand I would rather choose the battlefield myself. This afternoon has made me even more uneasy."

"If it's the lady you're worried about," Bright gave him a searching glance, "I wouldn't worry too much. He wants her money so he's not going to kill her. He might have another go at finishing you off."

"You may be right but I don't want him violating her."

"The Duke of Cathlay is powerful enough to make even Denby take care. Denby still thinks he has a chance of arranging a proper marriage so he gets all her money, I'll be bound. He's an earl after all. You're in his way."

"I'm sure you're right. I think I will try and warn Cathlay before the ball. How many men have you got working for you tonight?"

"Several but there are a couple of good footmen I can borrow as well. We'll keep an eye on this Comerford place and you, don't you worry. I don't intend to lose the best position I'm ever likely to get."

With that Bright waved him through and locked the door behind them. He led him to a servants' door in the basement. This one had an armed footman manning it. Bright followed Nat inside.

"Thank you for your loyalty, Bright. Stay safe yourself. If Jones is back would you send him up to my room? If not send Garner."

"Yes, Major." Bright saluted and sped off to the kitchen area.

Nat ran up the stairs to the main part of the house. He reached his room without seeing anyone to slow him up. He had taken his jacket off and was sitting on the bed trying to remove his boots when Jones ran in without knocking.

"Sorry to burst in but your groom said to make haste. Leave that to me."

Jones knelt down and dealt with the boots. A footman arrived with hot water and Jones set about shaving him.

Nat sat back and some of the tension drained away from him. He wouldn't be entirely happy until he could keep watch over Eliza.

"Any sign of the earl's footman?"

"I was about to give up when William appeared. He looked haggard. I bought him some drinks and he said he thought the earl was about to do a runner and he didn't think he would get paid. They've tried taking the knocker off the door but the duns are still coming."

So Milton's financial position was even more perilous than they'd thought. "Was he just speculating?"

"I don't think so. He said the coachman told him he'd been ordered to check over the old family travelling coach and enquire about the cost of hiring four horses."

Nat caught his breath. He didn't like the sound of four horses. Could Milton be contemplating a kidnap?

"Jones, if I dash off a note could you deliver it to the Duke of Cathlay? Insist on handing it to the butler. His name is Sayers. Tell him it's urgent. Your uncle can help me dress for the evening. Come on. We should find pen and paper in the library."

Nat ran down the stairs in his shirt sleeves, followed by Jones. He charged into the library to find Luke relaxing in an armchair reading a newspaper, already dressed for the evening.

Luke's mouth dropped open. "I thought you wanted to be at the ball early tonight?"

"I do but this is important. Jones will fill you in whilst I write the note."

Nat ignored their muttered conversation and quickly set out what Jones had heard. Luke joined him at the desk.

"Let me seal it for you."

Nat handed the note over. Luke was right. Sayers was far more likely to listen to Jones with a viscount's seal on the note. He gave Jones another guinea.

"Take a hackney and insist on seeing the Duke yourself if you can. Then if he wants to carry on to the ball you can stress how lucky I was to escape unharmed this afternoon."

Luke gave him a grim smile. "I hate to say it old man but at the moment the one in mortal danger is you."

"I know but I wish Eliza and the Cathlays would stay at home tonight. Somehow I don't think they will."

"Would you like me to take the note?"

Nat thought quickly. "No. I'm going to need you to get me into the ball. It's probably too late to stop them going."

Jones ran off and Nat scaled the stairs two at a time, calling for Garner as he went. He had to get to the ball so he could make sure Eliza was safe. Twenty minutes later he ran back down the stairs to find Luke waiting for him by the front door. Once outside he looked around in bewilderment.

"Where's the carriage?"

"Not coming. We'll get a hackney around the corner."

"Good notion."

They were in luck when a hackney came towards them almost immediately. Nat wrinkled his nose at the musty smell as they climbed in. He used his handkerchief to wipe the seat. It was a good job Jones had bought him plenty.

"It's not in the same class as your carriage but you're right, we'll be less conspicuous."

"I've told the driver to drop us around the corner from my club. It isn't far from there to the Comerford house and it will look as if we've walked from the club."

In what seemed like eternity to Nat, but in reality was no more than a few minutes, the hackney drew to a halt. Luke paid off the jarvey and they strode along the road. Nat took care to stay in the shadows. They soon reached their destination and ran lightly up the front steps to join the line of people snaking up the grand marble staircase to the reception rooms. Nat scanned the stairs but he could see no sign of Eliza. His mouth went dry and a bead of sweat trickled down his back. He could be back on the battlefield, awaiting the order to charge. He was used to facing danger but it was fear for Eliza's safety that threatened to overwhelm him. At last they reached the front of the line.

Lady Comerford simpered over them for several minutes. He forced himself to concentrate and smile in all the right places as she introduced her two eldest daughters. Finally it was time to move on. Nat sauntered into the room, determined to hide his unease. He turned to Luke.

"I seem to remember that Grace and Lady Grant won't be here tonight?"

Luke grimaced. "They couldn't get out of a promise to attend a card party given by one of Aunt Theo's oldest friends."

Nat moved close to him. "I can't understand why the Duke was happy to have Eliza so tightly protected last night and yet is happy to come here tonight without them."

"The Duchess has a lot of friends. I expect she will make sure Lady Eliza is always attended by some ladies. I can't see any sign of them yet."

Nat scanned the ballroom as they strode into it. "I can." He glanced at Luke. "They are sitting on the chairs along the far side of the room."

"Ah, yes. Lady Eliza is standing up and has taken the arm of a young woman."

Nat risked another look. "I see her. Let's find Cathlay. He said he would be here."

They strolled around the edge of the ballroom, being careful to avoid catching the eye of any proud mamas.

Cathlay joined them. "Would you care to join me in a game of cards?"

Nat was about to refuse when he felt Luke nudge him. They followed the Duke into an almost empty room and settled at a table at the far end. The Duke shuffled one of the pack of cards laid out.

"I got your message, Overton. I decided to risk coming anyway, despite what happened to you this afternoon. My wife will watch Eliza. Now what shall we play?"

Nat could contain himself no longer. "Shouldn't we be

looking for Milton?"

Luke gave a soft laugh. "You are not thinking in your usual clear-headed way, Nat. His Grace is right. As long as the earl thinks he has a chance with Eliza she is perfectly safe. He is here I take it?"

The Duke nodded. "Yes, he is."

Nat rolled his shoulders and drew in a deep breath. "But what about the chaise and four my valet says he's ordered?"

Cathlay picked up a pack of cards. "Vingt-et-un? I have men watching everywhere along this street and in the mews behind. They'll get a message to me if they see anything suspicious."

Nat nodded. There was sense in the Duke's reasoning. The earl might take fright if he saw them too obviously watching him. He settled down to playing cards and lost some of the money he had won off the Duke playing piquet. After an hour the room was quite full. The Duke was hailed by an old friend and Nat and Luke gave way to the newcomer after they had been introduced. They wandered out to the ballroom.

Blood thundered in Nat's ears. "There's no sign of Eliza and the Duchess is sitting on the seats for chaperones."

"I expect she's with some of her own friends. Let's split up and walk around in opposite directions until one of us spots her."

They had nearly finished their circuits of the room and Nat could see Luke coming towards him, when a faint cry caught his attention. There was an open door leading to an outside terrace off to his left.

Chapter Twenty Two

E liza insisted on sitting with Augusta amongst the chaperones. She wasn't in the mood for too much gaiety. The Comerfords' magnificent ballroom seemed dark and dreary, despite the sparkling chandeliers liberally sprinkled around the room. She sighed inwardly when an acquaintance claimed her company for a promenade about the room. It took a promise to consider working for a new charity for orphans to free herself from the company of Mrs Spencer. Was it possible to find a way back to Augusta without being intercepted? She couldn't shake off the feeling that people were talking about her behind their fans. Perhaps she should plead a headache, it wasn't entirely untrue and she longed for solitude. Or did she? She couldn't resist another scan of the room but there was no sign of Nat.

Her temper wasn't improved when Peregrine Dempster sidled up to her.

"Deserted by your heroic shadow I see, oh fair one. Why not make do with me instead?"

Lud, he was becoming quite the expert at playing the jealous, disappointed swain. "I don't want any shadows, heroic or otherwise, thank you very much. Especially not you."

Even in her distracted state she didn't miss a flash of anger harden his expression for a moment. She'd never taken much notice of his banter but clearly her sharp retort rankled. What if he always meant it seriously? That would be awkward. He wasn't a man to cross.

He pursed his lips. "Crotchety tonight are we? Backing off to keep you keen is he? The solid Major has more guile than I gave him credit for. Mayhap the gamblers backing him will win their bets. I wish you joy of him."

He turned on his heel and marched off. Her shoulders sagged. Whatever else you could say about Dempster, he always knew the latest gossip. She hadn't imagined being the subject of plenty of curious looks this evening. A retreat to Augusta's side was definitely the best course of action. She strolled along the edge of the room, being careful to avoid eye contact. She had kept her dance card free so far and the last thing she wanted was to be asked to dance. She was hot enough as it was. A current of cooler air wafted in through the door from the terrace. She paused to enjoy the feel of it play across her face. A hand landed heavily on her shoulder and propelled her through the door to the terrace.

She opened her mouth to scream. Another hand closed it and stayed clamped around her mouth and chin. She was lifted bodily out onto the terrace. Nausea threatened at the smell of unwashed male, overlain with a strong tang of a heavy cologne. Her feet hit the floor and she cried out as the hand over her mouth let go. The hand was replaced by the flaccid, drooling lips she remembered from the park.

"We have unfinished business you and I. Ignore me for a shipwright's boy would you?"

She struggled as the lips found hers again. The earl wrestled her underneath one of the sconces lighting up the terrace. If he thought he could force her into marriage by such tactics he was going to get a shock. She would die a once-married widow rather than submit to that. She stopped resisting and waited for their inevitable discovery. She caught a glimpse of Peregrine Dempster watching them through a window from the ballroom. He signalled to a group behind him. This would be a bigger scandal than Max refusing to marry Lavinia, especially with Dempster fanning the flames. Someone was coming out already.

She staggered backwards as the earl was wrenched away from her. Nat floored him with one punch to the jaw. The earl struggled upright and Nat ran at him again. He was held back by Viscount Enstone. She heard her brother-in-law telling four rather odd looking men to escort the earl away. They lifted him up by his arms and legs and ran down the steps connecting the terrace to the garden. Viscount Enstone followed them. Nat ran forward and steadied her with an arm under her shoulders as she swayed with shock.

He held her close to his side and she could feel quivers run through him. His jaw was set and his expression hard. The earl was lucky Viscount Enstone had held him back, although if Cathlay hadn't arrived would Nat have shrugged him off? He was a man of strong passions but with iron control, so perhaps not, even though he had looked murderous when he floored the earl. She shivered, despite the heat from where their bodies were joined. Nat's features relaxed and he pulled her into an embrace and stroked her back.

"You're safe now, sweetheart."

Her arms found their way around his neck.

Dempster's shrill tones came towards them. "I told you the smart money was on the Earl of Milton. We are to wish you joy then, my lord?" He halted with his mouth hanging open.

She heard Nat's laugh as if in a dream. "A case of mistaken identity I think you will find, Mr Dempster."

"But I saw the Earl of Milton with my own eyes, out here kissing Lady Eliza."

Cathlay raised a hand. "As Major Overton said it's a case of mistaken identity. Now I suggest you take your friends away and leave us to our family gathering."

"I told you it was all a hum and she would have Overton." A gruff voice behind Dempster said. "Come on man. Let's do what the Duke suggested."

Dempster's friends hustled him away. Cathlay broke the silence.

"We had better get you home, Eliza. You've had more than enough excitement for one evening. Do you want me to send Major Overton to fetch Augusta?"

"I'm perfectly able to manage." She broke away from Nat and walked along the terrace. She hesitated and then entered the ballroom, head held high.

Augusta wasn't far away. She tucked Eliza's hand through her arm and led her towards the exit. Eliza's face ached from smiling at all the people who wished her well. There was no sign of Nat or Cathlay to help deflect the attention. Augusta glided along at her side, a picture of serenity. At last they reached the sanctuary of the Cathlay carriage. She sank back against the squabs with a sigh.

"Lud, what an evening. How do you manage to stay so calm Augusta?"

Augusta laughed. "It comes from years of being a politician's wife."

"I wish some of your composure would rub off on me."

"You did well. No one would have guessed the turmoil you must have been going through. Cathlay said he had all the proof he needed to remove the Earl of Milton. I expect he has it all in hand tonight."

Eliza saw Augusta study her face in the dim light filtering into the carriage. "What is it?"

"I thought you would be excited now you can put that poor man out of his misery."

"Which poor man?"

"Major Overton, of course. It's obvious you're besotted with each other."

"I'm not sure I want to marry Major Overton."

"Ah." Augusta paused. "I'm sorry I mentioned it. You are too overwrought to think clearly tonight."

Eliza spluttered and straightened her spine. "I'm twenty five and I'm perfectly in control of my thoughts. I'm not sure we should suit."

Augusta caught her hand. "You might be in control of your thoughts. I don't think you are in control of your emotions. Mama would counsel you to think carefully before turning down a good man who is clearly besotted with you."

Eliza wrenched her hand away. "That's not fair. Mama would never want me to do something I don't care for. You're afraid of a scandal. Well I don't mind. I intend to set up my own establishment and spend my life on charity work if it comes to it."

"Oh dear, I should have kept quiet. After seeing you with your arms around Major Overton's neck I thought everything was settled between you."

Eliza shook her head. A rush of heat sweep through her. So Augusta had seen them together. Let her think what she liked. It was Nat's own fault if she had treated him badly. He shouldn't have tempted her as he had. That wasn't fair. She had tempted him in the garden. He'd said to take all the time she needed. She couldn't in all fairness marry him unless she could overcome her fear of remarrying. Until she knew him a lot better, how could she be sure of that?

"Eliza, my dear, take care you don't run away from your future. I'll say no more now."

Eliza followed Augusta up the stairs and watched her disappear down the corridor to her rooms. There was a batch of new novels in the library. She would be awake half the night and might as well find a book to keep her company. She retraced her steps and slipped into the library by the door nearest to the stairs. It was difficult to raise much interest in the books she had enthused about when they had arrived earlier in the day. Eventually she selected two. Reluctant to go straight to bed, she opened the curtains hiding the window seat that was her favourite daytime reading place.

She found the best position to catch the light from a candelabra standing on a nearby side table. There was no one to see her so she curled up on the seat with her feet underneath her and settled her dress around them. Alice would scold if the dress creased but she was past caring. She opened the first book and started to read but the words insisted on dancing around the page. She dropped it on top of its fellow at her side and leaned back against the cushions piled up on the seat. Twin fires were lit at either end of the room and the warmth was soothing. Lud, what a coil. What was she going to do?

Nat moved to follow Eliza into the ballroom. The Duke laid a hand on his arm.

CHAPTER TWENTY TWO

"She's best left to Augusta for now. Come, walk back with me."

Nat was about to protest but he was right. Eliza needed some time to herself. He watched her march into the ballroom with the queenly bearing that had impressed him so much when he first met her. This was his opportunity to ask the Duke, formally, for permission to address her.

"Thank you. Should we give them time to clear the ballroom?"

"I have a better idea. Let's slip through the gardens."

Nat followed him to the farthest door leading out to the garden. The sconce lighting the steps down had been extinguished.

"Ah, my men's doing I expect. If you keep to the right you will find a handrail, Overton."

There was no sign of anyone in the garden but Nat was sure someone was there as they approached the gate out to the street beyond. It was probably a guard but his breathing quickened until Luke materialised out of the gloom. He fell into step with them.

"The Runners have Milton banged up nice and tight. You've got the evidence you need then, Your Grace?"

"I have more than enough evidence to satisfy the Home Secretary. Any doubts he might have will be doused by the knowledge of the attempt on Overton's life earlier. The Earl of Milton will be put on a ship to the East Indies and told not to come back."

Luke grunted. "I can't see him taking any notice of that."

The Duke chuckled. "I don't suppose he will, but he will have no money and will be dressed in rough clothes. No one will believe any story he tells them. He'll be another drunk

243

pressed into crewing a ship. I've arranged for the captain to get a big bonus for making sure he stays there and doesn't hide on the ship when it returns. Half of it will be payable in six months. There will be more payments for keeping a watch on him. Don't worry. I'll know if he finds a way back."

"Thank the lord for that. I'll see you in the morning, Nat. Thank you, Your Grace."

Nat watched as Luke strode on ahead of them. "I was close to killing that scum of a man tonight when Luke stopped me."

"I know you were and I'm glad of it, although I think you would have stopped short of murder even without your friend's intervention."

Nat relaxed. "I expect you're right. He's not worth hanging for."

"True. Lord Overton must be happy to have found you to be a man of principle and intelligence. Your Uncle Charles was a rum customer and it was a lucky day for the estate when he drank himself into an early death. I didn't know your father but by all accounts he was of the same stamp as Henry. Come home with me and we'll have a quiet brandy together."

Two guards stationed on the gate, well hidden by shrubbery, let them out onto the street. They walked back saying little. Nat decided to wait to discuss Eliza until they were private. He had left his cane behind and stayed alert for any trouble. They reached the Cathlay mansion without incident. Sayers himself opened the door to them. The Duke ushered Nat into an impressive library, where shelves of books rose from floor to ceiling. It must be twice the size of Luke's and yet with fires burning at each end and freestanding candelabras dotted about it had a homely feel. The tension in his shoulders loosened a notch at the sight of a group of leather chairs arranged in front of the roaring fire nearest to them.

The sound of a door opening woke Eliza with a start. Cathlay's voice came to her.

"I'll have a decanter of the new brandy, Sayers."

"I took the liberty of leaving a tray with the brandy and the port out for you, Your Grace."

"Excellent man. I see it now. There is no need for you to wait up for us."

Eliza paused in the act of lowering her legs to the floor and quickly drew them back up. The last thing she wanted was to talk to one of Cathlay's friends. She had best wait until they were settled. With luck they wouldn't hear her leave. She heard Sayers's heavy tread and the sound of the door at the other end of the library shutting. She peeped around the curtains in case Augusta had come down for a late night drink with Cathlay.

A gasp escaped her. Nat had wasted no time in talking to Cathlay. She closed the curtains in front of her and held her breath. There was no sound of anyone walking towards her. They couldn't have heard anything. She ought to leave at this point but perhaps Nat would say something to help her decide. In the circumstances she could be forgiven for eavesdropping.

She shuffled to the end of the seat nearest to them. By dint of pushing the edge of the curtain forward an inch at eye level she could see them clearly, albeit at a distance. She watched them settle into the leather chairs in front of the fire. Nat sipped at a drink handed to him by Cathlay. How could he look so relaxed lounging in his chair, when she was so on edge?

Cathlay put his drink down on a side table. "Before we start I should perhaps inform you that Lord Hargreaves is Lady Eliza's nearest male relative. However, I'm sure he won't mind me deputising. You do realise that with Dempster bringing his friends onto the terrace the best way to avoid a scandal is an announcement of your engagement in The Times as soon as it can be arranged."

She stiffened. Cathlay was talking about her as if she was a chattel to be given away at the whim of her closest male relative. She risked pushing the curtain a little wider. Nat seemed to be almost grinning at Cathlay.

"I hadn't thought about that but I'm sure you're right. I don't understand how society works a lot of the time, which can be a problem. It's no matter, as I've been waiting for the right opportunity to ask your permission to address Lady Eliza for some time." He laughed. "I'm sure she's well qualified to help me find my way around the beau monde. Luke's term, not mine."

Eliza caught her breath on a sob. Her hands balled into fists. It seemed his first priority was to marry someone who understood how society worked. She couldn't face Nat tonight. Not after what she had just heard. She lowered her legs and stepped out from behind the curtain. A glance to the other end of the room showed Cathlay holding the brandy decanter. Neither of them was looking her way. She glided across to the nearest door. Fortunately, it was slightly ajar and it was an easy matter to slip into the corridor.

Nat downed the rest of his brandy and accepted a refill. He was making a mull of this. He was talking about Eliza as if he was considering the merits of a horse. The Duke smiled at him. The sort of encouraging smile he had often given to young soldiers who lacked confidence. He laughed softly to himself. This was what love did to a man. Lord, he was in love and he had better

246

start putting his case. He breathed in and returned the smile. He wasn't used to these sorts of conversations but it was time to be open about his feelings.

"I was attracted to Eliza from the first time we met and long to make her my wife. I'm not sure how interested she is in me." He paused. "I don't think she knows herself."

The Duke's shoulders started shaking. "Forgive me, Overton. You are in the right of it. An immediate announcement would be the sensible course but I don't think for a minute things will be simple for you with Eliza. Augusta thinks you are perfect for her, so do I as it happens, but she says Eliza is still suffering the after effects of nursing her mother for two years. She may be too unsettled to consider marriage for a while."

"I don't want to rush her."

"Very sensible. If you push too hard you will lose her. Whatever the scandal she will be free to make her own decision in this family. If it's any consolation, Augusta is convinced she is in love with you but doesn't know it yet."

Nat shifted in his chair. "I know I'm in love with her."

"Augusta said you were." The Duke laughed. "Don't look so glum. You'll come about, Overton. That said you have all my sympathy at the moment. I had problems with Augusta. She thought I was far too arrogant and sure of myself to make a good husband. I won her over in the end. I can't say it has always been easy, she's a fiery one, but I wouldn't change her for the world. Eliza appears much quieter but deep down she's the nearest in temperament to Augusta of all her sisters."

Nat laughed. "I've already come across Eliza's fiery side. We got off to a bad start. I'll visit her tomorrow and ask her to marry me. As you say, I'm not at all sure she'll have me, scandal or not, but I owe her a proposal. If she isn't ready to accept I'll go travelling for a bit to give her time and then ask her again."

Nat found Jones still up when he arrived back at Luke's house.

"You should have gone to bed. I don't expect you to stay up half the night for me."

"I couldn't do that, Major. My uncle said you would be late back so I snatched some sleep earlier this evening."

"I'm glad of it. I need to go out quite early tomorrow and I want to look my best."

Was he imagining it or was Jones scrutinising him carefully. He definitely had an expectant look on his face. Luke always said that servants knew what was going on well before their masters. He might as well tell him.

"I'm hoping to secure a wife tomorrow. It may be nothing will come of it, so please keep it to yourself."

Jones grinned at him. "Soul of discretion me, my uncle is too."

Nat sighed. Luke's entire household probably knew he had compromised Lady Eliza Wyndham.

Chapter Twenty Three

N at accepted his grandfather's huge diamond tie pin. He was too nervous to protest. In a way it was fitting. This was a moment his grandfather had been hoping for when he had insisted that he accepted all invitations to friend's houses. Ironic that if it hadn't been for an unusual set of circumstances he would probably be pursuing a vicar's daughter or some such now.

Jones stood back and studied him. "If I say it myself, Major, you're as fine as five pence. Your lady won't be able to resist you."

Nat nodded. His stomach was churning and his beautifully tied neck cloth felt too tight. Even the Duke thought Eliza would lead him a merry dance and he was inclined to agree. Still he could hope for a quick resolution. He decided to walk to help him relax. This felt worse than being called in to see the colonel over some misdemeanour or other. He decided to take a shortcut through the gardens. Bright saw him coming and let him through the gate.

"Still taking precautions, Bright?"

"Best to, Major, even with our friend locked up. We can't be sure it was him shooting at you and Lady Eliza is quite a prize."

Nat laughed. "Is there anyone in the household who doesn't know I'm on my way to offer for her?"

Bright grinned at him. "I doubt it. Viscount Enstone's coachman had the full story from one of the grooms at Comerford House, who saw it all from the gardens. He said you had a wonderful right hook. They're all wondering what happened to the earl afterwards. The groom was called back to the mews."

"The Duke had him taken away. I expect his men made sure there was no one around to witness what happened."

Bright nodded. "He's a downy one. Paying well too from what I hear. Anyways, I'll follow you at a distance to be safe. You won't know I'm there."

Nat looked at Bright's set expression and gave up all thought of protesting. "As you will."

By the time he had reached the end of the street there was no sign of Bright, but it was a comforting thought that he was watching him. He should have let him accompany him to the park and they might have caught the earl in the act then, saving Eliza all that upset. At the thought of Eliza he speeded up. He hoped she wasn't too shaken. Even a strong personality like Eliza could take a long time to regain their normal composure after bereavement.

Sayers opened the door almost immediately to his knock. He handed over his coat and hat to a footman and followed Sayers into a sunny morning room.

"Major Overton, Your Grace."

Nat bowed low over the Duchess's hand. He could feel Eliza's presence in the room. He glanced around as he straightened up. She was standing near to a window staring out at the garden. Her dark hair, piled on top of her head, gleamed in the sunlight. She was beautiful. As if aware of his scrutiny she glanced at him. She looked troubled and her complexion seemed paler than normal. His breath caught in his throat. She didn't have the air of a woman happily anticipating a proposal of marriage.

Augusta walked over to her and caught her hand. "Will you give Major Overton a moment of your time, my dear?"

Eliza glanced at him. Her almost wild expression suggested that what she wanted to do was run for the door. He had never forced himself on a woman in any way, shape or form and he wasn't about to start now. He walked towards her and stopped a few feet away.

"I would consider it a great favour if you would allow me an opportunity to speak with you but I won't press you if you don't want to."

She held his glance for a few moments. There was a grey haze in her normally bright blue eyes. She looked troubled. The Duchess let go of her hand and gave him a nod before slipping out of the room. Nat wanted to run to Eliza and scoop her into his arms. Instinct held him back. If the Duke was right about her not being ready yet, she needed to come to him if this was going to work. She gave him a smile but it looked as if smile was the last thing she wanted to do. A wave of nausea hit him. Her family seemed happy with him but could she be looking for a better match and not know how to tell him?

"Won't you take a seat, Major Overton?"

So formal. His heart skipped a beat. She was going to turn him down. He knew she desired him, so why? If she needed more time she could simply say so. He could see no reason why that would make her look as upset as she did. Surely he couldn't be mistaken in her goodness? He followed her to the chairs she indicated. They were facing each other and several feet apart. He lowered himself into the seat and averted his gaze as a spurt of anger ripped through him. Was he not good enough for her? If he was about to suffer the biggest disappointment of his life he'd be damned if he let her see his distress.

Eliza forced her shoulders back against the chair. He had sensed he was going to be rejected. The anger in his face as he sat down had shaken her. She had to be strong. After what she had overheard she wasn't sure he was truly in love with her. Even though she found him attractive, loved him even, the thought of full intimacy still terrified her. She needed to be sure he loved her to find the courage to explain it to him. She had tried so hard to tell him in Lady Grant's garden but the words wouldn't come. It wouldn't be fair to either of them to marry him and find she couldn't get over her difficulties. She bit back a sob. He had himself well in hand now. There was nothing to mar the placid set of his countenance. She took a deep breath and looked at the floor. No she couldn't do it.

"I want to thank you for all the help you have given me. I also want you to know that, despite any unpleasantness after last night, I don't expect you to sacrifice yourself to save my reputation. I don't think we would suit."

She held her breath waiting for him to say something. The silence stretched like the heat of a summer's day. She found the courage to look up. Nat was regarding her intently. There was a serious expression in his grey eyes, or was it contempt. He gave her a half smile and stood up. He swept her a magnificent bow.

"In that case, madam, there is nothing more to say. I wish you good day."

Eliza was mesmerised as she watched his retreating back.

Part of her wanted to run to him and say it was all a mistake. The sound of the door closing felt like a physical blow. She stood and walked to the window. Her hands fluttered at her sides and blood thundered in her ears. She had just made the hardest decision of her life. There was no going back.

She moved to the side of the window as he came into view. He marched down the street, with a rigidly erect posture. All too soon he had disappeared into the distance. Would this be the last time she ever saw him? Perhaps not, with him being Max's neighbour. Lud, how would she bear it if she kept seeing him at Hargreaves Hall? Her hands flew to cover her face and she turned away from the window. She heard Augusta's footsteps echoing along the corridor and getting louder. She gathered up her skirts and ran out of the room towards the stairs. A glance back showed Augusta standing outside the morning room, making no attempt to follow her. Still she ran as if hoping to escape the events of the morning.

Once she reached the sanctuary of her room she rested her forehead by the side of the door. She couldn't have risked saying yes. The more she thought about remarrying the more memories of Miles and the terrifying year of her marriage intruded. There was no sign of Alice. She locked the door and ran into her dressing room. It was empty thank goodness. The floor seemed to shift underneath her and she held onto a table and took some deep, shuddering breaths. Somehow she forced her heavy legs out of the dressing room and across to the bed. She threw herself down without even taking her dress off. She hugged herself, remembering the feel of Nat's strong arms around her and his lips pressed to hers. There was nothing to be done.

Eliza cried herself to sleep and awoke to the sound of someone banging on the door. The room was in semi-darkness. She turned over and buried her head under the covers but that didn't blot out the banging. There was nothing for it but to stagger over to the door and unlock it. A pair of arms wrapped around her and led her back to the bed. For a blissful moment, her sleep numbed mind thought it was Nat. Then Augusta's hand brushed a stray lock of her hair out of her eyes.

"The interview with Major Overton didn't go well then?"

Eliza chuckled. "I love your genius for understatement."

"Come on. Let's get you tidied up. Dinner will be ready in an hour. We're having a quiet night in. You don't have to talk about it if you don't want to."

Nat walked at a furious pace. He wasn't sure where he was walking to. It didn't matter as long as it was away from Lady Eliza Wyndham. At seventeen his pride had been hurt more than anything. This was far worse. He had guarded her, protected her and fallen deeply and irrevocably in love. It seemed she was hanging out for a better catch with her huge fortune. That must have been what she was too embarrassed to tell him in Lady Grant's garden. Lord he had made such a cake of himself, letting her know how much he cared for her. His dreams for the future were shattered. He doubted he would ever be able to settle with anyone else. It wouldn't be fair. What should he do now? Part of him felt like packing up his things and going up north to where he felt safe.

From there he could do another tour of his business interests and even take up the invitation to sail on one of the ships in the fleet of the shipping company he was part owner of. The problem was he would want to stay there. He was a man of his word and he couldn't go back on his promise to Uncle Henry to manage the Overton estates. He would have to return. What if Eliza moved back to Hargreaves? It would be hard to live so close to her. At the same time it would be torture if she married someone else. He turned a corner and nearly tripped over a carter standing by the side of the road soothing his horse. A grubby hand grabbed his sleeve.

Nat caught the man's wrist and then burst out laughing.

"Bright. What are you doing here?"

"I followed you for a bit and then went past in the cart to wait. You're fair game for anyone today. Didn't go well with the lady then?"

"No it didn't. I think I'll go travelling for a bit."

"What and run away from the chase. It took me five times of asking to persuade my Martha to marry me."

Nat stared at him. "You've never mentioned a wife."

"No. She died young and somehow I could never think of putting anyone else in her place."

"I'm sorry to hear that. No children?"

"I left my little girl with my sister and joined the army. She did well for herself, my Louise. She's married to an innkeeper on the Great North Road, not far from where I grew up. They own a posting house. Once you're safely married I'm going to ask for some time off to visit her."

"You should have said before. You could have visited her when I was with my grandfather. You must certainly visit her now. We could travel together until we reach her."

Bright looked at him with his head on one side. Like a great blackbird with his dark clothing. "You're a fool if you don't stay and fight. Mayhap the lass is too jangled up to think properly at the moment after being chased by that monster. Women can sense evil better than men I always think."

Nat shook his head. "She doesn't want me and that's all there is to it. I expect she is hanging out for a duke."

Bright snorted. "Not her. A real lady she is. Jump in. I had better drive you home before you get set upon by cut throats walking about in an area like this."

Nat glanced around him. He had strayed into a rough part of London. Two ragged urchins lingered on a street corner ahead and how had he missed the putrid smell coming from the mess of human waste, mud and animal remains clogging up the open channel running down the centre of the road. He climbed into the cart beside Bright. The best thing to do was to have a quiet day. He might see things more clearly after a night's sleep.

He sensed as much as heard a movement to his left and pulled his pistol out of his pocket. "Our presence has been noted."

Bright whipped up his horse and moved towards the centre of the road. Nat raised his pistol. Two roughly dressed individuals sloped off towards a side street.

Bright gave a bark of laughter. "I'm glad to see you still have some of your instincts for staying alive." He kept the horse going at a smart trot until they turned on to a better road.

Nat replaced the pistol. "I must remember to ask for my cane back from Comerford House. A pistol would have only saved me from one ruffian. Thank you for following me, Bright."

Bright snorted. "You'll be no use to anybody until you've married the lady, Major. That's a fact."

Nat sighed. "There is not going to be a marriage. I expect I will stay single."

Nat was staring into space trying to compose a letter to Mr Wright, the co-owner of the Armstrong and Wright shipping company, when Luke entered the library.

"So this is where you're hiding out. Don't look so down, you'll come about. We're invited to Aunt Theo's for dinner. She and Grace are having a quiet night in."

Nat smiled, but it felt more like a grimace. "Please make my apologies to Lady Grant. I'm not fit company for anyone today."

Luke pulled up a chair next to him. "It's no good hiding yourself away, Nat. It will get out if you don't mix and give the gossip-mongers ammunition."

"Let them talk about me all they like. I don't care. My grandfather was the social climber not me."

"Ah, so that's what this is all about." Luke glanced at the address at the top of his letter. "Bright said you were on about going on a tour of your businesses up north. I never had you down as a quitter."

Nat went to stand but sat back as Luke put a gentle hand on his shoulder. "It's not a question of quitting. I'll not stay where I'm not wanted. I don't care what society says of me."

"You might not but a lot of other people care, including me. Did you know that the Duke of Cathlay has spent the last several hours going around the clubs challenging anything said to your detriment? He told me Lady Eliza had sent you to the rightabout and he was worried you might take offence."

Nat snorted. "That's mighty kind of him but I expect he's more worried about Eliza's reputation than mine."

"I don't think so, even though that must be a consideration for him. He's more worried about her state of mind. The Duchess is afraid she is going into a decline she is so upset. What did you say to her?"

"Nothing, I didn't get the chance. She told me I needn't

sacrifice myself and we wouldn't suit."

"So you stormed off?"

"I took my leave but I was perfectly polite."

Luke put his head in his hands. "This is worse than I thought. Don't you know anything about women?"

"How should I? I'm not blessed with a sister and the only women I met as a stripling were the sisters of school friends. They thought I was beneath them and took great pains to make sure I knew how they felt."

"Lady Eliza isn't one of your simpering misses. You can't believe she would be influenced by any slight difference in your stations."

"I can't think of any other reason she would turn against me now Denby is out of the way. She responded to me enthusiastically in the coach when we had to drive around the other day. Let alone in Lady Grant's garden." Nat felt the colour rise to his cheeks.

He needed to keep his temper in check. That should have remained private. "Why suddenly go cold on me now?"

Luke shook his head. "I admit it's strange. By all accounts Lady Eliza is normally sunny tempered but she was devoted to her mama. Two years of nursing a declining invalid would upset anyone. Perhaps she doesn't feel ready to marry again yet." Luke held out his hands, palm upwards.

"If that was it why not say so. We talked in the garden. She said she wasn't sure. I said she could take all the time she needed. Today makes no sense unless she was trying to let me down gently in the garden."

Luke shook his head. "We have all been convinced she has fallen for you. Perhaps she feels she hasn't recovered enough to make such an important decision. Her first marriage was a disaster by all accounts. Be kind to her, Nat."

Nat banged the desk with his fist. "If you're so concerned about her, you marry her. I'm sure she would be happy to snare a viscount."

Nat stalked out of the library before he said anything to further alienate the best friend he had ever had. His head was thudding. He ran up to his room and locked the door. Jones came out of his dressing room. Damn. He should have checked in there.

"Good evening, Major. It's time to get you dressed for dinner."

Nat ground his teeth. Was he never to get any peace? "I have a sick headache and won't be going. It's nothing to worry about. I get them occasionally. You may have the night off."

Jones immediately ran to the windows and drew the curtains.

"My ma used to have those. You need it nice and dark. Let me help you undress. Then I'll go down and see if the housekeeper has a headache remedy."

Nat sighed. It was easier to submit to Jones's ministrations than argue. It was a relief to lie down in a cool bed. Jones tiptoed out of the room and returned carrying a drink on a tray.

Nat accepted it warily and took a sip. "I can't drink this foul tasting stuff."

"It will make you feel better, Major. Even the butler says it works every time."

Nat forced it down. "I may be going away on a business trip, Jones. I'll let you know tomorrow. I don't want to be disturbed by anyone tonight."

"I'll draw the drapes around the bed for you before I go."

Nat sat up in bed. "No you won't. It makes me think I'm

back in the army camped out somewhere."

Jones jumped back as if he had been hit. "As you wish, major. Goodnight."

Nat watched him go. That was someone else he ought to apologise to in the morning.

He slipped in and out of an uneasy sleep for a while until his headache eased. The headache cure must be strong. He didn't wake again until a footman came in to light his fire. He felt slightly limp, as often happened after one of his headaches, but otherwise quite well. He sat up and asked the footman to have a dish of tea sent up to him. Plenty to drink would soon put him to rights.

The footman returned with the tea, some freshly baked bread and slices of ham and beef.

"The housekeeper remembered that you had no dinner, Major."

Nat eyed the tray with appreciation. "Please give her my compliments."

"Yes, Major. Would you be wishful to have Jones sent in to you?"

"Not yet, thank you."

The footman nodded and withdrew. Nat poured his tea and chewed a piece of excellent beef. Luke certainly knew how to run a fine establishment. What had Luke meant by his comments about him not understanding women? Eliza, no he must call her Lady Eliza now, couldn't have been clearer in her dismissal of him. Perhaps he had overreacted but if Lady Eliza truly wasn't ready to marry anyone wouldn't it be kinder to disappear from her orbit for a while. That wasn't running away.

He put the tray on a side table and lay back against the

cushions. The next thing he knew was Jones opening the curtains to reveal a sunny morning.

"What time is it, Jones?"

"It's eleven o'clock, major."

"Good Lord. I must have gone back to sleep after eating that excellent breakfast." He pointed at the tray.

"We thought it best not to disturb you."

"Quite right. I feel much better. I would be grateful if you could persuade the housekeeper to give you the recipe for that headache cure. Nothing has ever worked half so well on me. I had better get up now and face the day."

Chapter Twenty Four

Eliza got up early and decided to breakfast downstairs. As she expected, Cathlay was already there. She sat down next to him. He lowered his newspaper and smiled at her.

"What are your plans for today?"

"I intend to accept an invitation from Grace Bamford to go shopping and then take tea at Gunter's."

"Very wise. There will be talk after the Comerford ball but it's always best to face down gossip. I went round as many clubs as I'm a member of or could persuade a friend to invite me to yesterday. The talk seems to be that Overton and I were together when we saw the Earl of Milton pulling you out on to the terrace and went to the rescue."

Eliza laughed. "If they didn't have that idea before they spoke to you I'm sure they did afterwards."

"Well I might have dropped a hint here and there. Augusta and Theodosia Grant were busy with their friends too. Peregrine Dempster is not well liked and people are inclined to discount his version of events as malice. It's well known he wanted you himself."

"I hadn't realised how serious Dempster was. I always took his protestations of undying love as his idea of fun before yesterday evening." Eliza felt her cheeks grow hot. "I'm afraid I lost patience with him and was rather rude. That put him in the mood for revenge I fear."

"He certainly didn't help but the Earl of Milton was the villain." Cathlay stroked his chin. "I think Milton wanted you because Overton had fallen for you as much as for your money. By all accounts Overton is a splendid young man and everything the earl could never be." Cathlay smiled at her. "Augusta tells me you and Major Overton have agreed you would not suit. A pity but never mind."

Eliza rose and walked across to the window. "It's no good Augusta thinking she can make a match between us." I could never marry such a passionate man."

"Good Lord. Has he tried to force his attentions on you? I wouldn't have thought it of him."

Eliza turned to face him. Heat flooded through her at the memory of Nat's kisses. Honesty compelled her to counter the suggestion he had tried to force her to do anything against her will. "Major Overton has never taken anything from me that wasn't freely given."

She looked away at the puzzlement in Cathlay's eyes and ran out of the room. She should have said nothing. Now she had admitted to her illustrious brother-in-law that they had gone beyond the bounds of propriety. She ran up the stairs and sought the sanctuary of her bedroom, glad Alice was nowhere to be seen. Light streamed through the window. It was a beautiful spring day, a perfect day to be out for a ride in the grounds around Hargreaves Hall. Somehow or other she would go back there soon.

Before that she owed it to Augusta to try and dampen down the inevitable scandal. Whatever Cathlay said there was going to be considerable gossip and not all of it favourable to her. Grace was a dear to offer to help and she would keep their engagement. As long as she maintained a dignified silence in relation to Major Overton she should be able to carry the thing off. Peregrine getting involved might well be a helpful distraction, especially after all the work Cathlay had done bringing his actions to the fore. A knock at her door cut into her thoughts.

"Come in." She expected Alice but it was Augusta who entered.

"Cathlay said you seemed rather overset. Would you like to return to Hargreaves immediately?"

Eliza smiled at her. "You're so kind but I couldn't use you so. I owe it to you both to do my best to scotch the scandal I've brought on the family."

"Nonsense. We don't care a jot for ourselves. It would help you though to make your peace with society. You may not think it now, but I expect the day will come when you want to consider another marriage and an unresolved scandal could be uncomfortable for you."

Eliza shook her head. A wave of sadness settled like a lead ball in her stomach. No man would ever match up to Nat. "No. I'm resigned to life on my own."

Augusta took her hand. "Eliza, my dear, I am convinced you are far from indifferent to Major Overton. I don't understand why you turned him away. He can't possibly be a fortune hunter if that's what you're worried about. I shouldn't say this, but we both saw he was enamoured of you early on and Cathlay had him investigated after Max's bitter disappointment with Lavinia. Overton is one of the richest men in England.

"Is he? I had gathered he was well off in his own right."

"So why?"

Eliza pursed her lips. "I have my reasons."

"I won't tease you any further. Cathlay has some plan of the two of you being seen together as friends, to silence any stubborn gossip-mongers. "Do you think you would be able to cope with that? I can tell him to forget it."

Eliza tossed back a loose lock of hair. "Of course I can cope. I'm a Lovell."

"Well if you're sure. Tell me if it gets too much and we'll invent an excuse to travel back to Hargreaves. I can hear Alice coming. I'll leave you to dress for your outing." She smiled at Eliza and walked out, leaving the door open for Alice.

"I think I will change into something better Alice. I need to make a good impression today."

She must face society and she wanted to look good. The truth was that would be a lot easier than facing Nat again. When Grace called for her, Eliza was impeccably turned out in a morning dress of deep blue with a matching fur trimmed pelisse. A groom handed her up into the Bamford carriage and she settled down next to Grace. She fixed a smile on her face as they greeted each other.

"What a delicious outfit, Eliza. Where would you like to go first?"

"I have one or two errands for Augusta in Oxford Street. Apart from that the only place I particularly want to visit is the new bookshop in Piccadilly, the one we visited with Augusta. What about you?"

"That's Hatchards. I would love to go there too. If we ask the carriage to wait for us in Oxford Street we can carry out your errands and then get it to drop us off at Hatchard's. Luke said he would meet us at Gunter's later. We can walk to Gunter's, it's not far from Piccadilly."

"That sounds perfect."

Grace gave her an anxious look. "We'll be seen by large numbers of people. Are you sure you're ready for this?"

"Best to get my first outing over, it won't get any easier. Cathlay approved my plans." Eliza straightened her shoulders. "Thank you for your support."

Nat dressed and made his way downstairs. He found Luke waiting for him in the breakfast room.

"Good morning, Nat. I'm glad to see you looking healthy. There's work to be done today."

"What sort of work?" Nat poured himself a cup of coffee and sat next to Luke.

"The Duke of Cathlay says the best way to deal with a scandal is to face it down."

Nat studied Luke's bland expression. "What is it you've got planned?"

Luke laughed. "Am I that transparent? Grace is going shopping with Lady Eliza today. I said I would meet them in Gunter's and escort them home afterwards. Why don't you join us?"

Nat raised his eyebrows. "Are you serious? Lady Eliza," he stressed Lady, "made it quite plain she didn't want to see me again."

"Did she? I thought she said you wouldn't suit? That's not the same thing at all, especially when you're going to be her brother's neighbour."

"If she sees me she'll lose her temper and how's that going to stop people talking? Sounds more like fanning the flames to me."

"True. She will know how to put on a good show but if she's caught unawares..." Luke scratched his ear. "We're too late to intercept Grace. I know. You could wait somewhere close. I'll suggest to Lady Eliza that you join us and if she agrees I'll step out and find you."

Nat shrugged. "Anything for a quiet life but I don't think for a moment Lady Eliza will agree. Let's walk. Bright can follow us if you like. We can send him for the carriage when Eliza and Grace are ready to go home."

Nat nodded. "We should be able to find him in the stables on the way out."

Luke set a fast pace, which Nat was glad to match. They reached the shopping area around Mayfair. Luke caught his arm and pointed to a row of shops leading off the road they were on.

"We should have time to stroll along Bond Street. There are bound to be people I know, especially men, who I can introduce you to. Just smile and do the polite when I introduce you. I'll do the talking."

Nat found himself laughing. "If you say so."

"I do and that relaxed look with you laughing is perfect. Don't worry we'll soon have plenty of people on your side."

Nat shrugged. "I don't care. I've done nothing wrong and I'll be judged on my merits or not at all. I'm not interested in cutting a dash in society."

"Trust me on this."

Luke seemed so anxious Nat went along with him. He smiled and nodded in all the right places to a stream of his friend's acquaintances until Luke declared himself satisfied.

"We've made a good start. Now it's time for me to go along

to Gunter's in case the ladies are early. Where do you want to wait?"

"There's no point me looking in clothes shops without Jones and Garner. I could do with some books for when I set off on my travels."

Luke sniffed. "I won't argue with you on that today. There's a new bookshop in Piccadilly. You shouldn't get into too much trouble there. I think it's called Hatchard's."

Luke soon found the bookshop and left him outside. Nat studied the display of books in the two bay windows visible from the street. His spirits rose and he savoured the smell of leather as he walked in. Reading was one pleasure he hadn't had much opportunity to enjoy for years. Luke's library was extensive but he hadn't found a book on its shelves less than fifty years old. He prepared to enjoy himself, glad he had a fair amount of money with him. He deserved a treat and it would surely be acceptable to buy books for Grace and Lady Grant as leaving presents.

He was drawn to a display of leather bound volumes with the titles picked out in gilt. A copy of Gulliver's Travels, by Jonathon Swift, sat next to Robinson Crusoe, by Daniel Defoe. They were both boyhood favourites and beautiful editions he had to have. An assistant came forward to help and suggested two books by Fanny Burney when asked what novels were likely to appeal to females. He added a book about the rights of women which might be an interesting read. He had heard Lady Grant talking about the author, Mary Wollstonecraft.

He looked about for something light hearted and spotted 'Les Liaisons Dangereuses'. A chuckle escaped him. That might be fun and was certainly apt given his current circumstances. He heard someone gasp and his gaze wandered around the shop when the assistant took his purchases away to wrap up for him. Two deep blue eyes locked with his. He stiffened and waited to see what Eliza would do. She seemed quite agitated.

He half expected her to run away but there were other people around and if she did all Luke's hard work would be for nothing. He bowed low. She moved towards him and gave him a polite nod in acknowledgement.

"Good morning, Major Overton."

"It is indeed, Lady Eliza."

The assistant returned with his books. He accepted the parcel and instinctively held out his arm. Damn, now he had put her under pressure. He held his breath until she slipped her arm through his. He smiled at Grace as she joined them.

"Forgive me for not greeting you properly. Luke is waiting for us at Gunter's."

Grace looked surprised but recovered quickly. "That's good. We have a couple of footmen outside ready to take our books."

Grace led the way outside. Nat glanced at Eliza but her expression gave nothing away. She was smiling and looked as if she was perfectly happy. But was she? Close to there were lines of strain around her eyes, or was that anger? Two footmen came to take their parcels. One of them stepped forwards and took Nat's parcel from him. He felt Eliza's arm tremble in his. He studied her face. With no one watching of import it had taken on a distinctly stormy expression.

She moved away from his side slightly but he tightened his grip on her arm. She had kept her temper well in Hatchard's and it would be a shame to ruin it now. He might be furious with her for leading him on but he didn't want her ostracised. From the level of Luke's concern that could be a possibility.

Could Luke be her target? If so it seemed he was already succumbing to her charm. A fresh wave of the anger he thought he had thrown off threatened to overwhelm him.

Chapter Twenty Five

Eliza felt Nat's grip tighten on her arm and his body stiffen. He was so angry with her but then he had cause to be. Why on earth had she fallen into his arms at every opportunity if she didn't want to marry him? When she had been in Nat's embrace all her fears had faded into the background. She should have realised that was because they were embraces and nothing more. Memories of Miles had threatened to swamp her after the interlude in the coach.

Grace accepted Nat's other arm and they set off towards Gunter's. The street was quite busy. She could feel all eyes upon them and the muttered comments, often behind hands, were impossible to miss. She kept her head high and a smile pinned to her lips. Nat was chatting to Grace and seemed to have relaxed. A matron she knew to have long been envious of Augusta's influence cut her dead. She trembled and would have stumbled if Nat hadn't held her up, with a smile on his face as he did so. Presumably he wanted to stay friends with the Cathlays. They reached a quieter stretch of pavement and he bent closer to her so only she could hear.

"Are you feeling quite the thing? I'll summon a hackney and take you home if you want."

Eliza sighed. His concern was genuine and it would be

wonderful to be happily engaged to a man like him. She dragged in a deep breath and forced a smile.

"I'll manage. People will have heard us mention our destination. It's best we do as we said."

Nat nodded and turned to Grace. "Are we nearly there?"

"Yes, not far now."

Eliza tensed as a group of acquaintances drew near. Nat changed course without seeming to do so and guided them across the road.

Grace snorted. "Why did you avoid those people? Just because that odious Mrs Smart cut Eliza it doesn't mean they would."

"Very likely not, but as a soldier I learned it's important to take on the enemy at a time and place that suits you. Eliza has had enough unpleasantness for one day so why take the risk?"

"I suppose you're right but we've still got to negotiate Gunter's."

"The people in there won't have seen Mrs Smart. There are always sheep like folk who will follow where someone like that leads."

Eliza straightened her back and held her head higher. She wouldn't let the likes of Mrs Smart upset her. Nat sounded so wise and so concerned. Lud, she had treated him so badly, a man with a dread of society women. Yet still he cared what happened to her. It was best not to think about that for now. She could see Gunter's coming into view. She must concentrate on surviving the next hour without providing any more ammunition for the gossipmongers. A laugh escaped her. She was starting to sound like she had been in the army herself. Grace had loosed Nat's arm to precede them into Gunter's. He patted the hand resting on his elbow.

"That's my girl."

She looked at the floor and hoped he wouldn't see the flush heating her cheeks. Once inside Luke hailed them from a quiet table set in a corner. Eliza found herself seated with her back largely to the room. Nat was to her right and would have a clear view of anyone approaching them. He had said he felt under an obligation to Max and seemed to have taken on the role as her guardian today. She must try not to feel too guilty or it would show in her face. It was comforting to have a measure of protection all the same. The tea and pastries Luke had ordered arrived almost as soon as they had taken their seats. So Luke had expected Nat to be in the party. She accepted a cup from Grace and selected a pastry.

"This is most welcome. How on earth did you arrange for it to arrive so quickly, Viscount Enstone?"

She saw Nat raise an eyebrow at him as if asking the same question. Her eyes narrowed.

Luke waved a hand. "I had someone lurking outside to let me know when you were all on your way."

He glanced at Nat, who gave no sign of having noticed. She looked across at Grace who wouldn't meet her eyes. She'd wondered before if the siblings were matchmaking. She must be right. There was no time to ponder on that now. She had better concentrate on getting through the next few minutes without anyone else giving her the cut direct.

Grace smiled at the group in general. "This is lovely. We ought to make another assault on the British Museum together," she lowered her voice to a whisper, "now there is no awful person ruining it for us."

Eliza couldn't help but laugh. She smiled at Grace. Her romantic turn of mind was something of a nuisance, but she didn't lack for intelligence and had realised there were people close enough to catch at least snippets of their conversation.

It was Nat who answered. She turned to look at him as she heard his deep tones.

"It would be a shame to leave so much of it untouched but I have to check on some of my business interests soon before returning to Overton Grange. I think you will have to visit it without me."

Grace looked crestfallen but brightened up when Luke addressed Eliza.

"Aunt Theo has invited Nat and me to dinner tomorrow evening. Won't you join us Lady Eliza?"

Eliza took a deep breath. Her hands were so tightly balled into fists under the table that her fingernails were digging into her palms. Nat had been so kind to her today. Was there a chance things could work out between them if she was brave enough to explain her difficulty? If she didn't accept this invitation she might never find out.

"Yes, I would love to come."

Grace beamed at her. "Excellent. Luke forgot half the message. Aunt Theo sent a note around to the Cathlays inviting them too."

Eliza spotted a matron she knew edging towards their table with two girls in tow. It was too good an opportunity to miss. She raised her voice as much as she could without appearing obvious.

"What a delightful gathering, Miss Bamford. You may be sure I shall be there tomorrow evening."

Grace grinned at her. "Aunt Theo will be so pleased to see you, Lady Eliza."

The matron passed by, tugging her girls along until they

caught up with another family. Eliza glanced behind her. There was no one close by. She smiled around the table and leaned forward slightly.

"That woman is a terrible gossip. It will soon be everywhere that I am engaged with Lady Grant tomorrow evening. Please give your aunt my thanks for arranging a reprieve before I need face the Ton."

She saw Nat look behind her. His eyes narrowed and he gave a slight shake of the head as she tried to angle herself to see what he was looking at. She turned towards Grace instead.

"This has been a delightful expedition but it's time for me to return home."

Nat finished his drink and jumped up. "I'll escort you."

Eliza was about to protest when a swish of silk and murmur of voices alerted her to the approach of another party. She saw Nat nod to a dark haired young man nearby as she quickly said her goodbyes. Nat tucked her hand through his arm as soon as she stood up and whisked her past the group. She fixed a smile on her face and matched her stride to his. He put his spare hand on hers where it nestled in the crook of his arm. A surge of awareness hit her. From his suddenly raised colour he must have felt it too.

The sharp voice of Mrs Smart came to her. A strangled sound, which had to be from Dempster followed. The dark haired young man reappeared and held the door to the street for them. They sailed through in time to see a coach draw up at the kerbside. The young man opened the door for them and then jumped up beside the coachman. Eliza gasped as she realised the coachman was Bright. She hesitated for a moment. Lud, Nat wasn't abducting her was he? Reason kicked in. Of course he wasn't. The last thing he would want to do was fall out with her family. She allowed him to throw her into the coach. He jumped in behind and it pulled away.

"I had Bright on standby. I had a feeling you might need to get away quickly."

Eliza shivered. "Who is the young man with Bright? I saw you signal to him."

"Jones, my new valet. His uncle is Luke's valet. An intelligent young man."

Eliza couldn't help but laugh. "A characteristic that will be honed working for you I expect. The look of amazement on Peregrine Dempster's face as you helped me evade him was comical."

"I had enlisted Bright earlier and we decided he should take Jones along in his Sunday best to act as messenger. He let Luke know when we were approaching so he could order for us. I had a feeling you would encounter problems and I'm not surprised Dempster was involved." He smiled at her. "He's not a threat like Milton but a rather spiteful man from what I've seen of him and today confirms that impression."

"You must have been a master strategist in the army."

"I had my moments and I learned a lot about men. I'm afraid I hadn't realised my views on aristocratic women had become entrenched. When I first met you I mistook a perfectly understandable anger with me for haughtiness and that coloured my dealings with you."

The coach turned a corner and Cathlay House came into view. Nat took her hand in his. She didn't resist.

"You must believe me when I say that my admiration for you was and is perfectly genuine."

The coach drew to a halt and Jones opened the door. Nat let go of her hand.

She took a deep breath. "Thank you, Nat. It was so kind of you to watch over me today."

"Think nothing of it." He smiled at her and jumped out.

She accepted his hand to help her down and smiled back at him.

"I will always help if you have need of me, Eliza. I shall look forward to seeing you tomorrow night at Lady Grant's."

She watched him stride off down the street. He had been so kind to her today. Jones knocked on the door of Cathlay House before climbing back up to his perch. Bright doffed his cap to her and drove off. The butler himself was waiting at the door but it was a moment before she could take her eyes off Nat's retreating figure. Had she made the biggest mistake of her life in refusing his offer?

Augusta was waiting for her in the hall. "I heard a coach draw up. How did you get on?"

Eliza shook her head. "Not good. That odious Mrs Smart gave me the cut direct. The rest of the expedition went off reasonably well but Major Overton had to rescue me from the woman in Gunter's."

Augusta stared at her for a moment. She couldn't face a conversation about it. "Augusta I'm too tired to go out this evening. I'll have a tray sent to my room. I think I will have a walk around the garden to clear my head and then go up. I'll see you in the morning."

Augusta laid a hand on her shoulder. "If that's want you want, my darling. I'll be at home this evening if you want to talk, or need company."

"Thank you." Eliza pulled away before tears overcame her and almost ran to the outside door.

She looked around for a footman to unlock it for her but for once there were none around. Moodily she tried the handle and it opened. That was odd but perhaps one of the footmen had gone down to the stables on an errand. She slipped outside and pulled in a lungful of air, grateful for some solitude at last. She wandered down to the bottom of the garden. Her peace was disturbed by the sound of hushed voices, the missing footman chatting to some of the grooms presumably. She might as well go back in. It was cold despite the sunshine of an early spring afternoon. The sound of footsteps approaching made her turn around to the sight of two men looming over her. Before she could scream one of them threw a rough brown sack over her head.

"Is this the one, George?"

"Yes that's 'er."

Eliza was bundled over the shoulder of one of her assailants, kicking and threshing her legs about as hard as she could. She tore off a glove and dropped it out of the sack. A split second later a hand clamped around the back of her thighs, making movement impossible.

"It was mighty obliging of her to make it this easy. Money for nothing."

They stopped and she heard the sound of the garden gate opening. She was dumped on her feet and the sack was pulled off so roughly it grazed her nose. Something cold and hard pressed against her neck.

"Now Missy, keep quiet or I will cut a piece off your ear." The smell of ale and onions hit her as her abductor leaned close. "Nod if you understand."

Eliza nodded slowly and gulped in a breath when the blade of the knife moved away from her neck.

"Good. I like nice, sensible women. We are going outside

now remember my knife and stay quiet. Got it?"

Eliza nodded again. A frantic glance around the garden showed two grooms and a footman trussed up behind a bush. A prod in the back propelled her through the gate. One of the grooms had seen her she was sure. She was lifted onto a cart waiting farther along the road, away from the mews. Her heart was thudding but she concentrated on dropping the second glove so the men didn't see it. The footmen would be missed soon and someone would come after her. She had to help them pick up her trail.

The cart started moving and she was shoved onto the floor with the sack thrown over her. The smell of rotting vegetables made her gag but she concentrated on opening her reticule and pulling out her handkerchief. The solid feel of the huge hatpin Grace had given her was strangely reassuring. It might buy her time. She pushed it back and closed the reticule. Nat would come after her. Somehow she knew that he would. He was a soldier and a good one. He would find a way to rescue her. She had to believe that because she needed to stay calm and help herself as much as she could.

After what seemed like an age, but was probably no more than ten minutes, the cart pulled up. She was uncovered and lifted out. They seemed to be in a dark side street. An all-black carriage with four showy black horses was waiting for them. It had to be the Earl of Milton. She shuddered. Brawny hands gripped her shoulders and the smell of ale and onions wafted down to her. She waited until they were right up to the coach before letting the handkerchief slip.

She held her breath but neither man showed signs of noticing it. One of them lifted her up and threw her into the coach when its door opened. Sure enough the Earl of Milton was waiting for her. Rough hands threw her onto the seat opposite to him and the door banged shut.

Lord Milton lounged in the shadows. "I do hope those ruffians weren't too rough with you, Lady Wyndham. I'm afraid I couldn't see any other way to steal you away from your bridegroom."

Eliza's heart thundered in her chest. She fought to keep her breathing steady. Her best hope was to try and keep him sweet in the way she had with Miles, when he was sober. The earl lifted his cane.

"I don't have a bridegroom to wrest me away from, Lord Milton."

He stopped with his cane half way to the roof and leaned forward to study her from narrowed eyes. "You don't?"

"Indeed not. I refused the major's so obliging offer. My sister is tired of being responsible for me and was quite angry but why should I settle for a mere baron?" She had his attention now. "I was hoping for something rather more." She gave a theatrical sigh. "I'm tired of her airs and graces but there don't seem to be any dukes hanging out for a wife this season."

He stared at her. Could she keep him talking a bit longer? Every minute of delay might help.

"According to Major Overton you are short of money, which rather put me off you."

"The Major has been far too busy in my affairs. Any diffi-culties I might have are temporary I assure you. It's simply a matter of putting my estates in order. My father was sadly negligent you understand."

He was taking the bait. Perhaps her time with Miles hadn't been wasted. She forced a smile and nodded at him. "I see. It seems Major Overton was seeking to discredit a rival then."

"I can assure you, Lady Wyndham, that my regard for you is quite genuine. You will come to thank me for taking you away so that brute can't keep importuning you."

He tapped on the roof of the coach and it set off.

Eliza was thrown back against the squabs by the speed of their departure. Either the horses were much better than they looked or they would blow up after a few miles.

She pouted. "I vow abducting me is all very romantic but is it strictly necessary?"

"Since your brother-in-law believed the pack of lies told him by Overton I can't see any other way to secure your hand. They had me thrown into detention. Fortunately I got messages out to my godfather and my maternal uncle, telling them how I was being framed by a jealous rival. It took their combined efforts to get me out."

Eliza dug her nails into her palms to stop from saying anything. So that was how he had escaped. Surely it wouldn't be long before Cathlay heard of his release.

"So it's to be a special licence is it?"

"There isn't time for a trip to Doctors Commons for one of those. We could go to my northern estate and get an ordinary licence from the bishop but even that would take time. It will have to be Gretna Green. Then we won't be found until we're man and wife." He smirked at her and his eyes travelled over her person.

Lud, was he going to try and seduce her in the carriage? Her chest felt too tight to breath. She closed her eyes and feigned sleep, straining her ears for sounds of him moving towards her. The coach was still bowling along at an impressive speed, far too fast to try and throw herself out. She heard him laugh and opened her eyes enough to see him open the window and lean out, pipe in hand. It sounded like they were still in London from the shouts of traders and carters.

The smell of tobacco wafted towards her, another potent reminder of Miles. Dusk was starting to fall so perhaps he wouldn't see that she was shaking. Eventually he shut the window with a snap. She tensed, waiting for sounds of an approach. None came and a quick peek showed the earl himself with his eyes closed. She was safe for a while. The coach was definitely slowing now. They would have to stop quite soon to change the horses. If he thought she wasn't antagonistic towards him he would be less vigilant and she might get a chance to escape.

Chapter Twenty Six

A servant entered the coffee room at Luke's club and stopped by Luke. Nat lowered the newspaper he was reading. The servant coughed to attract Luke's attention.

"A young man from your household begs a word with Major Overton on an important matter, my lord."

"Did he give a name?" Luke asked.

"He said his name was Jones, my lord, and that the matter was most urgent."

Luke glanced at him. Nat nodded. He had a great respect for Jones's intelligence.

"We'll come at once."

Nat and Luke followed the servant to the rear entrance of the club to find Jones in the hallway twisting his hat with both hands. Luke signalled for the servant to leave them and pressed a coin in his hand.

Nat raced up to Jones. "What is it?"

Jones glanced around but no one was in the hallway. "Bright sent me. He had a drink with his brother-in-law, the Bow Street Runner. The Earl of Milton has been released and Bright fears the worst. He reckons the earl will try and kidnap Lady Wyndham and flee to the border with her to get a ring on her finger. He says for you to go to Cathlay House and see where Lady Wyndham is. He's getting horses ready."

The ground moved under Nat's feet for a moment. He couldn't fault Bright's logic. "We're on our way. Go back and pack an overnight bag for me, with the barest essentials. Pack a bag for yourself in case we need you with us."

Jones nodded and ran out. Luke's grim expression did nothing to reassure him.

"Come on. Let's pray that Eliza is at home."

They hailed a hackney and were soon at Cathlay House. Nat ran up the steps, two at a time, and banged on the door. Sayers answered his knock himself.

"Is the Duke in, Sayers?"

"No, Major Overton. Let me take you to the Duchess."

"Thank you." Nat let out a breath. Eliza must be with her.

They followed the butler to a family sitting room. Augusta rose to greet them but there was no sign of Eliza. Nat rocked back on his heels as if he had been punched.

"I apologise for the intrusion, Your Grace, but we have news and I came to check that Eliza is safely at home."

The Duchess walked towards them, frowning. "I saw her when she came back from her outing with Miss Bamford. She was going to rest in her room and have supper sent up on a tray. The events of the last few days have tired her out."

"The Earl of Milton has been released and we fear a kidnap attempt."

She rang a bell which was answered by Sayers.

"Have Lady Wyndham's maid sent in to us, Sayers."

"At once, my lady."

Nat watched the butler scurry out. Worry gnawed at him. The Duchess put a hand on his arm.

"I'm sure all is well. Come and sit by the fire whilst we wait."

They did as they were bid but Nat couldn't help but leap up when a young maid followed Sayers into the room.

"Is your mistress at home?"

The puzzled look on the maid's face filled him with foreboding.

She shook her head. "I haven't seen her since this morning when she went to meet Miss Bamford."

The Duchess surged to her feet. "She came back. I spoke to her in the hall. She was going to take a turn about the gardens and then retire to her room."

Sayers stepped forward. "Her outdoor things haven't been left with me or any of the footmen. I'll have the head groom sent for."

Nat paced the room whilst they waited. At last the door opened but it was Sayers who entered. "We've found the grooms on duty this afternoon tied up in the garden along with a footman. Roberts here saw Lady Wyndham being carried out."

A nervous looking young man stepped forward. He was rubbing at his wrists and large wheals were visible below his sleeves.

"I rolled around so I could see. Lady Wyndham dropped a glove or something from the sack they had around her."

The Duchess went as white as chalk.

Nat groaned. "We'll go and look. Tell Cathlay I'm going after her. Milton's best bet is to head for the border with her. If she's left a trail we should be able to confirm that."

The groom caught his arm. "They was all bundled up like but I recognised the one from his voice. George Wendle, a bad lot he is. He hangs around the Three Pears Inn most days. Do

285

anything for money he would once he's carried his vegetables to market."

Luke clapped the lad on the shoulder. "Good man. I know where that is." He handed over a crown. "Come on Nat. You follow any trail and meet me back at Enstone House. If the blackguard knows anything I'll get it out of him."

"Take Roberts with you, Lord Enstone." The Duchess cut in.

"Send him with Major Overton. I have an acquaintance or two who will assist me with Wendle."

Nat followed Roberts through the garden at a trot. Sure enough there was a lady's glove lying near to the gate.

"You were right about the glove."

"I heard a cart rumble off." Roberts stopped at the road and pointed. "It sounded like they went in that direction."

"Is that the way to the Great North Road from here?"

"It could be. Follow me."

Nat watched the road as they ran and spotted a second glove a few yards further on. "This must be where they threw her into the cart."

They ran until they came to a junction with a larger road. Roberts pointed. "That way would lead you in the right direction."

Nat looked around. "They would have to put her into a carriage at some point. Before here I suspect." He looked back. "What about the road we just passed. It's fairly quiet around here."

They doubled back and were rewarded when Nat came across a handkerchief in the gutter. He picked it up and saw the initials EL. Of course her maiden name was Lovell! What a brave girl to lay a trail. An old man ambled up to them.

"You chasing after the eloping couple?"

CHAPTER TWENTY SIX

Nat's heart skipped a beat. He pulled out a shilling. "Yes I am."

The man took the coin and bit it. Nat jumped from foot to foot with impatience.

"Well?"

"Dark headed lass she was. They threw her into a big black coach with four black horses. I figured she expected to be followed when I saw her drop the handkerchief and hung around like."

Nat pulled out another shilling. "What about the man?"

"Never saw him. Foolish cove though."

"Why do you say that?"

"Let himself be palmed off with some poor animals. Looked good but they'll run aground in a few miles, you mark my words. You should catch them. They've been gone barely half an hour, seemed to take a long time to move off."

A sweat broke out on Nat's brow. Had he ravished her? It was best not to think about that. Concentrate on them not being much ahead.

"Thank you. If you remember anything else go to Enstone House and ask for the Viscount. Tell the staff Overton sent you." Nat handed over the shilling.

They hailed a hackney and arrived at Enstone House to find Luke waiting for them.

"Found that rascal, Wendle. It sounds like Scotland is Milton's destination."

Nat sent Roberts home with a message for the Duchess, filling Luke in as he wrote it. They went around to the stables to find Bright waiting with Pharaoh and his own horse saddled up.

Jones was there with two bags. He held one up. "This should

see you through, Major Overton. Do you want me to ride with you?"

Nat shook his head. "I have a better idea. If you go now, you should be able to get on the mail coach north with those bags. I've got some things in my saddlebag." He turned to Bright. "You're from north of London aren't you? Where would Jones be best to wait for us?"

"M'daughter's place. Get off at Brinkley and make for the Blue Boar. Tell her to have rooms ready for tonight. By my reckoning we'll overtake Milton either just before or just after Brinkley. Whatever happens we'll be safe at the Blue Boar."

Luke handed Jones some money. "Do you want me to come too, Nat?"

"No I think we are better travelling light. Stay in case any more information comes our way. Keep the Cathlays in check for me."

Bright knew the best ways out of London and they were soon bowling along. Nat remembered the old man who had seen Milton's coach.

"They may have been forced to stop for a change of horses quite quickly. Four black animals, pulling an all-black coach, shouldn't be hard to trace."

"I know where to look. We can't be more than an hour and a half behind them now. Don't worry we'll catch them."

Nat felt better now he was taking action but his stomach contracted when Bright drew a blank at the first inn they tried. They ploughed on and had better luck at the Red Lion in Latchford. Nat waited with the horses and tried to keep calm. He couldn't bear to think of Eliza in the earl's power.

Bright ran out to join him. "We're less than an hour behind them. The ostlers said they didn't take to the man in the coach and gave him awful horses. They haven't got much in the way of riding horses but, if we nurse these fellows a bit farther, I know a farm where we can borrow what we need. I grew up around here and the farmer is a big friend of mine."

Half an hour later Bright turned off the road and led them to a farmhouse down a quiet lane. Bright went in and returned within minutes with two strapping young men.

"Come on, Major. These two will bed our horses down and have new ones saddled up in a few minutes, in you come."

Nat gulped down some of the ale he was given by the farmer's wife but found he couldn't eat. Bright tapped him on the shoulder.

"Our mounts are ready. I've promised them a big bonus."

Nat managed a grin. "They've earned one."

He grimaced when he saw his mount. It wasn't far removed from a carthorse in looks but at least it would carry him easily enough. Bright surprised him by turning away from the main road and carrying on down the lane.

"Don't worry, with this full moon there's a shortcut through the fields we can take."

Once they regained the main road Bright checked at the first inn they came to.

"They didn't stop here but one of the lads in the yard said he saw them go past and was surprised they carried on as one of the leaders was hanging badly. He said there's an inn a couple of miles farther on that's just off the road and cheaper. I reckon they will be making for there. He said it's by some woodland and pretty secluded."

Nat's heart beat faster as they rode on. Would they reach the inn in time to catch them?

Chapter Twenty Seven

Eliza concentrated on breathing regularly as they pulled up in the yard of an inn. Would the earl do the same as the last time and carry straight on or would he get down and give her a chance to escape?

"We must be well in front of any followers by now, Lady Wyndham. I propose we stop for something to eat. This place is quite secluded so don't think anyone will come to your aid if you make a fuss."

She closed her eyes. He wasn't sure of her. "Now why would I make a fuss at the prospect of some supper?"

He jumped down from the coach and lifted her out. She tried hard not to flinch at the touch of his hands on her waist. He didn't seem to notice anything amiss and threaded her hand through his arm. She looked around in the moonlight. Her years of running wild with Max had left her good at tree climbing. There was woodland behind the inn and not far away. If she could reach it she might be able to hide until Nat got here. She was sure he would follow her somehow. Her spirits lifted.

She concentrated on the route they were taking. The land-lady showed them to a private parlour close to the exit. She left them to fetch the food the earl ordered. The earl let go of her arm and walked to the fire. He regarded her from under hooded lids.

"I think it's time you let me sample the goods so to speak. Then I won't need to worry about whether to trust you or not." He walked towards her.

Eliza strained every muscle in her body to keep herself still until he reached her. She would only have one chance at this. He reached her and lifted her chin with a finger. Eliza tightened her grip on the head of the pin through the cloth of the reticule. The earl lowered his face towards hers. Eliza stabbed him in the thigh as hard as she could. He let out a shout and staggered backwards gripping his thigh.

Eliza lifted her skirts in one hand and ran for all she was worth. There was no one in the hallway. She took in a great lungful of the night air once she was outside and ran towards the woods. The moon went behind a cloud but she kept running. She heard shouts behind her and the unmistakable tones of the earl calling for assistance. Her heartbeat roared in her ears but she kept running. If she could make the trees she had a chance of evading capture. The moon came out as she reached the woods.

She dived in and found a narrow pathway almost straight away. She ran until the pain in her side stopped her. After a moment spent doubled over she pressed on at walking pace. She must come out farther along the road soon. If she could climb a tree where she had a view of travellers she could keep a watch out for Nat. She heard a horse whinny. Panic ripped through her. Had the earl found her already?

She came to a bridle path and turned to double back as two riders appeared in the distance. Something made her hide behind a bush to get a better look at them. They came into view and joy enveloped her at the sight of Nat and Bright. They had caught them up! She called Nat's name and stepped onto the path. They quickened their pace and Nat stopped beside her. He grabbed her hand.

"Well done my clever girl. When I say the word use my thigh to try and scramble up. Now."

He pulled on her arm and she did as he had bid. She landed across his lap on her stomach. With the help of his hand around her waist she turned over and sat on the saddle in front of him. She lifted her skirts and threw a leg over the horse without being told. This time she was glad to share a horse with him. She leaned back against him and relief flooded her. His arm came around her waist and for the first time in years she felt safe in the company of a man who wasn't a relative.

Bright brought his horse alongside them. "Come on we had better get going. That beast will go for hours but you won't be able to go fast."

They turned their horses and trotted off the way they had come. Eliza tensed as she realised the truth of Bright's words. The horse was so wide it was easier to balance than on the previous occasion they had shared a horse. Even so they would never outrun a pursuit.

She grabbed the horse's long mane. "If I hang on to this we should be able to manage a slow canter."

Nat tightened the arm around her. "We'll try it."

He urged the horse on and their pace improved but not by much. Within a few minutes they heard a commotion behind them and the sound of hoof beats. Eliza looked back to see the Earl of Milton on horseback and making ground. Two other men followed but they were farther back. Her hands felt clammy as she tightened her grip on the horse's mane. Bright turned into a side path and beckoned to them to follow him.

"Keep going down here. I'll decoy them. Don't worry about me I played in these woods as a boy. You'll hit the main road in about a mile or so. The Blue Boar is a couple of miles farther on. If you hear the river then you've gone off course. Veer away from it and you'll find another path to the main road."

"We'll find our way out." Nat said. "Take care, Bright."

Bright saluted them and doubled back. Nat urged their horse on. At the increased speed its action jolted them around. Eliza kept both hands entwined in the horse's mane and Nat kept his arm firmly around her.

"Hold tight and don't worry. I'm carrying two pistols and so is Bright."

"I'm not worried now I'm with you."

She had been so frightened the first time she had shared a horse with him but now it felt so right. They heard shouting in the distance and she shivered.

There was a scream and Nat slowed the horse.

"Should we go back, Nat? Bright might be hurt."

"We'll wait here a while and see what happens." He edged the horse behind some bushes.

It wasn't long before they heard a horse coming towards them. Eliza held her breath as Nat handed her a pistol and pulled out another one. There was a whistle and she felt Nat relax. He gave an answering whistle and took the pistol off her. Bright pulled up by them.

"I led our friend towards the river. There's a section that runs through a deep ravine. I shouted insults at him and then turned at the last minute. His horse shied and he was thrown down into the ravine. His people are trying to get him out. You go on and I'll hang around to see how he fared."

"But what if you get caught?" Eliza said.

"I won't but it wouldn't matter. I'm riding a horse belonging to a friend and got lost on my way back to his farm. He'll vouch for me."

Nat laughed. "Bright is a master at this sort of thing, Eliza. Thank you, Bright."

He swung the horse back onto the path and set it to a steady trot. Eliza relaxed, with the Earl stuck in a river and his servants occupied trying to get him out they were safe now. They found the main road without mishap and she was nearly asleep by the time they reached the Blue Boar. She came to with a start when they turned into the yard of a prosperous looking coaching inn.

"Nat, what will they say about you turning up with a woman at this time of night? I have no maid or anything. They might send us on our way."

"Don't worry. Jones should be waiting for us with rooms ready. We sent him on the mail coach. Bright's daughter is the landlady here."

An ostler took the horses head and Nat swung out of the saddle. He lifted her down as if she weighed no more than a feather. The dark haired young man Eliza had seen at Gunter's came running out of the inn.

"You made good time, Major. I got straight on a coach and I've only been here a short while."

"Our quarry helped us out by driving the most useless horses. Have you made all good with Bright's daughter?"

"Yes. She's preparing a couple of rooms now. I'm afraid that's all they have free but I can sleep with Bright in the stables."

"You go on ahead and see if they can hide us in a private parlour. We'll go around the back."

Nat took her around to the back entrance and the door was opened to them by a cheerful looking woman with Jones following.

"I don't know what this is all about but I'll trust you, Major Overton." She laughed. "Never hear the end of it from my father if I didn't. He thinks the world of you."

She led them into the kitchens. "This is the best I can do I'm afraid. We're busy but there's plenty of food."

She showed them to a scrubbed table at the back and produced chicken and vegetable soup and a game pie, washed down with ale. Eliza was surprised to find how hungry she was. Jones went out saying he would wait for Bright in the stables. The kitchens were busy but no one was taking any notice of them.

"Oh Nat. I don't know how it was but I was sure you would come for me. I love you." There she had said it.

He took her hand and a frisson of excitement shot through her. She had never felt this exhilaration with Miles, not even when he was courting her and acting the gentleman.

"Eliza, if you love me why did you turn me down?"

His tone was so gentle she wanted to cry at how she must have hurt him. She owed him the truth.

"It wouldn't be fair to marry you because my husband treated me so badly and was so cruel in our coupling that I don't think I can ever be intimate with a man again."

He put an arm around her. "I wondered if it was something like that but at the time I was so hurt all my old prejudices against society women came back to me. At one stage I was half convinced Luke was your real target."

"I'm so sorry I upset you like that. Fear overwhelmed me. I needed a little more time to be sure of you. You were so kind to me this morning, even though you had every right to be angry with me after my summary dismissal. It was obvious you were acting from a genuine concern for me. I knew then I had made a terrible mistake in saying no and yet I love you too much to tie you to a woman who is too frightened to lie with you."

"Eliza, I love you with all my heart. If I could prove to you that lovemaking would be different with me would you marry me?"

"Yes, I would."

She put her hands on his shoulders and feathered a kiss on his lips. It was time to be brave. She pulled away.

"I don't think Bright and Jones should have to sleep in the stables."

Nat's mouth dropped open. "Are you saying what I think you are?"

Eliza trembled but it was partly a pleasurable tremble. "I love you, Nat and I want to marry you. I have to be sure I can be a proper wife to you and this is our opportunity to find out."

He dropped a kiss on her forehead. "That sounds logical. If you're sure we'll ask Bright's daughter to show us to our room."

Bright's daughter raised her eyebrows at Nat's request but said nothing. She offered to take them up herself, using a back staircase.

Nat locked the door and drew the bolts across. He turned to look at Eliza sitting on the edge of the bed, with her eyes closed. She looked exhausted. Tonight was not the time for her to face down fears that must have been haunting her for years. What she needed was time to get to know him but she was determined to put it to the test now. There didn't seem much point trying to talk her out of it. He grinned. Not that his body wanted to talk her out of it. Miles Wyndham had been a brute by all accounts. Once she could see the differences between them she would find it easier.

Bright's daughter had laid out a nightdress on the bed for her. Perhaps he could coax her to sleep and wrap her in it. A good night's sleep would restore her energy. He could judge whether to go ahead with her plan in the morning. He sat down next to her and put an arm around her.

"Relax. We needn't rush. Rest your head on my shoulder for a while. You've been so brave but it's not been a good day for you, has it?"

She smiled. "It started out mixed, then became horrendous but things are better now."

He chuckled. "That's my lovely girl."

She snuggled up against him. She felt so right in his arms. Heavy rhythmical breathing told him she was deeply asleep. He laid her gently on the bed and slowly, piece by piece removed her clothing. Her body was every bit as lovely as he had expected but now was not the time to look at her. He teased the covers from underneath her and bit by bit pulled the nightdress over her head. She mumbled something and he stopped and waited.

Good, she was still asleep. He could have put her to bed naked but somehow he felt she might find it unnerving to wake up like that. His hand caught the curve of her bottom as he pulled the nightdress down. He took a deep breath and gently pulled the covers over her. She was so lovely. Should he sleep in the armchair? She was so deeply asleep she wouldn't notice him. It was a big bed and it beckoned to him after an exhausting day. Besides he was a natural early riser and would probably be up before she stirred. He stripped his clothes off, donned his nightshirt from the bag Jones had brought for him and climbed in.

He fell asleep instantly and awoke to find Eliza curled up against him. He fought the temptation to wake her. It was only fair to give her time to decide if she was truly ready for intimacy with him. Refreshed by sleep, the temptation was much stronger than the night before when he was tired himself. He dragged himself away from her and out of bed. They had a lifetime to get this right as long as he could persuade her to marry him.

He threw on his clothes and walked to the door, carrying his boots in his hand. The bolts made a scraping sound but she didn't stir. The key turned silently in a well-oiled lock. He sat on the top stair and dragged his boots on. He found Jones and Bright already up and eating breakfast in the coffee room below. He ordered a mug of ale and joined them.

"Any news of our friend, Bright?"

Bright glanced around the room but no one was nearby. "He didn't survive the fall, but it was his own choice to chase me. The horse stopped at the top. He always was a bad rider."

Nat nodded. "Anyone notice it was you he was chasing?"

Bright shook his head. "I hid my horse deeper in the woods and walked back on foot to see what happened."

Nat sat quiet for a moment. "At least Eliza will have no more trouble from him. Jones, we need to get you back to London to reassure the Cathlays."

"There's a mail coach leaving for London in about half an hour. The landlord reckons I'll get a seat."

"Good man. I'm glad I took you on."

Jones beamed at him. "Thank you, Major. I've time to help

you get ready."

Nat's mouth curved into a smile. "I don't think that will be necessary, Jones. The most important thing is to get you on the coach. I'll see you off."

His ale arrived together with a plate of ham and eggs.

"Your daughter and her husband keep an excellent inn here, Bright. I don't suppose they have any carriages for hire do they?"

"They do. I'll go and find out if they have one free."

"There's no rush. Finish your breakfast first. I'm happy for you to spend another night here once you've reclaimed our horses. Have some time with your daughter. There's a big bonus for them as well." He handed Bright some more money.

Bright grinned at him. "Generous of you. Are you feeling in a good mood?"

Nat grinned back. "I think so. I'll let you know for sure when you're back in London."

Nat saw Jones onto the mail coach. He collected a tray with tea, toast and eggs and carried it upstairs.

Eliza awoke with a start to see sunlight streaming around the edges of the curtains. Where was she? She heard Nat moving around and it all flooded back.

"Lud, she must have fallen asleep in his arms. What must he think of her?"

She sat up in bed to see him coaxing the fire back into life.

"Nat, I didn't fall asleep on you did I?"

His deep laugh rang out. "You did, Madam. You can make it up to me later. I've locked the door and pulled the bolts so we are safe from disturbance."

"What about Augusta? She'll be so worried."

"I've seen Jones onto the early morning mail coach. He'll go straight to Cathlay House once he arrives in London. I've brought you some breakfast. You need to eat it before the tea goes cold."

He poured two cups of tea and sat down on the edge of the bed by her. There was something so companionable sharing breakfast still in her nightgown. Except it wasn't her nightgown. She looked at the food. Lud she was hungry.

He put the tray with the eggs and toast on the bed by her. "I had some food in the coffee room."

They chatted away as she ate. There had never been companionable moments like this with Miles. She must stop thinking about him. She was with Nat now. They chatted for ages about nothing in particular. Nat collected cups and plates and loaded the tray. He got up and placed it on a table by the window. Her pulse raced when he turned around and smiled at her.

"Would you like me to leave you whilst you get dressed? I can send a maid to help you."

Eliza shook her head. "I want to carry on with our plan. Don't you?"

He laughed and took her hand. "I do, as long as it's right for you. I don't want to rush you."

"I will feel so much better once I know I can do this."

"If you're sure."

Eliza nodded. She allowed Nat to remove her nightdress. His hands were gentle, so unlike Miles when he was in the mood to tumble her. Thinking of Miles made her shiver.

"You're cold. Let me pull the covers over you. I'll join you in a moment. She watched, fascinated, as he removed his clothes and stood naked before her. His muscular body was so well honed. He was truly magnificent and definitely aroused. The room suddenly seemed dark, despite the fire burning brightly and the light creeping around the curtains. She concentrated on breathing steadily and the moment passed. The bed shifted as Nat climbed in beside her. He pulled her close and held her gently in his arms. Every nerve in her body tingled. She wanted more of him despite her fear. This was Nat, the man who had ridden to her rescue.

She took a deep breath and turned onto her back. Her body tensed as she waited for him to mount her. Instead Nat's hands started caressing her breasts and warmth flooded through her. He pulled her towards him until they were facing and pressed his lips against hers. She responded instinctively. Some of the tension left her. The kiss deepened until she was aware of only the two of them and their breathing. One of his hands reached lower and stroked her belly before finding its way between her thighs. He stroked her until she writhed with pleasure.

Her hand found his erection and she held him gently. Miles had never let her touch him there. He kissed her again and she ran her hand along his length. His back arched and he groaned. It was his turn to writhe. Slowly he slipped a finger, and then two, inside her. She caught her breath. This overload of sensation was new to her. The throbbing between her legs became nigh on unbearable. He removed his hand and she tried to push against him.

"You're ready now. Relax. He kissed her once more."

She braced herself for his weight to land on top of her but instead he rolled onto his back and lifted her on top of him.

"I'm all yours whenever you're ready."

"With me on top?"

"Why not? Then you will have control and feel safe."

She gasped. Nat was right. It was completely different with

him. Carefully she guided him in. Sensations shot through places she had never felt before and the rhythm of it came naturally to her. A scream escaped her as sensation exploded into fierce contractions inside her. This was the wonderful feeling she had heard her sisters talk about. Nat groaned and his hips bucked until he subsided and she felt his seed spill inside her. He kissed her forehead.

"That was wonderful. Now will you marry me?"

"Yes please, Nat."

"Thank goodness for that."

They lay side by side, holding hands, for some time. Nat seemed to have dropped off to sleep. Excitement shot through her. She had enjoyed herself with Nat, more than enjoyed. It had been wonderful.

After a short while Nat sighed and opened his eyes. "Did you enjoy that?"

"Yes I did. I'm so happy."

He smiled. "I'm glad. We had better get you back home now. We're supposed to go to Lady Grant's for dinner tonight."

"I expect Augusta will have cancelled that. Even if she hasn't I don't suppose Lady Grant will mind if we excuse ourselves." She smiled up at him. "I'd rather you came to us for a family supper, if we're back in time."

"If your sister doesn't mind I would like that. We should be back with time to spare if we start soon."

"I'm sure she won't mind."

"Good. We can tell them together then if you want."

"I would like that. It will serve them right to wait for the news after the way they have pushed me towards you."

"Have they indeed. To think I was afraid they would think I wasn't good enough for you."

CHAPTER TWENTY SEVEN

Eliza caught his hand. "You're more than good enough for me."

"Thank you. I'll go down and find Bright. If they can do it I'll have a hot bath sent up for you."

He threw on his clothes and ran out. Eliza hugged her knees, a bubble of happiness inside her that she hadn't felt for years. Nat was soon back.

"Hot water is being heated up for you. I'll shave in Bright's room."

"Did Bright find out what happened to the Earl of Milton?"

"He didn't survive the fall." He sighed. "What a waste for a man to be like him. He could have had a good life and done so much good looking after his tenants and servants. We don't need to worry about him anymore. I've hired a closed carriage to take us back."

Nat hesitated when Jones handed him his grandfather's diamond tie pin. A laugh escaped him and he accepted it. Grandfather had been just as bad as the Rees when he thought about it. He ought to wear his diamond tonight of all nights, in his honour. Even the terms of Grandfather's will had been designed to push him towards taking his place as Lord Overton eventually. Perhaps he had been right though. The businesses were in good hands and he could reap the benefits of his shares in them without any input if he wanted. Managing the Overton estates felt right. It was the nearest thing to looking after a troop of soldiers he was likely to find in civilian life. With Eliza by his side he would relish it.

It was raining so Luke's spare carriage, driven by Bright, dropped him off at Cathlay House. He was shown into an elegant drawing room where Eliza was sitting with the duke.

"Good evening, Overton. It's just the four of us this evening it seems. I apologise for my wife not being here to greet you. Can't imagine what's keeping her. I'll go and find out."

Eliza's eyes flew to his face. "That was subtle. I swear I never said anything to them. Won't you have a seat?"

Nat laughed. "Would you mind if I shared the sofa with you?"

Eliza's brow let go of its wrinkles and she smiled at him. "If you want to."

Nat flicked up the tails of the beautiful black evening jacket and sat beside her. He breathed deeply to settle his nerves and the smell of roses and lavender swept over him. She seemed to be studying his tie pin.

"The pin was a present from my grandfather on my twenty first birthday."

Why should that make her blush?

"It's a bit too showy for my tastes, what do you think?"

To his amazement her blush became deeper and she gave a strangled cry. He leaned closer and he could see she was trying not to laugh.

"I'm so sorry. I have a lot to explain. You have to understand I didn't want to be attracted to you. I wanted to hang on to my nice ordered, safe existence so I tried to convince myself you were a fortune hunter like Miles. When I saw that tiepin I took it as proof, reasoning that you were trying hard to impress people by wearing a fake diamond."

Nat put an arm around her and drew her close. "You thought it was a fake."

"I'm afraid so. It must be worth a king's ransom."

Nat laughed. "It probably is."

Eliza smiled up at him. "I heard you talking to Cathlay on

the night of the Comerfords' ball. I was reading in the window seat of the library."

Nat frowned. "You must have heard me admit that I was madly in love with you."

She shook her head. "I slipped out of the bottom door after I heard you say I would be able to help you know how to go on in society."

"Ah! So did you convince yourself it was your position in society I was after?"

She nodded and he dropped a kiss on her forehead.

"Now of course you are so mired in scandal you have no position and I still want to marry you."

She laughed up at him and tapped his arm. "If you are going to tease me I might take fright again." She ran her tongue around her lips.

A powerful urge to kiss her shook him but first he had to reassure her.

"I don't want you to be frightened ever again. If you want to wait a few months or even a year until you know me better you only have to say."

She met his gaze and smiled. "It's a bit late for that now. Besides I've realised I always feel safe when your arms are round me. That frightened me more than anything at the start I think."

Nat opened his arms and she snuggled into them. When she kissed him more firmly he responded with enthusiasm, pulling her against him. A flash of green silk, quickly removed, caught her eye and she pulled away with a sigh.

"I think I just saw Augusta coming in and then going away again."

Nat laughed. "You have very understanding relatives but

perhaps we had better tell them the good news before the Duke calls me out."

Augusta reappeared on the arm of the Duke. Both of them were smiling and Eliza ran across to them.

"We have a wedding to arrange, Augusta."

"That's wonderful. We can discuss the details over dinner."

Nat joined them and Eliza smiled as Cathlay slapped him on the back. Augusta led them to the small family dining room. She placed them side by side on a table with as many leaves removed as possible. There was a large candelabra standing in the middle of it and a blazing fire added more light to the cosy scene. Nat held her hand under the table and a deep contentment washed over her. Her fear of the future had melted away and now she felt happy anticipation. The footmen left them to their soup.

"How soon can we organise the wedding, Augusta?"

Augusta put her spoon down. "It would be lovely to have everyone down for it but that could take a while. I had a letter from Max this very morning, as it happens. The friend he visited in Edinburgh has to come to London, so they are making a holiday of travelling down together. He should be at Hargreaves for a few days stay in a couple of weeks or so."

Nat joined in. "My business up north is with a shipping company I am part owner of. I could arrange to have the Scottish family travel down by ship."

Eliza felt like bouncing with excitement. "Oh that would be wonderful. We don't see Diana often because she has a young family. Would they be able to stop off for the Northumberland family too?"

Nat laughed. "You will have to give me the numbers and I

will arrange for however many ships are needed to be at the family's disposal. I should like the wedding to be at Hargreaves so Uncle Henry can attend."

Eliza sighed. "Yes please. I would much rather have a family wedding with close friends and family retainers. I should hate to marry in one of the fashionable London churches."

"So would I. How would you like a sailing trip all around Scotland afterwards if the weather is favourable?"

Eliza was too happy to say anything for a moment. She glanced at Augusta who was smiling at her. "Very much. I would love you to see Cathlay Castle."

"I would like that. It will be wonderful to meet the rest of your family at the wedding. Uncle Henry is my only family now and I am hoping to share yours."

The Duke laughed. "We've been waiting to welcome you to the family anytime these past few weeks, Overton. We're thrilled to have you."

Nat smiled down at Eliza. "That means a lot to me but nothing compares to winning Eliza's hand."

Epilogue

The sound of the church bells and the cheers of the villagers faded into the distance. Eliza turned and accepted a kiss from her new bridegroom. Heat washed through her. She had been longing to get him to herself for weeks. The more time she had spent with him the safer she felt.

"Oh Nat. I can't wait for a repeat of our morning at the Blue Boar." Snatched kisses have been nowhere near enough."

He smiled. "I'm glad. I don't want you to be afraid. There is no one to see us here. I could give you a foretaste."

"What do you mean?"

He grinned at her and bent down to lift the hem of her gown. His hand found its way up her leg and between her thighs until his fingers reached her groin. She wriggled as a finger massaged the nub at the centre of the sensations sweeping through her. Her hand found its way to the buttons of his falls. He stopped her with his spare hand.

"Best leave me for now. Sit back and enjoy yourself."

He leaned over and kissed her and she concentrated on kissing him back. His finger speeded up and waves of sensation exploded through her. She laid her head on his shoulder and shuddered. His arm went around her and held her close as she collapsed limply against him.

"Oh Nat. That was wonderful but what about you?"

He drew in a breath and blew out his cheeks. "I'll survive for now, I think. Talk to me about something boring."

She giggled. "What would you like? Crop rotation?"

"That's not boring."

"I thought the idea was to distract you."

He laughed. "It is. I think I'm alright for now. I'm a bit worried about leaving Uncle Henry at Hargreaves but I need to get you to bed as soon as we possibly can. The servants went back an hour ago so I expect you will have to go along a receiving line first."

"Very probably. Don't worry about Uncle Henry. He was enjoying himself with all my sisters to fuss over him."

"Yes he was."

"Tell me about the shipping line. Diana's children loved their journey down."

The journey soon passed. They pulled into the drive of Overton Grange and Eliza burst out laughing.

"What is it?"

"You were right. Look, the servants must have had a lookout. They are all lining up on the drive."

Mrs Ambrose was waiting to take them along the line.

"I know everyone is familiar with you my lady, but we like to do things properly at Overton Grange."

"Of course, Mrs Ambrose. I do appreciate the trouble you have gone to."

They stopped to chat to each person waiting. Mrs Ambrose walked them up the steps afterwards.

"I know I shouldn't say this, my lady, but I can't help it. I knew as soon as I saw the two of you together that you were made for each other."

Eliza laughed. "That's exactly what my sister, the Duchess of Cathlay, said."

The butler overtook them and threw open the front door. "Welcome to Overton Grange, Lady Eliza. I hope you will be very happy here."

"Thank you. I'm sure I shall be."

Mrs Ambrose joined them in the hallway. "I'll have tea and cakes sent to the drawing room, my lady."

Eliza was hard pressed not to laugh at Nat's comical expression.

"That's kind of you, Mrs Ambrose, but after so much rich food in the wedding breakfast I don't think I can eat another thing." She turned to Nat who shook his head.

"I'm not hungry either."

She dragged her gaze away from his. "I would like to change into something more comfortable. Perhaps you could have tea sent up to my room."

Mrs Ambrose curtsied. "Of course, my lady. I'll see to it at once."

Nat held out his arm to Eliza. "Allow me to escort you."

They walked slowly up the stairs, arms linked.

Nat leaned close to her ear. His breath sent shivers through her.

"Send your maid away as quickly as you can and then open the connecting door. No one is seeing us again tonight and I don't care what the servants think."

Eliza giggled and went through the door he opened for her. She wanted him as much as he wanted her and she was so happy.

Afterword

If you loved 'A Good Match For The Major', I would really appreciate a short review. This helps new readers find my books.

This is the first book in my Reluctant Bride series of stand-alone novels linked by character. The next two are:
   The Viscount's Convenient Bride
   The Marquess's Christmas Runaway

Look out for Grace's story which will be book 4

For more information please visit my website:
   https://josiebonhamauthor.com

You will also find me on:
   Facebook @josiebonhamauthor
   Twitter @BonhamJosie

Printed in Great Britain
by Amazon